THE DANCE OF CREATED LIGHTS

OTHER TITLES FROM NEW FALCON PUBLICATIONS

THE
DANCE OF
CREATED LIGHTS

A Sufi Tale

JAY BREMYER

NEW FALCON PUBLICATIONS
TEMPE, ARIZONA, U.S.A.

International Standard Book Number: 1-56184-084-X

Library of Congress Catalog Card Number: 96-67335

First Edition 1996

Book design by Sekhmet Books
Cover by Nancy Wasserman

The paper used in this publication meets the minimum requirements of the American National Standard for Permanence of Paper for Printed Library Materials Z39.48-1984

Address all inquiries to:
NEW FALCON PUBLICATIONS
1739 East Broadway Road Suite 1-277
Tempe, AZ 85282 U.S.A.
(or)
1605 East Charleston Blvd.
Las Vegas, NV 89104 U.S.A.

I DEDICATE THIS BOOK to Sheikh Nur al Jerrahi Lex Hixon, whose example I greatly appreciate, and who has allowed me to use his translations from the Koran; to Fred Stocking, without whose help and encouragement I would have given up; and finally to my wife and writing-partner, Sara, who made this story worth reading.

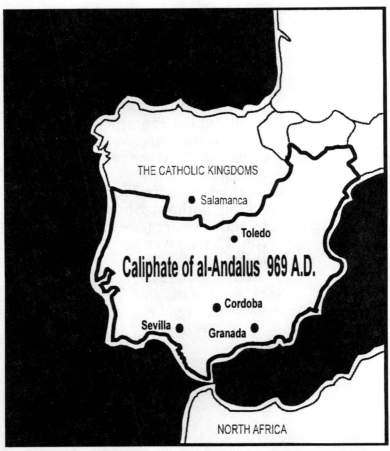

THE CATHOLIC KINGDOMS

Salamanca

Toledo

Caliphate of al-Andalus 969 A.D.

Cordoba

Sevilla

Granada

NORTH AFRICA

"Without the arcane and esoteric, the body of science is like flesh without bones." — Rabbi Alpha ben Hebaron to al-Kiran Kamir Kirian, Cordoba, Spain, 969 A.D.

TABLE OF CONTENTS

Tell all the truth but tell it slant —
Success in Circuit lies
Too bright for our infirm Delight
The Truth's superb surprise

As Lightning to the Children eased
With explanation kind
The Truth must dazzle gradually
Or every man be blind —

Emily Dickinson, # 1129 (1830–1886)

PREFACE

Within a century after Mohammed, Prophet of Allah, had received the first phrases of the Holy Koran from the lips of the Archangel Gabriel in 610, the Islamic empire had spread from India through Central Asia and across the Middle East and North Africa into southern Spain. Here the kingdom of al-Andalus had become, by the tenth century, one of the greatest kingdoms in the world, strong enough to host and protect scholars, musicians, poets, physicians, scientists, theologians, philosophers, and heretics of all persuasions.

Hakam II, who inherited the Caliphate in 961, encouraged diversity and freedom of thought in his kingdom, sponsoring twenty-seven free universities in which Greek and Roman culture, science, and speculative philosophy, as well as traditional Islamic subjects, were studied. By the year 969, however, fundamentalist sentiments were on the rise in al-Andalus, and a plot was being organized to take the throne from young Hisham, the only heir, upon the death of his father in order to re-impose Islamic purity on the kingdom.

It is against this background that the following story takes place. Its central event is the All Faith's Festival, celebrated every ninth year at the winter solstice in Cordoba and culminating in the Dance of Created Lights, during which, if the prophecy is fulfilled, two dancers will fly.

TIME LINE:
Common Era

570 — Mohammed's birth in Mecca

610 — Mohammed's first vision, begins his mission as Prophet of Allah

632 — Death of Mohammed

644 — Othman becomes 3rd Caliph in Medina, founder of Omayyad Dynasty; capital subsequently moved to Damascus

711 — Tariq conquers Visigoth Kingdoms in Iberia; Moslem empire stretches from India, through Central Asia, the Middle East, North Africa and into Spain

749 — Omayyad Dynasty overthrown by al-Saffah, "the Blood-spiller," founder of the Abbasid Dynasty; capital moved to Baghdad

755 — Abd-er Rahman I conquers al-Andalus (Moorish Spain) and establishes Omayyad dynasty in the West

883 — School of Ibn Massara established in Cordoba

969 — The great All Faith's Festival celebrated at winter solstice in Cordoba — the Dance of Created Lights

GLOSSARY

(Note: Arab and Andalusian words are spelled and pronounced in various ways. I have attempted to stay consistent within the text but have not followed any particular school. In my opinion, the pronunciation which sounds most melodic should be used. The following definitions are according to the usage in the text.)

Abd-er Rahman I: founder of Omayyad dynasty in Cordoba, al-Andalus in 755 A.D.

Abu El-Ali Misram: father of al-Kiran, cousin to Hakam II, married to Mershi Kamir Kirian.

Al-Andalus: Moslem Empire, Moorish Spain, 711 to 1492, established as an independent Kingdom or Caliphate in 822 under Abd-er Rahman II.

Alansha: al-Kiran's Sudanese nurse, cook.

Alborak: white mule with head of a woman and tail of a peacock on which Mohammed rode to the Heavens from Mount Moriah.

Ali: son-in-law of Mohammed, husband of Fatima, the 4th Caliph, following Abu Bakr, Umar, and Othman.

Allah: al-ilah, "the God."

Al-Kiran Kamir Kirian: 17 year old Cordovan in 969 A.D., son of Abu el-Ali Misram and Mershi Kamir Kirian.

Al-Mansur: Abi Amir, Chamberlain to Caliph Hakam II.

Al-Rusafa: royal retreat N.W. of Cordoba, founded by Abd-er Rahman I and named for the Omayyad retreat on the Euphrates

River where he had been sheltered when, as a youth, he had fled al-Saffah.

Al-Saffah: "He who spills blood," founder of Abbasid Dynasty which deposed the Omayyad Dynasty in the East and moved the capital from Damascus to Baghdad.

Amu Darya: the river known to the Greeks as the Oxus, on the northern border of Afghanistan.

Arians: early Christians who were displaced by Catholics in a doctrinal dispute over the nature of the incarnate Christ.

At-Talibin, Mesire: Northerner, associated with a Christian mystical order, meets al-Kiran at Taifa ibn Massara.

Ben Hebaron, Alpha: Jewish rabbi, Kabbalist, teacher of al-Kiran.

Caliph: leader of the faithful, secular king as well as religious head of state.

Cordoba: capital of al-Andalus, Moorish Spain.

Dance of Created Lights: three day dance or dromenon, celebrated during Festival of All Faiths at winter solstice every ninth year in Cordoba, based on the vision and prophesy of Mohammed at Medina.

Hakam II, al-Mustansir: Omayyad Caliph of Cordoba, succeeded Abd-er Rahman III in 961.

Hajj: pilgrimage to the Ka'ba in Mecca.

Hasdai ibn Shaprut: the Jewish Prince of Cordoba, physician and adviser to Caliph Hakam II.

Hisham II: son of Hakam II, heir apparent.

Ka'ba: the house of the black stone in Mecca.

Kabbalah: Jewish system based on the paths of the splendid rays as related to the world tree and sacred alphabet.

Karobla: dragon creature, related to Alborak.

Kemi: blackbird, nickname for al-Kiran.

Kerm-oak: evergreen on which scarlet insects nest; in ritual linked to terebinth-oak as twins, respectively, the evergreen ruling during the waning of the solar year, the terebinth during the waxing.

Kristien: Nubian slave, princess and priestess of Oshiwah, student of ben Hebaron, al-Kiran's partner for the Dance of Created Lights.

Madrasah: place of study, college.

Mershi Kamir Kirian: al-Kiran's mother.

Mershi Khayam: Mistress at Taifa ibn Massara.

Muezzin: the caller to prayer.

Mullah: Moslem devoted to religious scholarship and practice.

No'Koonja Naqsch: enneagram, a ninefold emblem associated with the Sarmouni and other orders of Central Asia.

Oshiwah: Nubian Goddess, Isis, line of the Black Madonna and Magdalen.

Othman: 3rd Caliph following death of Mohammed, of the ancient Omayyad family of Medina.

Orwan Kamir Oshiwah al-Kirian: al-Kiran's grandmother, mother of Mershi Kamir, initiate of school north of Pyrenees.

Shariah: the five practices of Islam: ablution, prayer, pilgrimage, fasting, and alms giving.

Sheikh ab-Dar Il'ium: Sufi chief of Taifa ibn Massara.

Shi'ite: Moslems who trace descent of the true Caliph from Ali, cousin and son-in-law of Mohammed.

Subh: Hakam II's favorite wife, a Basque, mother of Hisham II.

Sufi: generally a Moslem with a mystical orientation.

Sunni: follower of the traditional succession of the first four Caliphs and the Sunna: the custom or way of life according to the example of Mohammed.

Taifa ibn Massara: esoteric school in Sierra Morena mountains northwest of Cordoba.

Tekke: a Sufi school for spiritual development.

Ulama: doctors of Islamic theology.

Ziryab: assistant to Mershi Khayam, al-Kiran's friend, whose name means blackbird in Arabic, gold water in Persian.

Zikr: silent communion, remembrance of the divine.

CHAPTER ONE

"THE PROPHECY"

Seventeen years old, kin to the mighty house of Hakam II, the Omayyad Caliph of Cordoba, al-Kiran gazed toward the sun through closed eye-lids. Seeing a magenta corona, he recalled the nine couples ritually dancing for three days in and about the great Plaza, moving toward the rainbow bridge prophesied by the Blessed Mohammed, Messenger of Allah, upon which the dancers would rise, thus marking the beginning of a new age.

He had been eight years old. There had been no eclipse and the dancers had not flown up into the sky, at least in the outer-world; but watching the dance from his father's shoulders, he had experienced reverence and awe.

Since the last All Faith's Festival, held every ninth year to commemorate the Prophet's vision, he had pursued his studies and the freedom of the city while secretly dreaming of the next Dance of Created Lights. This was the year.

Lying in the sun with Marik, his best friend, high on the bank above the Guadalquivir, shirts off, soaking in the heat, listening to the great, slow waves of the river, al-Kiran fantasized about being selected to dance.

They had just come from wrestling. Both were Arab, high born, and handsome, but unlike olive-skinned and raven haired Marik, al-Kiran was blond and blue eyed, a peculiarity made attractive by the fact that Caliph Hakam II was also blond and blue eyed, as had been the great Abd-er Rahman before him.

An outstanding athlete and scholar, al-Kiran was nevertheless shy and reserved. Recognizing his own lack of experience, particularly regarding politics and young women, he looked to his friend for advice. Whereas his father was a teaching mullah, a mystic by nature, Marik's father served Hakam II at the Royal Court.

Following the last All Faith's Festival, he and Marik had shared an excitement based on the belief in miracles. They had dreamed of great spiritual adventures. But when, three months ago, al-Kiran left the academy to study with the Alpha ben Hebaron, Marik had warned that the rabbi had links to a Sufi conspiracy and should be avoided. Since then, much to al-Kiran's disappointment, Marik had been reluctant to discuss the mysteries which had sustained them and should now, he believed, form the platform for their spiritual quests.

While they watched royal barges, loaded with silks and spices from the Orient, moving steadily toward the Roman bridge connecting the central city to the palace on the other shore, he attempted to relate some of the details of the rabbi's lecture that morning, leading up to his interpretation of the prophecy. But Marik turned away, disinterested.

As the indigo sail of a royal pleasure-boat approached the caravan of barges then disappeared through the arches beneath the bridge, al-Kiran told himself he would never accept Marik's fear that things were about to change for the worse. A devout Moslem, he believed in the future and in the miracle of the rainbow bridge.

"Okay," Marik rolled grudgingly onto his side, "tell me what the rabbi said about the prophecy."

The sun sparkled in al-Kiran's eyes. During the years since he had witnessed the long dance, he had queried his parents without much response; but Alpha ben Hebaron had been explicit. Leaning forward, excited, he began: "According to my teacher, a school of dervish mystics had arranged . . ."

"Dervishes?" Marik interrupted, upset. "I've warned you about ben Hebaron. He's teaching false doctrine. There were no Sufis until long after the Prophet's death."

"According to him," al-Kiran paused, well aware of the doctrinal conflict but surprised by Marik's reaction, "there have always been Sufis."

"They're heretics, Kemi," Marik responded, using his friend's nickname, then rolled back and gazed at the sky. Al-Kiran leaned forward after him.

"Heretics in Baghdad are not heretics in Cordoba."

"Not under Hakam II, but if 'al-Mansur' has his way . . ."

"The Victorious," al-Kiran, startled by Marik's tone, translated the name, knowing he was referring to one of the Caliph's advisers. He assumed Marik's attitude and concern came from his father's knowledge of the Court.

"Why do you flinch?" Marik turned back to him. "You know the fundamentalists are gaining power."

"Cordoba is based on tolerance," al-Kiran asserted.

"Things are changing." Marik spit to the side.

River sounds floated up toward them. Drawing back, al-Kiran reminded himself Marik was an alarmist. His own parents had encouraged him to explore Sufism and study with the rabbi. His mother's mother was an initiate of an esoteric sect, although he didn't know, or even want to know, the details.

Tentatively, al-Kiran said: "Don't you even want to hear what he's teaching?"

"If it's just between us," Marik conceded.

"Aren't you at least curious about the secret school founded in Medina following the Prophet's last vision?" al-Kiran tried to incite the old interest.

"Did the Prophet dance?" Marik grumbled.

"No. He was over sixty years old by then. Two of his grandchildren, a young girl and boy, were the dancers."

"Just two dancers?" Marik seemed surprised then picked up a stone and tossed it. A group of soldiers strolled past and waved at them.

Once the soldiers were a safe distance away, al-Kiran whispered: "He had them dance for three days and nights, in a carefully arranged pattern."

"What did the Prophet do?" Marik responded, reluctantly.

"According to the Sufis?" al-Kiran tested.

"You know none of this is recognized by the traditional schools." Marik sat-up. "But . . . tell me."

Warming to the story, al-Kiran said: "The Prophet was with his grandchildren during the entire dance, focusing their energies. As they grew weary, he fed them from his own strength. During the final day, the sun was totally eclipsed.

"The Prophet watched the children dance as if in a dream.

As light returned, the children embraced him. All three collapsed. When the Blessed Messenger finally awoke, the children were stretched out next to him on the sand. Then he gave the prophecy recorded by Ali."

"'This is the morning. Next time it will be the day.'" Marik quoted the words as handed down from generation to generation, which were the basis for popular speculation and excitement before each Festival.

"When we were young," Marik leaned forward earnestly, "we believed. But now we know there have been over twenty Dances here in Cordoba and nothing extraordinary has happened. There's been no eclipse, no miracles. According to al-Mansur it's all a pagan long dance designed by Sufis to subvert the True Faith."

Hesitating slightly, then plunging ahead, al-Kiran quoted his teacher: "The actual words were: 'The morning has begun. Rainbows will flow from the dark.'"

"Forget it, Kemi." Marik frowned. "You'll only get in trouble believing such things.

Al-Kiran wanted to share the prophecy the rabbi had uttered, but was uncertain. Then, certain that he shouldn't, he repeated the words to himself, wondering at their meaning:

"When the moon eats the sun between
earth-base and stars, Venus, a white owl,
beckons to the black snake, Mars.
Spinning in violet rays, they
revolve through the violent sky.
Dancing on a rainbow bridge, they bear
dark-light while the old world dies."

CHAPTER TWO

"The Princess Slave"

Alpha ben Hebaron was lecturing on divine proportion and the building of the cosmic temple; but al-Kiran couldn't take his eyes off the new student. Black and mysterious, she was dressed in white robes, a laurel wreath about her forehead. Luxuriant hair, shining in sinuous plaits, each with a jeweled bauble at its end, danced about her shoulders. Her whole presence expressed a unique balance, grace and strength.

Hasdai ibn Shaprut, the Jewish adviser to the Caliph, had interrupted the lecture earlier to present her to the rabbi, explaining that the Royal Uncle had received her as a gift from the chief of the slave merchants. Ben Hebaron had, in turn, introduced her to the students as Kristien, Slave Princess of Nubia.

They were in the Rose Park, east of the madrasah near the central mosque, the students sitting on the grass beneath the trees, the master on the stone retaining wall which encircled the kerm oak. Normally al-Kiran would have been intent on every word; but this morning, since the Nubian's arrival, he couldn't concentrate.

"She's got them; that's for sure," Sa'id whispered confidentially, grinning, broad and square faced.

"Got what?" al-Kiran asked, puzzled then irritated. Sa'id, almost four years older than himself, generous and self-assured, had an easy way with girls which al-Kiran wished to emulate. But Sa'id's tone bothered him.

"The curves and symmetries our teacher refers to." Sa'id laughed quietly.

"Sacred geometry?" He gazed at Kristien. "She's got more than that, something I've never seen before."

At that moment, the rabbi stopped and stared at al-Kiran, then glanced at the Nubian. Pushing thick fingers beneath his cap, through granite-gray hair, short-cropped like his beard, his eyes the color of fire agate, he shifted topics: "Following the

19

Prophet's death, the 'faithful' swept out of the Arabian desert in a violent wave." Folding his hands behind his back, he circled the kerm oak. Of medium height, stocky but agile, tough and demanding, he was in his mid-fifties. At times, he seemed to be giving instructions for a military campaign but without letting his students know more than necessary to perform their part. Perhaps, al-Kiran speculated, he had been a military commander before appearing in Cordoba some twenty years earlier.

Nonetheless, the material was exhilarating and the rabbi friendly, in a gruff way. His sudden shifts, during lectures and discussions, disturbed but also fascinated al-Kiran. He was determined to apply himself until he was ready to confront the teacher with his questions.

Pacing through the group, now, he stopped next to al-Kiran and glanced up at a tall cypress, green against the bright blue of the sky. "Would that be a fair description?"

"Yes," al-Kiran responded, slightly off guard.

"Othman, of the ancient House of Omayyad, initially fought to preserve the sacred sites. In the early years he resisted the Blessed Messenger — is it not so?"

"Yes, master," he answered, stronger now.

As ben Hebaron turned away, al-Kiran glanced around the group. All, except the Nubian, had passed through the Cordovan academies, or similar systems, before seeking out the Jewish master. Each felt they would receive knowledge and technique beyond that available through any other teacher.

Including Sa'id and himself, four of the students were Arabs. Additionally, there were five Jews, three Celts, two Slavs, one Frank, one Italian, one Visigoth, and one native Iberian. The black princess slave was the first African. Females and males were equally represented.

Reflecting back to an earlier occasion on the river bank when he had mentioned the absence of Berbers and Yemenites to Marik, he remembered Marik staring at him a moment before saying: "They're descendants of the warriors who established Islam in al-Andalus. Don't you understand anything?" Offended, and not seeing the relevance, he had protested that ben Hebaron only required that the student "sincerely wants to learn. Nothing else matters!"

"It matters to them," Marik had declared, exasperated. "They're not about to pollute themselves with false doctrine."

"In order to save his own head," ben Hebaron's deep voice jolted al-Kiran back from his reflections, "Othman converted to Islam, bowing to the Messenger of Allah.

"Following the assassination of Umar, the six surviving companions of Mohammed appointed Othman supreme Caliph — Leader and Protector of the Faith.

"As the Islamic warriors spread across North Africa," he glanced at the Nubian princess, "Othman ruled from Medina, a good and devout man, seldom leaving except to visit the black stone, housed in the Ka'ba at Mecca, most sacred of Arab shrines, preserved and protected now within the new faith. Yet Othman's reign was plagued by conspiracy and unrest. Is it not always so?" Pausing, his gaze fell on one after another of his students. "Particularly in Iraq, the cry was raised that Ali, son-in-law of the Prophet, husband of Fatima, was the only rightful Leader of the Faithful."

He lowered his voice: "Ali, great be his memory, refused their overtures, but," beginning to pace, voice raised, "Aisha, widow of the Prophet, conspired with Bakr. In the eleventh year of Othman's reign, while he prayed in the mosque, the conspirators broke in upon him, demanding that he abdicate in favor of Ali. How did Othman respond?"

One of the Arab students, a beautiful young woman in her twenties, held up her hand. "That he could not put off the destiny which Allah had laid upon him."

"And what did the partisans do?" Disgust showed at the corners of his mouth. "They stoned him." A hush fell over the students.

"Yes . . ." ben Hebaron sighed, "in the mosque. But Ali intervened, forcing Aisha to flee to Mecca while, unconscious and covered with blood, Othman was carried to his home." World-weary, tugging his beard, he envisioned the scene. "When Othman revived, he called for the Koran and dropped into prayer. But Bakr waited outside the gates." Emphasizing each word, he backed up slowly. Watching him, al-Kiran sensed the rabbi was preparing a field in which he would eventually plant something — that the tensions between the sects, following Mohammed's death, had to be understood before real work could be done.

"Why would they attack Othman?" He pointed to al-Kiran.

"They did not understand the Prophet's message." He stood as he answered.

"Has it been understood, even in our day?"

"The Ulama understand," al-Kiran blurted out, feeling Kristien's eyes on him, wanting her to know that his father was revered as a teacher, even among the Ulama scholars — then regretted his statement.

"Do they always?" ben Hebaron asked gently.

Shaking his head, embarrassed, he re-seated himself. He had wanted to impress her with his answer, but the rabbi had caught him. She had smiled when he had risen. He had made a fool of himself.

"Who are the saints, Kemi?" ben Hebaron asked.

"Those who are vehicles of God . . ." he answered, tentatively.

Turning back to the group, ben Hebaron said: "Words are truth carriers or betrayers. Al-Kiran says that the Ulama are vehicles of God, and we understand. In another mouth, those words may carry a different message."

He paused while a group of students, led by another teacher, wove down a path, shaded and at ease in spite of the sun blazing in the distance above them. It was mid-morning.

Sitting and lowering his voice, ben Hebaron forced his students to listen carefully. "Bakr killed the guard left by Ali. Scaling the wall, he approached the royal family. Nailah, ancient and frail, threw herself between husband and assassin. Struggling to protect him, she lost three fingers. Her blood mixed with Othman's, the supreme Caliph, pooling in her lap, spilling from his noble throat."

Standing, he continued: "Othman's bloody shirt, with

Nailah's three fingers, was hung above the blood-stained Koran in the mosque in Damascus. The Omayyad loyalists rose up in horror. Wouldn't we also rise? Walking to the fountain spewing water across tiers of granite into a pool, beneath the surface of which golden carp circled, he tossed a stone, throwing the surface into turmoil. The point of impact spread in widening circles. "Doesn't disaster fall like a stone from heaven into our midst?" Arms crossed over his chest, he waited for an answer.

"We must prepare," the Nubian stood, an unrippled flow upward, "for the unforeseen."

"It is so." A finger resting on his top lip, which was clean shaven, he returned to the kerm oak. "Ali took the sword to restore order. That spring, he led 50,000 Iraqis against the Syrian army. He became the fourth Caliph. Everyone, on both sides, fought in the name of the Most Blessed Messenger. What of the Ulama saints then?"

Sa'id stood to answer. "There was no Unity, master, therefore there were no Ulama."

"There were saints, rabbi." Kristien asserted, her voice sensual and husky. "The divine impulse, male and female, split or integrated, flows through the veins of all who dedicate themselves as vehicles of the one God."

"Were there saints on both sides then? Devoted to the theology of Holy War — spilling each other's blood?" Ben Hebaron addressed the Nubian.

"The light incarnate, master, is a rainbow split from darkness. There were saints on both sides."

"But they were half-saints or less, surely," Sa'id commented, seating himself. The Nubian smiled and raised her hands, locking them above her, palms upward, stretching her svelte body beneath silk, a dancer ready to spin, gold and silver bracelets sliding earthward along her black, glistening arms, in the dapple of sun beneath the trees.

"Half-saints or less?" ben Hebaron asked, echoing Sa'id.

"Full saints, master." Kristien spun, bringing her arms down parallel with her shoulders, shocking al-Kiran by her casualness, a playfulness uncommon in their group, her lips sparkling.

"Foolish saints, or so they are called in the desert, among my people — Fools for God."

No one else played with the rabbi, offering puns, skewing the seriousness of the lectures. Al-Kiran felt that he should be apprehensive, or embarrassed; but he was fascinated. He could not take his eyes from her as she re-seated herself and the rabbi turned back to his subject.

"According to the Shi'ites, Ali guards the Gates of Heaven. The mightiest of the companions of Allah, Ali stands above Mohammed, the Messenger, and Jesus, the Savior.

"Who among us would challenge the Shi'ite doctrine?"

A Jewish girl, an advanced student, answered: "To challenge a doctrine, teacher, one must fully understand it."

Ben Hebaron leaned forward, cupped a hand-full of red dust and tossed it into the light streaming from an opening in the leaves, watching the spray dissipate. "Like history, blood spreads in the air." He slapped his hands clean. "Dark and light dance together." Then, as if reciting from one of the books of the official scribes, he went on:

"Ali died five years later. The descendants of Othman regained the throne, moving their capital from Medina to Damascus, tolerating diversity and enjoying the flesh as well as scripture, ruling for 189 years, until al-Saffah, 'the blood-spiller,' of the House of Abba, raised the black flag, invited the Omayyad princes to the feast at Jaffa, and slaughtered them all, save only blond and blue eyed Abd-er Rahman I, the only surviving heir of the House of Omayyad. His descendants rule in Cordoba, city of rainbows, thanks be to Allah." Ben Hebaron paused, surveying his students. "Do what you must to preserve his line." Turning away, he signaled that the lesson, for the day, was over.

"What was that all about?" Sa'id asked. They were following a group of students toward the plaza.

"The shift from geometry to history?" al-Kiran responded, thinking he wanted to find Marik and introduce him to Sa'id. He hoped that by listening to their conversations he might better understand the political currents beneath the rabbi's references. He was confused and uneasy.

"It related to the Nubian princess," the older boy commented while choosing an orange from a merchant's cart.

"You can't be serious."

"Can't I?" Sa'id grinned. "Think about it."

Seeing Kristien in his mind, al-Kiran said: "She's beautiful, isn't she?"

"The Nubian? She's magnificent, but she's for the Royal Uncle." Smiling, as if he guessed how taken his young friend was with the black princess, he turned toward an Arab whose almond eyes, framed in a white scarf, lingered suggestively in his direction, and followed her back into the park.

Al-Kiran walked further into the bazaar, his hunger stimulated by black and shiny dried dates, plums lavender and moist in the sun, tart red blood-berries, earth-brown walnuts, roasted acorns, orange and golden spices piled tantalizingly in aromatic swirls on long tables, past fruit stalls beneath canopies, merchants busy as Cordovan shoppers jostled each other, all races friendly and at ease, pleased with the abundance, selecting their favorite goods for the home pantries and snacking while gossiping about the latest news.

He pushed forward, pondering what Sa'id had meant in regard to the rabbi's sudden shift to history and politics. It had occurred shortly after the Nubian was introduced.

He had hoped Sa'id and Marik would become friendly. With either alone he was often too tentative to ask questions which nagged at the edge of his consciousness, unformulated but urgent. He wanted to listen and gain knowledge without revealing the depths of his ignorance.

But he knew Sa'id might not be comfortable with Marik, who criticized the "esoteric group" and claimed it was dangerous to even associate with the rabbi.

Ben Hebaron had never directly prohibited discussions of his lectures with outsiders; but he had cautioned them about the teachings which were being unfolded a piece at a time. He had said: "The parts reflect the whole for the initiated, but may mislead those who are outside our path. The key, students, is in silence."

Wandering ahead, puzzling over the connection between words as carriers of meaning, and the rainbow warriors or — he stopped himself in mid-thought, uncertain what had been said. Had the Nubian referred to wars fought by foolish saints or saints for God? Pulling himself up onto the wall, he rehearsed the rabbi's lecture, looking for strands crossing what had seemed to be the main points.

In an earlier lecture, ben Hebaron had explained that the descendants of Abd-er Rahman ruled al-Andalus "with an open palm." Moslems, Jews, Christians, and sects more ancient than the three Religions of the Book, mingled easily in the bazaar, across the plaza, throughout the city. Al-Kiran felt secure among the Cordovans. The fertile plains supported them all. The sun-swept skies shined for everyone.

Nevertheless, something was wrong. He was adept at astronomy, math, and music, wrestled well, and excelled at swordsmanship, foot and horse racing. An aristocrat with the blue eyes and blond hair which marked the Omayyad bloodline, the world should be his for the taking — yet he often asked himself questions which he couldn't answer. At times he feared that the answers would reveal nothing but wars, and slaughter, and blood-letting.

When they were young, al-Kiran and Marik used to lie with the girls, nearly naked, along the banks of the Guadalquivir, their bodies hardened in the sun, uninhibited, happy, curious, and full of adventure. Now they played with veils, silk scarves accentuating eyes, suggesting beauties which might be revealed in moonlit gardens to the right suitor — yet these girls, young women now, frightened him. He wanted to know hidden curves, softening hips and thighs, breasts — but dared not approach. Something awaited him in a future he could not see.

New mysteries surrounded him, exciting yet disconcerting. In his dreams he caught glimpses of another world, or of a time he couldn't remember, or, perhaps, of a future which approached from a sanctuary on the east of a hill while he waited on the west, still in shadow. Stopping at a brazier, he bought a lamb-kabob, basted in mint and honey, then meandered through the streets, absorbed in his thoughts. As he approached his family's villa, the muezzin called for prayer. Licking the last juice from the wood skewer, then tossing it aside, he hurried through the gate and waved to his mother.

Entering his room, he spread his prayer rug, sprinkled water, and faced Mecca, his heart open in the anticipation of union with the highest good, submission to the will of Allah, the presence everywhere around him of millions of the faithful, all equal in the sight of God, reconstructing together, just after dawn, then shortly before mid-day, during late afternoon, immediately after sunset, then again following nightfall, the bridge of their faith built on the message of Mohammed, Prophet of Islam:

la ilah illa 'llah wa Muhammad rasul Allah —
There is only one God and Mohammed is the Messenger.
Nur Muhammad, the Muhammad of Light.

Reoriented and peaceful, he folded his legs under himself and practiced, as the rabbi had suggested, letting the thoughts and images slide across his inner vision. The sounds outside his window grew distant. In memory, he watched while his mother worked with her huge broom.

"What are you doing?" he heard himself ask.

"Pushing the phantoms from the corners and out into the garden." She moved like a young woman, black hair shining to her waist over a blue silk tunic. "The sun changes sour memories to pure nectar, sweet promise."

Turning suddenly, she patted his head. "Transubstantiate the monsters. That's what the Christians say."

"What do the Christian's know?" he asked, petulantly.

"Spiritus Mundi." She made a playful sweep at him with the broom. "The Christians don't know what they know."

"You confuse me, Mother," he heard himself complain.

"No, son." She looked at him severely. "I knock cobwebs from your head." He fell asleep as she faded.

Rising an hour later, he remembered a dream in which he had been wrestling in the heat, unable to get a hold on his opponent. He was still bothered by the shift in the rabbi's lecture that morning. It was like the time when, in the middle of an eloquent discourse on astronomy, ben Hebaron had suddenly, without transition or explanation, recited several poems about love-making and wine-drinking.

Afterwards, while the group was dispersing, he had asked the rabbi why he had not finished his lecture. His teacher had replied: "I did. Understand the poems. Understand the lecture."

Frustrated, he had told himself: "The stars move in steady courses because they are guided by a steady hand. Thus does Gabriel, through the Prophet, prohibit excess."

But at home his parents often recited Sufi poetry full of sexual allusions, images of wine-drinking and spiritual energies suffusing the physical body, the types of poems frowned on by the Ulama.

Brushing his hair, he repeated what he had said to himself that day: "The Sufis, having heard the Holy Koran, are true Moslems now. The Ulama, in condemning them, miss the message behind the verse." But he was still bothered.

Re-rolling his prayer rug, he wondered whether he might find Marik and discuss ben Hebaron's abrupt change, this morning, from sacred geometry to the fire and blood of early Moslem history. He couldn't understand why the rabbi had tolerated the Nubian's impertinence when she answered, like a dancing girl, his question regarding saints and war.

Shaking his head, he gazed into the basin. Watching his features spread, he felt the world he had known was swirling away. The steady practice of the five pillars of Islam — beyond question prior to his studies with Alpha ben Hebaron — was being cast in a different and unsteady light.

"Allah is more interested in souls than religion," he quoted his father, searching for a bridge from what he had known to what was apparently now expected of him, but immediately lost the thread.

"The Koran is the vehicle of the eternal, the message toward which all faiths struggle," he reminded himself. "Through submission to the divine will, we devote our lives to universal peace.

Why then," he puzzled, "does he allow me to study with a rabbi who challenges the foundation of Islam?"

Not finding anyone else in the house, a chill ran up his spine. He thought of Orwan Kamir Oshiwah, his mother's mother. This had been her home, before she entered a secret order north of the Pyrenees. Her influence was unspoken but ever-present, particularly in the labyrinth in their garden.

Glancing from the patio over the links of bright green hedge lining walkways, fountains, and rock gardens, reflected and heightened by vines and baskets hung against the patterns worked into the stones of the outer fence — he saw Alansha, soft and black, her old wrinkles like folds of warm night, working with his mother among the red and yellow flowers.

Cook and family member now, Alansha had come from Sudan to be his nurse. Her songs had been his introduction to the world of spirit, long before he could understand the words. Coming closer he could hear his mother humming, Alansha responding in counterpoint. Laughing contentedly, their work a natural rhythm, they didn't seem to notice him.

Looking at the labyrinth, he wondered about a secret connection between the Sufi Moslems and ben Hebaron, a Jew. When he had asked, his mother had said: "The important thing is to study with the best teachers. The fruit can not fall far from the tree. The truth to be discovered by Moslems, Christians and Jews — must ultimately be the same."

Unsatisfied, he had responded: "But couldn't I be misled by a false teacher?"

"If your fire is tended well, my son," Abu el-Ali had interjected, "the light will reveal the errors."

Shrugging at his thoughts, he waved to the women.

"Be back for supper," Alansha called after him.

Making his way between the white walls of the courtyards, he kept returning to the moment when the slave-princess had been presented to the group by Hasdai ibn Shaprut, physician to the Caliph, political if not religious leader of the powerful Jewish community in al-Andalus.

His mother said that the slaves in Cordoba are better educated than the judges in most of the world. That would be true for this slave, he thought while hurrying through the food market, the crowd thinner now, some merchants having already closed their stalls and gone home for the evening.

Entering the plaza where Marik often loitered watching the girls and engaging in mock arguments, he waved to his friend then joined him to walk toward the river, determined to relate his experiences and ask about the Nubian princess and the circumstances of her introduction to Alpha ben Hebaron.

True to his knowledge of the city and the affairs of the Palace, Marik said she had been captured by corsairs and then traded to a local merchant. "Apparently she is the daughter of a Sudanese King and a Nubian high priestess. The merchant made a gift of her to the Royal Uncle, who is well pleased.

"I hear she is unusually beautiful." Marik leaned back, hands behind his head, and stared into the sky from their favorite perch above the Guadalquivir.

"Is she to be a wife?" al-Kiran asked, self-consciously.

Glancing at him, a blade of long grass between his teeth, Marik said: "The Uncle offered her whatever education she might choose among the Cordovan masters."

"How do you suppose ibn Shaprut got involved?"

"What happens without his advice?" Marik responded with a question, implying by his tone that he didn't quite approve. Al-Kiran didn't answer.

"She might return to the Uncle's harem, but there are other possibilities." He paused. "She could be granted her freedom. But more likely she'll be married to one of the Nephews who guard the border. An allegiance with the Sudanese King would be helpful. Why don't you ask her?"

"I couldn't do that."

"Why not?" He teased. "She's in the class, isn't she?"

Al-Kiran hoped Kristien would be released from the harem. He fantasized that he and she might one day become friends and more — but he didn't dare admit that to Marik.

Lapsing into silence, they followed their own thoughts while the day drifted toward evening.

CHAPTER THREE

"THE PROMISE OF THE DANCE"

It was the day following spring equinox. Al-Kiran gazed toward Kristien. During the month since her arrival, he had grown increasingly attracted to and fascinated by her.

Aware that Alpha ben Hebaron was weaving some thread through his history of various sects competing for dominance within Islam, he tried to concentrate, but his eyes were filled with the Nubian Princess.

Abruptly dismissing the students, the rabbi indicated al-Kiran should walk with him toward the synagogue.

"'Kemi' — 'little black bird' — a fitting name, isn't it?" Ben Hebaron drew him closer while crossing a sun circle which broke through the high trees.

"Yes, master." He glanced up nervously. He considered his teacher to be fairly severe and extremely concentrated. Even though he feigned casualness or humor, he scanned each passer-by, referring information back to an inner catalogue.

His arm, lying across al-Kiran's shoulders, was strong and muscled, not at all the soft bulk of a scholar. His short, cropped beard was steel gray, like the swords of Damascus, with black flecks matching his eyes.

They had walked some five minutes when, halting at the gate to the central plaza, he moved out of the traffic. "Kirian," he used the family name, "you are to compete to be among the final eighteen in the great dance."

His heart leapt skyward but, outwardly, al-Kiran caught his excitement, thinking already of the control which would be required, dedicating himself immediately to the task.

"We begin tomorrow," he added after a slight pause. "Kristien will practice with you — as your partner."

Lowering his head, his mind whirling, al-Kiran muttered: "I will do my best to represent your school."

Ben Hebaron laughed, a happy roar rumbling up from his belly, legs apart and squared, then raised al-Kiran's face to his own, two strong thumbs under his chin. "You will do well, Kemi," he whispered, then turned and crossed through the gate.

Racing back through the park hoping to find Kristien, pounding through the trees and along the trails, his heart flying ahead of him, he remembered that he had seen ben Hebaron take her to the side during a break in his lecture.

She had seemed momentarily pleased, had even glanced at him but — he slowed to a walk — had rejoined the group without further acknowledgment of himself. Then the rabbi had begun a discussion of something wholly beside the point.

"She'll speak to me," he told himself. "We'll plan together. If we're chosen, we'll dance for three days, weaving about the plaza, moving toward ecstatic flight."

But, when he rounded a turn in the path and spotted her standing alone near a fountain, he immediately lost his resolve. She turned and acknowledged him in a friendly though diffident manner — offering no more than a slave in the Royal Uncle's household would owe to the son of Abu el-Ali, respected mullah and kin to Hakam II.

"Hello, Kristien," he managed to say as if he just happened to be walking through the park.

"Hello." The pool swirled at the foot of the fountain, just like his heart was swirling.

"It's a beautiful day, isn't it?" he added awkwardly.

"Indeed." She lowered her eyes.

"I'll see you tomorrow?" He took a few steps to pass by.

"I look forward to the master's lessons," she responded without looking up.

Al-Kiran walked on. Kristien had made no reference to the Dance of Created Lights. Or had she? Had she not at least referred to the lessons in the context of seeing him?

A safe distance away, he left the path. Crouching against a tree, forcing his mind back toward the master's lecture, he tried to remember what had been said; but his consciousness filled with images of the dance, his heart repeating the chase toward

Kristien in the park, with the news, then pulling back, uncertain and afraid.

Yet, even now he could see her, as he had while the rabbi had declaimed the lineages of the sects vying for control of Islam. She had been sitting at the other side of the group, back straight, her gown, opened in the front from her neck, folding gently across her breasts, her attention on the rabbi. A silk scarf, draped over her shoulders, rested beneath the dangle of braids, the tip of each a jewel.

The birds hovered like angels in the high branches above him. Suddenly he felt as if he were in the great mosque, amidst the forest of stone pillars which supported the separate domes, within which the faithful dedicated themselves to Islam while celebrating the most sacred space in Cordoba.

He started jogging, breaking into a slow run, then sprint, weaving in and out through shade and sun tunnels, moving deeper and deeper into the park, hearing great, invisible birds flying above him. Heart pumping, a new dimension seemed to shift into place. He could feel it in his legs and feet pounding and lifting from the ground, leaping forward, carrying him into the air. It was as if he had never been fully within himself before, solid and yet filled with light, as if this was what his body was built for.

He had not consciously dared to believe that, of the thousands who aspired to the dance, he might be selected. Yet he had glimpsed it around the edges of his dreams ever since the last All Faiths Festival, when his father had hoisted him on his shoulders and he had breathed in and out with the rhythm of the great dance.

The final selection would be made at summer solstice, less than three months away. The eighteen remaining dancers would be paired for the final six months of training. He wanted to believe that he and Kristien would be chosen.

The great dance would reach its climax at noon on winter solstice. Ben Hebaron had predicted that there would be a solar eclipse. "At that moment two of the dancers will fly."

Slowing to a walk, he turned back toward the plaza, anxious to find Marik or Sa'id. He thought about the astrological and prophetic context of the All Faiths Festival. During that lecture the rabbi had said that Kabbalah and astrology were necessary stages but that, incident to the Dance of Created Lights, intellectual skills would fall away and an entirely different consciousness would take over.

"Yet to reach the level where the disciplines can be dropped, we must pass through them. You have completed the traditional courses, thanks to the academies of Hakam II. Let those disciplines drop away. We approach the next stage. Eventually you will drop my teachings as well."

Walking into a market, passing colorful booths and tents billowing in the late morning breeze, the sun nearing mid-day, merchants hawking their wares, competing for his attention, he thought back to the day Kristien had been introduced by the Caliph's physician. Lost in thought, he turned toward home. "Ben Hebaron referred to my mother's line and to the black bird." Suddenly feeling unprepared, al-Kiran paused near a neighborhood mosque. Returning to the day Kristien had first joined the class, he remembered that after summarizing the slaughter of the princes at Jaffa, and Abd-er Rahman's escape, ben Hebaron had said:

"'From this gentle prince the present Caliph comes to power. This will be the year when the birds fly.' But," al-Kiran puzzled to himself, "he also encouraged us to question his history of the warrior saints of Islam. Why?"

He had wanted to ask whether the reference to birds flying related to the Dance of Created Lights, but had been too shy and distracted. He recalled a description of the movements of geese in the far north, and a statement that "the coming regime will be connected with a sky religion, which will eventually, even if only for a day, displace the fundamentalists in Baghdad — opening a hole in the sky."

Al-Kiran realized that most scholars maintained that no actual eclipse had occurred during the Dance of Created Lights, although the celebrants could, in the course of the ritual, experience an internal transformation. Nevertheless, ben Hebaron had suggested that this year the objective event would occur.

Taking a stick which had fallen from one of the cypress trees, he poked at the dust. When the muezzins called from the minarets, he made a circle around the bird in flight, which he had traced on the ground, then hurried off to his prayers. His heart aching, he swore that, if selected, he would experience the flight prophesied by the blessed Mohammed.

Mershi Kamir and Abu el-Ali seemed pleased when al-Kiran announced the news that he would be competing for selection for the dance — but they didn't say much. Alansha, who was in the kitchen with them, clapped her hands and beamed, but said nothing. He assumed they didn't want him to be disappointed if he wasn't within the final group of dancers.

The next day, ben Hebaron told the group that al-Kiran and Kristien would be working with him to learn certain skills related to the dance. Kristien glanced at him, but hurried away after the announcement.

That afternoon he began teaching al-Kiran movements related to the inner organs, breathing, and the phases of the moon. Instructing him to envision certain stops, then jumps while moving his arms and head, his legs and torso, in patterns identified in the Kabbalah, he explained that the sacred alphabet represents patterns brought out of the desert by the ancestors of the tent-dwelling Semite nomads, Arab and Jewish: "At the beginning of time, after the first day — after the God's work was done."

Al-Kiran remembered a statement to the entire group that morning, which had seemed out of sequence with the rest of the lecture: "Jews and Arabs are blood kin, originally followers of the mother ways, led by the moon, working the sheep, goats and wild asses, unable to endure the blazing sun and heat of the first days."

The rabbi had paused, studying each student, then added: "Throughout most of the world, the voice which sustains us has been divided into derivative alphabets, torn fragments of a lost language, each tribe coveting its own recollection."

In response to a suggestion during an earlier lecture, al-Kiran had borrowed his father's books on ancient alphabets and

Kabbalah. At first it had made no sense, though his parents had encouraged him, even suggesting certain other books of which they were particularly fond.

Now, however, while he practiced the movements in the hot sun and ben Hebaron seemed to doze in the shade of the kerm oak, he was thinking about the patterns in those books and the flight of birds. He felt that at some time in the future what he had heard in the lectures might fall into place — that the postures carried something of the "lost language."

"The Nubian may join us tomorrow." Ben Hebaron rolled onto his elbow to watch. "Turn left, Kemi. Now, right," he instructed. "Hands out and up, that's it." Then he lay back again, leaving him to his practice.

He wondered whether ben Hebaron realized that his heart had almost leaped out of his chest at the mention of the black princess. He hoped that she would come, even though the prospect frightened him. But when they met again, she did not appear and the teacher made no further mention of her.

As the private lessons progressed, however, he came to accept that although he and Kristien were both competing to be among the eighteen dancers selected at the summer solstice, they were receiving separate instruction. He saw her each morning in the park, but she paid him no particular attention except for casual salutations and, occasionally, what he felt, or hoped, were more intimate glances.

One afternoon, following a particularly difficult movement, ben Hebaron pointed at the Fountain of Ur and said: "Look through the waters to the energies upon which they ride." Then added: "Kabbalah is the tradition that in our bodies the sacred parts remain intact. Our bodies know this and are capable of reassembling the pieces which our minds have scattered. Our purpose, through the dance, is to express the true roots, to reassemble the original language."

"At times," al-Kiran responded, "I do feel . . ."

He broke off, his attention moving from the patterns in the water to the crows-feet wrinkles at the corners of his master's eyes, tying the tight gray and black bristle of his beard across skin leathered by the sun to dark pools peering out from a deeper space.

"Certain formations," he searched for the right words. "Just as I'm doing a move, I feel it . . . but then I can't remember what the feeling was."

"Hold the postures, move with care." Ben Hebaron slid his hand into the water. As the sun glanced off the surface and the pool swirled in widening circles, the hand and wrist seemed to glide off at an angle.

"Hold your mind suspended — then give it up," he added, each word clipped. "The magic is not in the surface, though you must pass through that. Do the exercises, align your vision, your breath, then release.

"As the worlds break apart, the light will find you. The Magdalen of Isis will spin between you and your self. At that moment, let go. Don't let your mind impede your body. Learn to ride that which flies."

"The Magdalen of Isis will spin between me and my self?" He pondered each word while walking home that evening. Crows flapped noisily in the pale branches of the olive trees separating his route from the royal gardens beyond which the Guadalquivir wound deeper into the city.

He had been to the wrestling arena, hoping to find Marik but, as had been the case each day since the rabbi had told him that he was to prepare for the dance, Marik had been too busy to come to the river where they could have lain back, gazing at the river, giving him time to unroll his feelings and speculate.

He was distressed by the distance which had arisen between himself and Marik, as well as Sa'id. They were the only friends with whom he might attempt to piece together the instructions given in the afternoon sessions.

When he had approached Sa'id following the group lesson that morning, the older boy had seemed friendly. But as they had entered the market afterwards, and he had mentioned he wanted to talk about the dance, Sa'id had responded: "That is your assignment. I have my own."

"What is that?" he had asked, eager for discussion.

"To keep my mouth shut and my eyes open." Sa'id had grinned affectionately, then boxed his ears. "What you're learning is between you and him."

"The rabbi told you that?" He had been shocked.

Ignoring his question, Sa'id had shrugged noncommittally, then, pointing to a girl, left him alone.

"The Magdalen of Isis must be Kristien," he reasoned, dismissing his thoughts about Sa'id. Marik had told him that the Nubian slave princess was the daughter of, or was herself, a high priestess of the cult of the Black Goddess. He considered asking his father whether there was a connection between the black Madonna, identified with the mother of the Christian savior, and the Magdalen of Isis.

As a part of his duties to the Caliph, Marik's father had made a study of the African cults and their potential impact on the Islamic world. But Marik had seemed uncomfortable with such discussions and had told him to distance himself from the teachings of the Rabbi Alpha ben Hebaron.

When he had insisted that he had his parents' full support, relying on his father's reputation as a scholar and priest, Marik had said: "Your father can't always protect you." Afterwards, however, they had grappled, rolling on the ground, the warning forgotten while they enjoyed matching strength and balance against each other.

"If Kristien is connected to the Black Goddess, and She to the Magdalen, then," he moved into the alleyway winding up toward the Kirian villa, "the rabbi must be referring to my dance with her."

Rounding the last sentinel, he turned through the gate to his mother's greeting: "Ben Hebaron was here. He predicts you will do well." Mershi Kamir pulled him to herself. "Through you, may the Vision at Medina come to all people of good heart and strong will."

Reluctantly breaking her embrace, he stepped back to look into her eyes. "But I don't know what any of this means."

"Have faith in your teacher," she responded quietly.

After the evening meal, al-Kiran sat cross-legged on the floor in the central room. He was thinking of the Chaldee letters while watching the moon move beyond the window, a bright sickle, a cup for water in the heavens. Ben Hebaron had called it "a memory of the tribes." He was pleased when his father suggested they walk together.

The faint yellow glow from the lantern, hung from trellises filled with plants and vines, glanced off the rosary which Abu el-Ali worked, telling the stones, each "a prayer, a memory, and a promise," as they walked into the Kirian gardens.

"Your mother told me of the rabbi's prediction." Abu el-Ali paused. "Through you, may we all experience the miracle which Mohammed, Blessed Be His Name, saw for his people. May we be worthy of the trials which lie in our paths."

Al-Kiran looked up to his father, tall and solid, revered throughout Cordoba. "If I am able," he lowered his eyes, "it is due to your guidance."

They walked toward the rose bush which had been brought from Mecca and planted near the entryway to the labyrinth which defined, within its turns, the pattern of their family seal.

Servants maintained the grounds, but Abu el-Ali and Mershi Kamir, with al-Kiran's help in recent years, were the only ones who worked within the juniper-hedge maze his grandmother had established long before his birth. Unless one knew the pattern of the interior gates, even having reached the center, he would have gotten there by chance without understanding the embedded figure which, his parents had explained, was the key to the labyrinth.

The bells of the Christian church rang in the distance. Light shimmered across the pools beneath the winged fountains which framed the entryway. Streams meandered toward the fruit, nut, and olive orchards along the back wall, some fifty yards beyond the maze which, like an anchor, held the center of the gardens.

Pausing, with a hand movement, Abu el-Ali indicated they should enter the maze.

The hedge, stretching upward from the mineral rich clay,

smelled solid and dark-green. At each step, the mat of dry needles sliding beneath his feet, al-Kiaran felt he was passing through a narrow channel carved deep into the earth.

When he was younger, he had imagined entire armies lost within the maze. Tonight it seemed that something real and dangerous might lie beyond the next turn.

Shuddering slightly, he asked: "What trials, father?"

Long fingers wrapped over al-Kiran's shoulder, Abu el-Ali directed his son through the gate, crossed to the other side, then faced the portal to their left before speaking:

"Does the kemi on the ledge have the heart for the flight?" He pointed into the next passageway.

Startled, al-Kiran recognized the line from a popular folk-tale, but saw it in the context of ben Hebaron's prophecy.

As they crossed back to the first gate and retraced their steps to the point behind the entryway, Abu el-Ali matched his words to his steps: "Encircled by rays of hope and fear, finally we leap onto the bridge rising from the Ka'ba."

The sky dark except for needles of light, they moved in silence along an equilateral triangle which overlay the six other passageways, then entered the clearing in the center.

The next afternoon, after an hour of strenuous exercises, ben Hebaron stopped him with a question: "Have you studied the eight paths of the splendid rays which cross the world tree?"

"Yes, teacher," he answered, pleased with himself for having gone beyond the references and explanations the rabbi had given to the group. "My father has shown me the system preserved by the Faithful Brethren of Basra."

Ben Hebaron nodded approvingly, then added: "Each day, as you prepare for the dance, walk the pathways within the labyrinth which you have walked since you were a child."

"The maze in our garden?" al-Kiran asked, stunned, having assumed that the labyrinth was a family secret.

"In the garden, and in your body. Walk those patterns which your parents have taught you, but rise up at the same time so that you see yourself from above."

"How can I do that?" He took a drink from the flagon.

"Start in imagination." Ben Hebaron fixed his gaze, holding his attention. "With practice, the technique becomes a vehicle. Hover above yourself as you move forward. Look down. See the pattern within which you move. See your self within a nine-pointed star which is the emblem of your blood." Al-Kiran froze, a shudder moving up his spine.

"The Kirian line preserves one of the patterns associated with the energies of the dance. Study it well. Follow it from your self into your self — into the sky."

He wanted to ask his parents to what extent the rabbi shared their knowledge of the Kirian seal. But he decided to wait until he gained a better understanding of the labyrinth through the technique his master had prescribed. He spent as much time as possible walking and meditating within the maze, paying attention to the energies which accompanied him while he walked the corridors, particularly at the gates where he crossed the inner paths leading to the center.

He felt as if a memory were being awakened, a knowledge and certainty which he couldn't describe in words but which seemed to grow within his body. One afternoon while tracing the corridors, he remembered his mother had referred to the pattern of approach to the center as "The Memory of Home."

During the hurry of his days, his mind teased him into spasms of excitement and dejection, exaltation and fear: "Will we be selected by the Caliph? Will there be a physical eclipse? Can we endure it? Will the new day come?'

One morning, exactly one week before summer solstice, he woke with a start. Scrambling to focus, he realized he had been frightened by a dream, a fragment of which still hovered within his room, then fled through the window. Rising quickly, he chanted stanzas from the Koran. Walking through the hallways, then crossing to the garden, his heart settled into an excited determination.

The first suggestion of dawn creating shadows around him, he moved to the center of the Kirian seal. Alone, holding his posture, watching his body, his breath flowing in and out in waves, conscious of the pattern in the labyrinth, seeing it from above, he heard a strange and distant music rising toward him from within his body.

The nine-pointed star, traced through the channels he had followed in entering the clearing, defined a boundary in the center of which his body resonated between earth and heaven allowing new and different energies to enter.

As the world spread with light, muezzins called to the faithful from minarets throughout the city:

"Arise, prayer is better than sleep.
Arise, there is no God but Allah,
And Mohammed is his Messenger."

Al-Kiran hovered above himself. Hundreds of thousands of the Faithful, Devotees of the Divine Messenger, inhaled together — a unified body within the faith, ready to form, through prayer and prostration, a bridge to Mecca and beyond.

Falling back into himself with a jolt, almost tumbling to the side, he breathed in, stretched, and re-oriented. Excited by the energies and purposes he had glimpsed, he hurried back through the maze, across the garden, and into the kitchen.

Alansha and his mother stood together, nodding in his direction. Taking his rug, he joined his father in the prayer alcove, facing the rays of clear sun streaming through the window. Together they entered the rhythms of prayer, celebrating the unity of the faithful, devoted to the vision of Islam realized upon earth:

"la ilaha illa-llah
There is no reality apart from the Ultimate.
la ilaha illa-llah Muhammadun rasulu-llah
Divine Unity alone exists, eternally
revealing the drama of Love."

Repeating the refrains of the sacred prayer, timed to their

prostrations, aware of the radiance of the morning sun, al-Kiran envisioned the bridge by which the splendor of the divine infuses the world.

Nodding to the angel on his shoulder, a representative of Gabriel who had delivered the scripture, Abu el-Ali rose and went to the table upon which the Koran was displayed, saying: "I've found a passage which may interest you."

Savoring the peace following prayers, al-Kiran smiled. A passage, "which may interest you," when pointed out by his father, would be of great interest. Abu el-Ali's voice filled the room:

> "'While chanting the affirmation illa-llah,
> the dervish gazes inwardly toward the true Ka'ba,
> the most precious Human Heart,
> whose secret is Muhammadun rasulu-llah.
> The heart of tender emotion
> contains the royal garden.
> Tracing the essence of awareness there
> among radiant flowers, resonant fountains,
> the dervish comes to the sublime spiritual Heart,
> the translucent emerald palace of the King.'"

He paused before adding:

> "'Waves of Love in the Stormy Ocean of Love
> break in ecstasy against the Throne of Allah.'"

Listening to the stanzas, al-Kiran's heart pounded as if physically assaulted. Yet, at the same time, the images rising with the Messenger's vision, calmed and reassured him.

Walking together to the kitchen, where his mother and Alansha were busy preparing the morning meal, he slowed and, when his father turned back to him, said:

"There are eight worlds through which the dervish passes?

"Yes," Abu el-Ali affirmed.

"And the Prophet, Blessed Be His Name, rode the white mule through the heavens?"

"Your question, son?"

"But the Kirian seal, father . . ." he paused, "is an enneagram — nine-pointed. The rabbi links it to the Kabbalah and the eight stations which cross the tree of life."

Abu el-Ali searched his face, then smiled. "The Prophet, Glorious and Sublime, Messenger of Allah, speaks of further heavens to be discovered when the dervish swirls beyond those of his earlier disciplines."

CHAPTER FOUR

"THE SUMMER SOLSTICE"

Al-Kiran hardly slept the night before the summer solstice. His mind was full of the tangled imaginings. In a dream he saw Hakam II, Great Caliph of al-Andalus, leaving the Medinat al-Zahra on red carpets, then passing down through the olive and fig lanes to the banks of the Guadalquivir, along the highway beside the river, across the Roman bridge to the Alcazar of the Ancestors and the Great Mosque, to the central square where the aspirants waited.

He watched Hakam II select nine females, then eight males. Then as Alpha ben Hebaron's will stretched like a pathway between the monarch and himself, he was gazing into the Caliph's blue eyes, descended from blond and brilliant Abd-er Rahman.

"Kiran! Kiran!" The boy jumped from his bed in a sweat, his mother's voice ringing down the hall.

"Yes, Mother. What is it? I was asleep." But he knew it was something more than that. Before finally falling into the dream, he had been considering the pathways of the world tree and the corresponding letters. He had seen something. The rabbi had been with him. The Caliph.

"Didn't you hear the call to prayer? Come quickly. You're to meet the Caliph today."

Slipping into his best tunic, he hurried to the kitchen.

"Mother, don't worry," he insisted, a little irritated, then looked around the big room for Alansha. Light was starting to define the shapes of trees beyond the patio. He saw her shadowy figure moving toward the labyrinth in the garden.

Grabbing an apple from the pyramid in the center of the long table, he turned back to Mershi Kamir. "I heard the muezzin's call, but was thinking . . ."

"Child of the Dervishes, son," she threw her arms up as if grieved, "where's your head!" but laughed.

45

Surprised by her mood, he replaced the apple and stooped at the basin along the wall, noting his hair, reflected in the ripples of the water, illumined by the glow of the oil lamps, red-blond like the Caliph's — reminding him of the choices which would be made that afternoon.

Straightening, as if to justify his tardiness, he said:

"The sun is just now catching the old muezzin's eye."

"Today is summer solstice — have you forgotten?" She moved gracefully about the room, like a dancer, knowing full well that he had not. He was struck by how much younger she looked than Abu el-Ali. Her gown, a luxuriant blue, brocaded with golden designs, fell to her feet from black flowing hair. Her eyes sparkled with mischievousness.

"Of course not," he responded, wondering whether his father was already in the alcove.

"May Allah be praised," she feigned relief, then took her broom and pretended to rush a ghost out of the corner, chanting: "Harushsss, to the east you go, to be eaten by the bigger goblin. Harushsss, you go to the east to be changed."

Al-Kiran hurried along the winding cobblestone streets, taking a short cut through the tanners' market toward the neighborhood in old town, beyond the central Mosque, where ben Hebaron and many of the wealthier Jews lived. Suddenly the Nubian was facing him. She had emerged from the Arian church.

"Al-Kiran . . ." her palm on his chest, she made sure no one overheard, then whispered: "I have been instructed in a form of intimacy which withholds itself, related to what the haremji are taught at the Academy in Medina. Ben Hebaron has suggested to me that now, beginning today, I may share these experiences with you."

He was lost in her dark eyes, high cheekbones, and full lips. Her words floated to him: "Ben Hebaron tells me that the Caliph will select both of us for the dance. We will be paired, I for the dark mother and you for the sun."

Speechless, he gazed at her, his heart racing.

"These six months may be all we have." She moved closer, her voice full of excited breath. "Let us use them well!"

Three Berber soldiers turned the corner into the lane. Her sparkling eyes merged into the shadow beneath the arch. Holding a finger across her lips, she turned and was gone.

Walking past the soldiers, his hands tingled. His blood waited for her touch. He glanced over the tile roofs of the adjoining buildings. A pale moon faded into the morning sky. Where the traditionalists saw an old man's face, he saw the peacock, then the Nubian princess he yearned to hold.

He slowed his steps. The rabbi had told him to come early, but his longing for the black dancer overshadowed all else. The knowledge that he would dance with her, somersaulted through his chest. "She's dedicated to the Uncle's harem; but perhaps, following the dance, she will request her freedom. Perhaps she will choose me. I am of the Omayyad blood."

But the further he moved from the Arian church, the more her image faded and the grand procession, in preparation at that moment, occupied his attention. He passed the street of the silk merchants and the old synagogue, where Hasdai ibn Shaprut, the Caliph's physician and confidant, had first come to prominence. Suddenly, he knew he must hurry.

"Where have you been, Kemi?" ben Hebaron boomed from his upper window when the boy turned, at a trot, toward the rabbi's home. "I sent Kristien for you an hour ago!" But the master was laughing. Much relieved, al-Kiran waved at ben Hebaron's wife and bounded up the stairs toward the study.

"Have you lost interest?" Turning from the window, ben Hebaron seemed sad, as if he had been alone all night, praying. "I have waited for you and now neither I, nor your partner, can call to you without slowing your steps."

Al-Kiran was shocked. His chest heaved where Kristien had stopped him with her touch. He was dizzy.

Alpha ben Hebaron came across the room and fixed his eyes into al-Kiran's. "You are so young to have so much expected of you. I am sorry the princess touched you so soon." Folding his hands down over al-Kiran's head and shoulders, he whispered: "Be at peace. We are here for you."

Al-Kiran slept, exhausted, on the rabbi's couch, surfacing

intermittently to the soft breeze from the window, the reassuring warmth of the sun, then sliding back into sleep.

When ben Hebaron's wife woke him, it was nearly time to leave for the plaza with the other students. He could hear the master talking to someone. Descending the stairs, he saw the Nubian princess.

She wore a long white robe. A brilliant indigo and green scarf covered her shoulders. He tried to remember when he had last seen her. His heart was pounding.

"Kristien? . . ." His voice broke as he tried to speak. They were approaching the Great Plaza.

"We will dance." She smiled, then dropped her eyes.

"You told me we have only six months. Is our work only for the Dance of Created Lights?" The words tumbled out, shocking him by their directness and urgency. He saw the Royal Uncle looming in their future, ready to claim her.

She raised her head slightly and whispered: "You are my true partner." They were nearing their assigned places in the Courtyard of Oranges. "But . . . Kemi, we are not dancing for ourselves." Her eyes deep with yearning, she reached for him, then withdrew her hand, her chest swelling then receding as she struggled to say something more.

Trembling, he felt the prize had been gained and lost between two breaths, and forced his attention back to the plaza. Two lines were being formed: the males on the north, symbolizing the warriors, the females on the south, for the home, fifty candidates in all. He and Kristien stood at the ends of their respective columns.

The morning breezes dropped into a quiet stillness. The hot Andalusian sun neared its summer zenith. Ramadan, the sacred month of fasting, had just ended. The celebration of the feast of the sun would begin as soon as the Caliph selected the eighteen who would dance at winter solstice.

In the heat now, he recalled ben Hebaron's statement: "We only emerged into day at the beginning of the present age. The followers of the blessed Mohammed recall a time when they couldn't face the sun and survive. Even Moses, the Lawgiver, could not, at first, face the God."

The sacred feast following the fast of Ramadan would be exuberant. Out of respect for the discipline of their Moslem neighbors, even the Jewish and Christian cafes had been shut during the hours of sunlight. Regardless of religious affiliation, everyone would celebrate together.

At that moment the trumpets announced the approach of the royal procession. The Iman, high priest in the lineage of Ali, walked through the eastern gate, followed by the Ulama, the Sunni doctors of theology. The crowd in the great square divided, opening a channel to the lines of the aspirants.

Sudanese warriors on prancing stallions, carrying the banners of the Omayyad dynasty, followed the scholars. The ceremonial guard rode behind them in blue uniforms, carrying silver shields reflecting the sun, on white mules.

Palace slaves rolled out a red carpet upon which Caliphs, from the time of Abd-er Rahman I, had received envoys from Damascus and Baghdad, or the Christian north.

The procession moved between the lines of the dancers, splitting at the far end and curving back around the candidates to form a circle, still open where the carpet extended into the path between them, upon which the Caliph would walk — coming to them as if he were the supplicant.

At Kristien's signal, the dancers bowed and touched their foreheads to the carpet, eyes to the ground.

Caliph al-Mustansir Hakam II moved through the gate and along the carpet on foot, bareheaded, golden hair loose to his shoulders. The crowd hushed in anticipation. Drums, like heart beats, sounded from the perimeter. Ethiopian pipes rippled, like the cries of mountain eagles, into the silence.

"Children of Light, arise! I am but a representative of the Sun. By the Prophet's message, I come to you. Today, as we emerge from Ramadan, as the sun welcomes us and the Earth sends us forth, Oh My People, may the blessed Mohammed's vision be in me that I may see."

The voice rose, deep and profound, the words a summons to the dance. Al-Kiran was awestruck as he and the others stood along each side of the carpet and received his message.

"Among these dancers are those who may fly. Arise that I, in the name of the Blessed Prophet, may choose among you."

The Caliph was midway along the line of the applicants, his voice strong with ritual assurance. Although al-Kiran remembered the ceremony from the summer of his eighth year, hoisted onto his father's shoulders in the crowd, there was no comparison. That was the outer ceremony. This was the inner.

The aspirants rose and faced each other across the red carpet. The Caliph was kneeling in the center, dressed in a simple white robe with a black waist-sash.

The soldiers dismounted. The entourage shifted and reassembled. The Sudanese warriors closed at the west end of the lines, forming a semi-circle, their scimitars held aloft and flashing in the sun, each waving a white banner in the other hand.

The royal guard in white turbans completed the inner circle, the crowd at their backs. The guards held golden shields, embossed with the crescent moon, off center, opposite the Seal of Solomon.

Consorts of the royal harem stood between each of the guards. Eyes, full of delight, peered through green veils. Sheer silk flowed over their shoulders, hanging loosely to rich gowns, sensuous and evocative, covering yet suggesting the secrets of the royal bed. A eunuch, bald and bareheaded in the sun, stood behind each woman.

Hisham II, just past two years old and dressed in a red uniform, golden haired and full of promise, heir to the throne, moved forward along the carpet toward his father, Supreme Caliph of al-Andalus. Subh, his mother, favorite of Hakam II, the only consort on whom he had sired a son, escorted the boy. She was dressed modestly, like the Caliph, her auburn hair flowing across the back of her gown, her walnut eyes lowered.

This was little Hisham's first appearance in a great assembly. A handsome child, he conducted himself with maturity beyond his age.

While Hisham and his mother approached the Caliph, al-Kiran sensed a new level of excitement, related to the future of al-Andalus, rising from the crowd, and within himself. The appearance of the favorite consort with Hakam II, as well as her child, heir to the throne, boded well for the kingdom.

Like most of the congregation, he had only seen Subh from a distance. She was "Aurora" to the confederacy of Slavic tribes north of the Rhine who had sent her to al-Andalus, a token of peace and alliance. Like many of his ancestors, apparently Hakam II was drawn to the princesses of the north. The Cordovans had rejoiced that their Caliph, so prone to study, abstracted, and apparently unconcerned with siring heirs, cared for this woman.

At that moment, while everyone waited in hushed suspense, a tall, dark man — turbaned like a master of the laws, his beard black, nose hawked and prominent, mustache bold and twisted, eyes severe and small but dominating and quick, full of secrets — stepped on the carpet and walked forward, joining the royal family between the lines of aspirants. With a chill, al-Kiran realized that the Chamberlain, al-Mansur, "the Victorious," was favored by the Caliph.

Called the Jewish prince of Cordoba, Hasdai ibn Shaprut, the Royal Physician, stood at the east end of the line of dancers, in the first rank of witnesses. Folding his arms over his chest, he turned and whispered something to the rabbi. Ben Hebaron nodded then looked directly at al-Kiran.

Glancing across the line to Kristien, he wondered what she might have seen. As if she felt his question, the sun dancing off her face and bare arms, she lifted and shook her left foot. The small bells attached to her ankle rang a subtle message, lovely and chilling at the same time.

The Caliph spoke:

"The light is present, even in the dark.
By the school of Abraham, by the line of Jesus,
By the message of Mohammed,
By the mothers who guard the Ka'ba in which the Prophet's seed is treasured,

May I now see in the darkness,
May I choose the created lights."

A flutter went through the crowd. Bells rang from the four corners. Each eunuch released a white dove.

Al-Kiran exhaled deeply, held, then breathed in as his master had taught him. His eyes, which had been fixed on Kristien's, closed. Pierced by an inner fire, amethyst flashing at the top of his head, he rode a flame downward, spiraling into a red snake coiled at the base of his spine.

The snake stretched and started weaving upward. Seeming to turn within himself, his eyes joined with the snake's. Alpha ben Hebaron was whispering something. A memory rose out of his heart. Breath racing outward, exploding in an indigo tongue projected from the point above and between his eyes, he gazed outward, steadying himself, then saw Hakam II, as in a tunnel, gazing into him.

"Kemi." The Caliph spoke as his hands closed on al-Kiran's temples, fingers in his hair, blue eyes looking affectionately and reassuringly into his. "By the Prophet, I bless and thank you. You do well, my son."

He stood in trance before Hakam II, his heart pounding. The snake within him shimmered, seemed to transform into a caduceus with wings. New circuitry, a rainbow flowing up and down his spine, flickered into stillness.

Looking into the Caliph's eyes, he felt Kristien smiling across to him. He managed the ritual answer: "Your Majesty, by the grace of the Blessed Messenger, I am your servant."

"Al-Kiran, son of my honored cousin, the Mullah Abu el-Ali Misram; of the mother house of Bethsheba; student of the revered ben Hebaron — in the promise of the Prophet, and by the line of our ancestors, you are the last of the dancers I select. You will dance for the created lights with the dark princess opposite whom, as of this solstice, you stand."

CHAPTER FIVE

"The Circuit of the Sun"

That night, following the solstice ceremony, the longest and warmest day of the year, al-Kiran dreamed he was walking with his parents on the banks above the Guadalquivir. He was talking about having been selected as one of the participants in the Dance and he explained that on the previous night he had dreamed it all in advance.

Then he said: "The rabbi scares me. He has something up his sleeve — something related to Kristien, the Nubian slave dedicated to the Caliph's uncle."

His mother responded: "The Nubian is ben Hebaron's concern, not yours. She is lovely, but let her be as she must," to which his father added: "She is of the mystery. For you in this dance, but after that . . . only the Prophet knows." Then Abu el-Ali pointed to the mountains to the west of the city. Following the line of his father's finger, al-Kiran was propelled through a rose crack between the worlds.

As he tumbled forward, a voice followed him: "The great angel of Allah, touched the desert and made it bloom. The sun is covered by black birds so that the dead may rise."

Struggling to turn back, his words sputtering in blue and silver streaks through the hole in the sky, he cried:

"She stopped me this morning . . . Arian church . . . a fire in my chest . . . I love her . . ."

Al-Kiran woke anxiously to the clank of the old Christian farmer who brought their milk to the door and was squabbling with the servant girl over the measure. His bed clothes were soaked with sweat. He panicked, realizing that those familiar sounds could be just a figment in another dream.

Turning quickly about his room, he realized that it was light outside. Somehow he had slept through the first round of prayers. Embarrassed and inwardly shaken, he hurried to the basin, cleansed himself, spread his rug and began prostrating and chanting quietly, trying to concentrate upon the rainbow bridge which stretched from the hearts of the devoted to the Ka'ba.

But the bridge flickered in his mind, displaced by dream images of people who had been talking to him. He saw himself with Marik, lying on the river bank, the sun rising behind them. Marik was saying something about al-Mansur — evil purpose . . . capturing the royal heir in a net of lies . . .

Pushing the images away, he rose, wanting to talk to his parents, not wanting to admit he had overslept, patches of song, strange poems, caught the rhythm of his thought, skewing his attention, disorienting him:

> Friends come from gentle streams,
> Wake like fish within your blood,
> Fly the sky within your dreams,
> Sail the days while flowers bud.

"Mother," he rammed through the door to the kitchen, "did we walk together last night, with Father?"

"Don't you remember?" Breaking from her chores, she looked puzzled.

"Did he speak of black birds covering the sun?"

She hummed a desert melody, then paused. "Aren't you a little late for the rabbi's lesson?"

Reluctant to answer, he reached for a warm bread loaf. Holding him in a lingering hug, she whispered: "It's a strain, isn't it? Go." She released and shooed him away. "I'll get my broom if I have to."

That morning ben Hebaron spoke about the roots of the Arabic language. He made no reference to the dance.

After the lecture, Kristien hurried away. Calling al-Kiran to himself, the rabbi said: "From now on, following mid-afternoon prayer, come to my home for instruction."

He approached Sa'id. But his friend was preoccupied, unavailable for private conversation.

Before going to ben Hebaron's that first afternoon, al-Kiran hurried to Marik's parents' villa. He was bothered by the memory of a dream in which Marik had warned him about al-Mansur's designs upon the young heir. But Marik was gone.

When he approached ben Hebaron, apparently busy with other matters, the rabbi left him in the courtyard while he stepped into the street to visit with callers.

"You're doing well, Kemi," he observed, his voice gravelly, upon returning; then walked in a circle, observing al-Kiran's posture and the correspondence of his breathing to the steps he had explained before going out. "You're through the first hoop. The second might not be so easy."

Breaking his exercise, a flame swelling up through his calf, he said: "I wish I understood, rabbi."

"There is no understanding. Not at this stage."

"The Kabbalists say there is a fire in the world tree." He had practiced that sentence, hoping for an explanation.

"So they do." Ben Hebaron nodded, then turned away.

That evening, while he walked with his father, he explained that he had dreamed that he would be selected for the dance, then he had re-dreamed it following his selection, and in the second dream he had told his parents how accurate the first dream had been, particularly the bridge of light between Hakam II and himself. "In the second dream you spoke of birds covering the sun and threw me into a gap in the sky."

Abu el-Ali, who had been listening carefully, indicated they should sit on the stone bench near the labyrinth.

Patting his beard down over his chest, he looked up, then lapsed into silence.

Al-Kiran had been disappointed they had not made time to talk to him. Following the great feast, they had walked through the royal gardens, but other people were around. Then he had gone off hoping to find Marik. After searching through the crowds of revelers, he had returned home and fallen asleep without seeing either of them again.

Abu el-Ali spoke quietly. "Some things can not be expressed in words." He worked his rosary. "Your mother and I have attempted to create an image within you, from which you can draw."

"You wouldn't answer my questions."

"Steady your heart, Kemi. Ride on the love you feel."

"Are the dreams real?"

"Some are." Abu el-Ali stood and pointed toward the villa. Inside, al-Kiran recognized the voice of the uncle who had warned against public involvement with a Sufi teacher.

That night he prayed alone in his room, then slept fitfully, anxiously listening for the muezzin's call. The next morning, he joined his father for ablutions. He struggled to focus while reciting the sunrise prayers.

After Abu el-Ali left for the madrasah, he rushed through the streets toward the park. But just as on the previous day, nothing was said of the Great Dance. Kristien hurried off. Turning to find Sa'id, he found that his friend was also gone.

He went home, hoping to visit with his mother, but she was gone. When the muezzin called for late morning prayers, he faced Mecca, and tried to steady himself. Praying alone, he imagined himself to be the head of a household, setting the example for his family. But no knowledge of the unity of Islam buoyed him up. He was determined to do the Messenger's work, but felt that he was not worthy.

That afternoon ben Hebaron had several visitors. Drawing him aside, he said: "Practice the same exercises as yesterday, then review what you have learned of the sacred alphabets, especially in relation to the reign of Hakam II."

Not much later, while he worked his way through the movements, observing the relationships among his body, his surroundings, his state of mind, and his breath, the rabbi returned. "I am very busy," he said. "You may leave early."

Back home, while his mother and Alansha worked in the kitchen, and the smells of spiced lamb curled through the rooms, he thumbed through the book on Kabbalah which his father had suggested; worked on a long poem he had begun some months before; then reviewed the diagrams he had made, correlating certain teachings with the movements ben Hebaron had set him to practice. But nothing held his attention.

That evening, Abu el-Ali brought a colleague to supper.

Alansha served them at the table in the reception room. His father seemed less at ease than normal, communicating somewhat formally with the mullah whom al-Kiran knew to be one of the more conservative of his father's friends. Neither he nor his mother joined in the conversation. No reference was made to the All Faith's Festival or the role which Abu el-Ali's son had been selected to play in the Dance of Created Lights.

As soon as the meal was over, he excused himself and wandered through the neighborhood where, as a child, he had played with friends at military campaigns, organizing the mighty armies of Islam for holy war, holding back the infidels and converting those who were prepared to hear the Message. When he and his playmates had run in groups between the great villas, some of which were replicas of the homes of their Roman predecessors, he had thought of himself simply as a servant of Allah, charged with responsibility for bringing the peace and security of Islam to the world.

Winding through the hills now, dusk spreading around him, he listened to chanting from hundreds of minarets. Making a place for himself beneath a stand of cedar trees, he looked out over the valley. Blue-pink shadows swept down, spreading like cloaks from the Sierra Morena mountains in the west.

Turning to face Mecca, he gave himself to the invisible line of the Prophet's messengers. In the silence, the whole of Cordoba, pagan, Jew, Christian, and Moslem, fell under the hush of evening prayer.

Rousing himself, somewhat encouraged, he followed the cobblestone paths to the road leading down into the markets and great squares of the central city, hoping to find Marik. Going to the river first, he watched pleasure boats slip in and out of the huge pylons, the noble families visiting pleasantly against the backdrop of the sunset. But his friend wasn't there.

Shrugging, he tossed a stone toward the river and turned back toward the markets. He wondered why, when they had been youngsters, he and Marik had almost inevitably found each other when either had any news or adventure to share — but ever since he had joined the rabbi's group Marik seemed insensitive to his need for companionship.

He took a short cut through a park. Peacocks sent their raucous screams heavenward, while their keepers scattered the evening meal. Passing into the fruit market, empty now, he wove toward the main plaza, wondering whether there ever had been real miracles, events which broke through from other worlds, or even real friendship.

He had been selected to dance with a priestess of the Black Goddess. He was being instructed in occult traditions so that with the right combination of energies, he would be lifted into a new level of knowledge — "From which," ben Hebaron had said, "you will know what actions are necessary."

But this evening, for reasons which he couldn't fathom, he felt as if he had been abandoned. No actions which he had mastered seemed capable of even bringing him to a friend.

During the ensuing weeks al-Kiran would occasionally recall the dreams around the summer solstice when he had been selected by the Caliph, but mostly he concentrated on the studies ben Hebaron heaped upon him. That seemed to be the only way he could hold off his mounting sense of doom.

The dreams had made him excited and apprehensive. But they seemed to fade as the work became more demanding. On two occasions, Kristien joined them during the exercises, but ben Hebaron never gave them an opportunity to talk privately.

He was vaguely aware of a destiny yearning in his heart for realization. But as weeks wore into months, even though his teacher seemed solicitous, al-Kiran felt increasingly detached from, even puzzled by, the interest shown in himself.

He remembered the nights preceding his selection for the dance when he had read from the sacred books, drafted diagrams of the alphabets of various languages, and meditated in the labyrinth before sunrise. But that excitement was gone.

On the evening preceding fall equinox, he walked back to the plaza. He was thinking about Kristien. Other than the mornings with the entire group, and the occasions when she appeared at ben Hebaron's for private instruction, he never saw her. He knew she had other duties, but he longed to just walk with her in private and ask her how she really felt.

Wandering past the food market, closed now, the stalls folded shut for the evening, he thought of Subh and Hisham II, a small child standing bravely in the center of the great plaza, and al-Mansur, hawk-like, a favored adviser to Hakam II, who had hovered behind the royal consort and her son.

"What is expected of me?" Kicking the gravel, he turned to cut through an old neighborhood then out onto the Street of Roses. Merging into the stream of evening strollers, the cafes full of conversation, he walked forward, head down, scowling.

"Kemi," a hand touched his shoulder, "are you lost?"

Marik laughed, then pointed to the table in front of which he had just walked.

"Who's she?" al-Kiran asked, noticing the young lady.

"That's what I'm trying to find out," Marik whispered. "Join us. Maybe we can find someone for you. Maybe a walk in the Royal Gardens a little later?" He grinned.

"I don't think so." Al-Kiran felt shy and awkward. Thinking of Kristien, he backed away.

"Come on, Kemi." Marik followed him a few yards along the street, but looking back at his female companion to assure her he wasn't leaving. "Don't be morose."

Backing against the whitewashed wall of the cafe, they let a group of young people stroll by, arm-in-arm, toward the singing which flowed from the courtyard at the next corner.

Looking into Marik's eyes, he pled silently for a return of the friendship which had once been theirs, when they had speculated about the city and its future, excited by the adventures which they had expected to share.

"What's wrong?" Marik lowered his voice.

"I can't understand what is happening to me — or around me," he answered, surprised by his own words.

"I can't say much," Marik lowered his voice. "But there are problems in the Palace."

"What problems?" al-Kiran asked urgently.

"Al-Mansur is pitting faction against faction. He says that

the All Faith's Festival should be suppressed." Al-Kiran's stomach tightened into a knot as Marik glanced around. "He's demanding an inquisition against the heretics."

"Surely Hakam II supports . . ."

"The word is out," Marik leaned forward, "that 'the wise' should not associate with the dancers or their teachers."

"'The wise?'"

"Those of us who follow the Sunni disciplines. It's a designation al-Mansur is using."

"But you drink wine. You always say we should take chances, explore the changing world. I'm more traditional than you . . ." al-Kiran protested, genuinely upset.

"Not in public." Marik drew back.

"But," al-Kiran reached for his arm, "no one will talk."

Apparently troubled, Marik said: "I have to go." Then: "I've told you . . . but you won't listen."

"You're my best friend . . ."

"And still am," Marik responded, earnestly. "But try to understand that . . ." His eyes dropped to the pavement.

"What?" al-Kiran asked, alarmed.

"I have responsibilities," his eyes came back up, "to my father."

"So we are not friends?" The words stuck.

"No." Marik glanced toward the table. "We are friends. But let's do the things we should." He forced a laugh. "Let's chase girls and . . ."

"But tomorrow's the equinox," al-Kiran tried to hold his arm. "I only have three months before the Festival. I have to concentrate and prepare."

"What you prepare for, I can't support." Shaking his head, Marik turned back toward the girl.

The next morning, deeply conflicted, aware that the energy which had surrounded him when the Caliph looked into his eyes and appointed him to the Dance, at summer solstice, was fading — al-Kiran determined to confront his teacher.

Ben Hebaron was addressing the students assembled around him in the Courtyard of Pomegranates to the west of the Great

Mosque. "The Holy Koran is the public proof of the experiences of the Prophet. But what else can be known? Tonight," he glanced at al-Kiran, "observe the equinox, look for the balance in all that is. Life and death, sunrise and sunset, supernatural intercessions and the tasks of a householder — all are components in one seamless web."

"Rabbi," al-Kiran spoke, suddenly aware of Kristien watching him, "how do we know that we experience the truth?

"What else can be experienced?" Ben Hebaron paused. "Your experience is beautiful, if understood. What you deny of your experience, appears as ugliness and delusion."

"Are we free to choose?" The Nubian interjected.

"The Creator has choice. You are the created who may become creators of yourselves."

"But Rabbi," al-Kiran asked, "are there others, on this earth, who create us?" He was thinking of the extraordinary moments when Kristien seemed to change him fundamentally.

"There are those who provide circumstances by which we may create ourselves. You can choose to see who you are. In that you find truth and beauty."

During the exchange, for a moment, he experienced some of the old excitement. He recalled ben Hebaron's statement on an earlier occasion: "Enthusiasm is the experience of the divine breath, the first leap from clay to consciousness."

But it passed and, even while accompanying his parents to the mosque that evening and hearing the recitation of autumn:

la ilaha illa-llah Muhammadun rasulu-llah
it is not what you are given but how you react
the sun dies toward winter to be reborn through death . . .

The Iman chanting in the slow rhythms of the ancient tongue; it was as if al-Kiran could only comprehend intellectually, not with his heart.

After returning from the mosque, al-Kiran stayed in his room for a while before joining his father in the library.

Seated near the lamp, at the low table, Abu el-Ali looked

up when al-Kiran spoke: "Father, how have Moslems, Jews, and Christians in Cordoba avoided violence and hatred?"

"The cycles of this world are the same for all of us," Abu el-Ali put down his papers, "regardless of the specific details of the faiths. It would be tragic not to celebrate together. We are children of the one God. May Allah, the most merciful, preserve us in tolerance."

Al-Kiran walked to the window facing the patio and garden, then asked: "Do you believe that there will be an actual eclipse during the Dance of the Created Lights?"

"The question is whether you believe."

"I prepare . . . but what will others see?"

"Through you, the vision will come. People of good heart and strong will are preparing with you."

"But what if my vision is not what the Prophet saw?"

"Whether it is the Prophet's truth, or just your own, we won't know until the Festival. But what we do know, you and I, at this moment, is that you have been selected."

Following the equinox, knowing he had less than three months to prepare for the Dance, al-Kiran attempted to re-dedicate himself. He yearned to merge with the divine will, but struggled with how to identify that will. Often thinking of the rabbi's statement that the Koran contains the public proof of the experiences of Mohammed, he worried about the fact that the Vision at Medina was not recorded in scripture.

"But what other proofs could there be?" he wondered while the weeks passed. "Would there actually be an eclipse? Would it be in the sky? What would others see?"

He cultivated his powers of concentration, practicing what ben Hebaron called "right effort — focused, yet receptive, attention," and learned to project consciousness into exquisite visualizations. At times, while revolving in a circle, his psyche would become fixed on a point just above his head and he would see himself floating above the ground.

So long as he held a visualization, it seemed real. But then it would fade. He couldn't distinguish between true vision and something he fabricated from his imagination.

When he pressed the question, ben Hebaron explained that at a certain level of imagination, through a slight shift, one can see into the spiritual worlds. "At first it only comes at unexpected moments. Some of the exercises are designed to nudge you toward that shift." He paused, studying al-Kiran.

"Eventually you will recognize the technique. Be patient. See yourself and then see yourself seeing yourself. Only then can you begin to act objectively."

But al-Kiran could only see that during his dreams he did not know he was dreaming.

Following instruction in ben Hebaron's courtyard one afternoon, while they were walking into the house, al-Kiran raised a concern which had been bothering him for months:

"You told me to concentrate on the relationship of the sacred alphabets to the reign of Hakam II."

"Yes." The rabbi pointed to the oak table, filled a clay mug with water, and poured himself a cup of wine. Rebecca, his wife, a strong and beautiful woman with luxuriant black hair streaked with white, wound up on her head in the fashion of the Jews, patted al-Kiran on the back and left the room.

"And what did you find?" the master asked, his eyes dark, rubbing his short beard with a large, weathered hand, then placing the wine decanter between them on the table.

"That there is a relationship between the Hebraic and Arabic letters. Both contain sequences which build . . ."

"Then fall away. Our cultures contain the seeds of dissolution." He completed al-Kiran's thought.

"Yes." Sweat from the afternoon exercises trickled down his back, staining his shirt, chilling him.

"And of the chamberlain?" ben Hebaron asked.

"Is 'al-Mansur' so powerful?" He was startled that the rabbi had leaped to the heart of his own concerns.

"It is a power, Kemi," ben Hebaron said, his voice softening. "It is not his power."

"He claims the Dance is a heresy?"

"From his viewpoint, it is."

"But the Festival has been celebrated for over two hundred

years," al-Kiran protested, upset that his teacher had not reassured him.

"It's for All Faiths, Kemi. Al-Mansur works with the dissolution of the alphabet, although he doesn't know it."

"That would be against the Omayyad Dynasty."

"Precisely." Ben Hebaron seemed strangely casual. "He has his own work, his own view, and it is opposed to the splendid diversity which has been the strength of this city."

Sipping his wine, he watched al-Kiran walk to the window before turning back. "Then have we come to the end of the sacred letters? Is this to be the last of the great dances?"

"The Blessed Messenger foresaw that a new level, a new Dance of Created Lights, would be experienced."

"Did the Divine Messenger see that?" Al-Kiran's throat tightened. A lump in his chest needed to escape, but was caught. "Or is that what the Sufis have made of what the Prophet, blessed be his name, said?"

"Sit a moment, Blackbird." Holding his arms out, his robe open across his broad chest, he accepted the veiled accusation. "I'll tell you a story."

Re-seating himself, al-Kiran realized he was questioning everything, including his teacher.

"Once there was a mullah who had been, at an earlier stage, highly regarded by the college of scholars and the teachers of the law, but who had grown old and feeble."

He looked up into the cross beams of the ceiling while al-Kiran listened. "According to many of the Ulama of his day, ibn Massara was at best eccentric and at worse a heretic. But they tolerated him for the sake of his former reputation."

Recognizing the name, al-Kiran asked: "Wasn't he a philosopher who founded a school here in Cordoba?"

"I am referring to his ancestor." His voice almost a whisper, he continued: "One night the old mullah, who lived north of the Amu Darya, called upon one of the foremost scholars of his time, and found the household in an uproar. The signet ring of the scholar had been lost. He had been resting near the fountain in his garden. The sun was setting.

"The scholar was upset because he always led his guests in the evening prayers, after which he would hold this ring to a candle and seal the names of all who attended into a book, assuring them that they were among the elect.

"While the sky grew darker and the chants of the muezzin spread across the city, the scholar, his entire family, all his servants and guests combed through the garden as if some catastrophe would befall them if the ring could not be found. Exhausting all possibilities, in fear that the prayers would be missed altogether, the scholar hurried everyone into the prayer chamber, directing them to immediately take their places on the rugs facing Mecca.

"Laughing distractedly, the mullah hobbled around dragging a dirty rag, peering under cushions, still looking for the ring. While the others anxiously fell to their prostrations, the scholar reprimanded him, exclaiming: 'I am outraged by your behavior, ibn Massara. The ring is lost in my garden. Tomorrow we will search for it there.'

"But the mullah, scratching himself immodestly, continued the search, looking for all the world like a senile old man who couldn't be expected to pray.

"Upon completion of the prayers, while some twenty persons remained obediently bowed to the floor, having performed as required in order to be entered on the rolls of the elect, the scholar cleared his throat and marched toward the sacred niche. Pushing ibn Massara to the side, he opened his book and declared: 'But for you, old crazy man, this household would now be in order.'

'But your ring?' The mullah spread his dirty rag before the scholar's feet, then looked up, glazed-eyed and humble. 'You said the ring seals the elect. Should I have not searched for it on your behalf, while you, Master, and your faithful flock, prayed?'

'Can the blind find a ring for those with practiced sight?' the scholar huffed. 'In this book I write the names of those who performed the prayers. In arrogance, you err. Had you followed me, you would have been saved.'

"What happened to the old mullah?" al-Kiran asked.

"As he struggled to his feet, to everyone's shock the ring was uncovered beneath his rag. Picking it up reverently, he handed it to the scholar, then started to limp away."

"What did the master do?" al-Kiran asked, puzzled.

"In a rage he shouted: 'This is a fake! Go back to the dark, fool, where the real ring may be found.' He flung it through the window into the night."

"Was it the real ring?"

"Yes, certainly," ben Hebaron answered gravely. "And as to the mullah ibn Massara?" he paused.

"He was trying to help, wasn't he?"

"Yes," the rabbi nodded, "but all that was left for him was to scratch himself and pretend to be senile."

"How had he found the ring?" He imagined the scene.

"The scholar screamed that very question in his face." Ben Hebaron chuckled. "Ibn Massara said: 'Where the light was, Master, it is now dark. In my search, I followed the changing light.' As you can appreciate, he was ordered out of the house and declared doomed for defiling the prayers."

"What does that mean?" al-Kiran asked, even more puzzled; but before the rabbi could answer Rebecca re-entered the room and announced that another visitor had arrived.

"Think about it, Kemi, then give me your answer." Ben Hebaron nodded, the lesson over for the day.

While winding his way through the park, on his way to his teacher's the next day, al-Kiran reviewed the story of the old mullah. He knew Sufi stories were meant to be paradoxical. He assumed it related to the failure of the sacred alphabet at the end of a cycle, and to al-Mansur's movement to suppress the great dance — but he was uncertain what was meant by finding the ring in the changing light.

Despairing, he concluded he had been chosen by mistake. His ability to leap from insight to insight was lost. He wanted to return to the public schools where he had excelled, and content himself there — but it was too late for that.

He believed that he would never be able to act "objectively, with force," as ben Hebaron had told him he must. Whereas he had once thrilled in what had seemed to be his own grace and speed, now he saw how clumsy and distracted he really was and suspected that he had never been competent, that others had let him win, that the competitions had been controlled by his parents or someone else so that he had seemed to have won — that he had been coddled as a member, although not in the direct line, of the royal family.

Even while he had practiced the slow steps, then stops, the inner grandeur of the progression through the sacred alphabet had become simply a memory of how he had once imagined it to be. The movements, at first easy, had become ever more tortuous, as if he were losing his natural rhythm.

Lost in thought, turning in at the gate to ben Hebaron's courtyard, he almost collided against the Nubian, who had apparently been waiting for him. Beckoning him to enter quickly, gold and silver wrist bands sliding together on her arm, she pointed toward the rabbi then pulled the gate shut.

His foot tapping impatiently, his arms folded over his chest, ben Hebaron said: "What did the story mean?"

"The fool found the ring," al-Kiran answered awkwardly, aware of Kristien's breath on the back of his neck now.

"And the fool was cuffed for it!" Ben Hebaron stamped the ground, worn smooth in a circle, then slapped his abdomen. As if a drum had been struck, his laughter came from deep within him, contrived by technique.

Pushing his cap back, sweat beads glistening on his top lip, he hunched down and started shaking a tambourine, studying something at ground level. Then, scanning their bodies, he chanted: "New steps, new letters, new alphabet, still sacred — practice now, circling slowly, watching yourselves watching each other."

His dark eyes glared red in the center, like an animal's. "Get to it!" He pointed to the perimeter. "Oppose him."

Kristien bowed deeply, her blouse billowing beneath the gap at her throat, her eyes up, reaching for him. His breath caught just above his solar plexus. Blood surged into the maleness between his legs.

"Dance," ben Hebaron shouted, ringing a bell. Laughing, he slapped his diaphragm like a drum, causing a flock of rooks to rise from the olive and fig trees forming a ring within the high walls of his courtyard.

Al-Kiran moved sideways. Kristien straightened, her mouth open slightly, tongue against shiny lips, her arms spreading, blouse clinging to firm breasts — mirroring his steps; smiling gently, graceful and sleek, her movements uninhibited, inviting. Green fire built in his solar plexus, flickering toward her, blinding him to everything but the black princess, as the rabbi had explained that it would.

"Forward, face each other, come near." The voice pushed him. Chest heaving, he twirled slowly, arms extended then hooked upward, bent at the elbows, energy flowing with his breath through his fingers.

Seeing her, he knew they were balancing to come forward, steps precise, each posture a drum beat, a sound and a form pictured within, reflected in their bodies, his maleness on fire, her feet bare on the earth, his rhythm complementing hers, moving toward each other, moving together.

"Reverse!" He felt nothing but her body leaning into his, pulled away suddenly, something ripping from him, the fire which had burned from him to her screaming for satiation in her dark depths, screaming to burst into flight.

"Harooosh, harroosh, you go to be eaten. Harooshhh," a voice whispered, "you go to be eaten by a bigger goblin. Dark Mother comes to eat you while you fall." A finger at his heart, like a spike, he crumpled to his knees.

"Students, freeze."

Ignoring the command, Kristien kneeled to him and whispered: "I go now until I find you in the dark before the light."

Tears flowing down his face, he tried to reach for her, but she flowed backwards and was gone. Looking into the sky, his vision was obscured by a dark figure, framed by the sun. His voice steady, ben Hebaron bent forward:

"Your clumsiness moves you toward truth. You fall. You

believe you ruin the dance. That is a step toward being able to act, toward building a permanent self."

Sweating and weak, exhausted, he wanted to convince the rabbi that he was incapable, that he should be released.

"Master . . ." He struggled to control the sobs, the words burning in his throat, "every movement is an effort."

"We move through a bag filled with sand," ben Hebaron spoke gently. "Your clumsiness is the key. Watch for the fire in the sand. It's been suppressed, but is not dead. While you watch yourself struggle, it will come to you."

Sniffing, rubbing his arm across his mouth, he looked for Kristien. Angry now, wanting to fight off the rabbi's expectations, he said: "The dance at Medina isn't recorded. I don't believe it happened."

Sitting back as if wounded, the red in the center of his eyes soft now, ben Hebaron said: "Never stop doubting. First doubt, then know. Then doubt again."

His heart going out to his teacher, he felt he had violated his trust. He hadn't meant what he had said.

"We are in this world, and another." Ben Hebaron spoke quietly. "You are correct to question my teachings. We must question, and then question our questionings."

"I didn't mean to question you, rabunni." He wanted to hold to something steady, to re-establish his faith that at least his teacher was invulnerable.

"No, Kemi." Ben Hebaron held him by sight alone. "You must question. Ultimately you must ask who is asking. We all walk the sword's edge between the worlds."

They were alone, beneath the sun. Ben Hebaron reached across to him. Al-Kiran saw infinite care and tenderness etched through the weathered lines of his face as he said: "You are young for this work, but we support you."

He scratched his head, then, looking tired and decrepit, leaned to his side and pushed himself up. "Learning to fly isn't easy." He bent over and attempted to brush the dust from his robes.

Raising his eyes as he spoke, he toppled over. Grunting, frustrated, he scrambled to his feet, bringing his right hand to his forehead to catch his cap but knocking it off, leaving his face smeared. Sounds drifted across the walls into the courtyard as he hobbled away, then, turning abruptly, with his cap dangling in one hand, his tambourine and bell lying in the dust, crouched and scanned the ground.

Al-Kiran wanted to run away. He had destroyed his chance to dance with the Nubian. He had ruined his opportunity to grow beyond himself and participate in the realization on earth of the Great Dance prophesied by the Most Blessed Prophet. He had betrayed his parents, who believed in him, and had taught him the way. He had challenged and failed his teacher, whom he loved and who had loved him.

"I'm so sorry, rabunni," he whispered, moving into ben Hebaron's arms, crying within himself. Then, suddenly, with a force greater than seemed possible, the rabbi caught and held his eyes with his own, saying:

"Tomorrow you move to the Hermitage Ibn Massara. By this pain, and hope, you search for then find the dark light."

Like lightning, he felt Kristien's promise pulsing through him, then started to black out, ben Hebaron's hands under his arms as he slumped to the ground, catching then dragging him gently toward the grass near the Jericho rose. Falling into the dark, he dreamed again, as he had dreamed before, that the black goddess was at his throat, her kiss pulling blood from his heart, a claw deep within his groin, pulling him toward, then into herself.

He woke just before the evening call to prayer. The moon shone, a faint sickle above the last embers of sunset, suggesting a globe at a deeper, darker level. The rabbi was wringing his hands and shaking his head, in mock despair. "What are we to do with you?" He smiled approval.

"We leave tomorrow. Tonight, ask your parents for your history. Honor them, for they have given much."

CHAPTER SIX

"SONGS OF THE KAROBLA"

M other," al-Kiran glanced up, relieved, as she moved toward him from the dark outline of the trees, "I'm to leave tomorrow for ibn Massara."

She nodded then slid onto the bench where he sat and patted his knee. "Your father is with ben Hebaron now, and the Jewish Prince, discussing the terms."

Surprised, he asked, "Hasdai ibn Shaprut? Why is the royal physician involved?"

"There are problems in the palace." She stroked his hair while the melancholy questioning of an owl floated through the sky. "Al-Mansur is making a play for power." She paused. The bells of the old Christian church rang through the valley.

Studying her, he pushed forward: "Ben Hebaron said to ask you about our history."

Taking a deep breath, she considered a moment before speaking: "By your father's mother's line, you are Sunni and kin to the House of Omayyad, favored and protected within this city. By descent from Ali and Fatima, on his father's side, you are heir to the Shi'ite revelation." She paused.

"By my mother's father's line, you carry the knowledge of the Yemenite Kings, from before the time of the Most Blessed Prophet, supporting civil obedience and good order, but leaving the correction of doctrine to the judgment of God."

"King Marthad of Yemen lived long ago, Mother." He remembered Marik's statement. "The tribesmen who followed Abd-er Rahman were fanatics and their descendants not much better." He had not intended to sound so critical.

"Some were fanatics, and are," she spoke cautiously. "Some are not. Some are here to help you."

"What does that mean?" He sat up straighter.

"My mother . . ." She broke off as he looked away, uneasy whenever she spoke of Orwan Kamir Oshiwah al-Kirian.

71

Turning back to her, he said: "I need to know."

"Having studied with the Essenes of Judah, she is an initiate of the cave mysteries and Mistress of the Temple of Isis. The Magdalen spoke to Jesus of Black Isis, consort of bright Heaven, but it is not recorded. She is not easily accepted by men, though all are drawn to her."

"You said we should never speak of Grandmother. " He had always been uncomfortable with the knowledge that she had pursued such a bizarre course.

"My mother's blood in you is of great interest to the rabbi and the physician." Mershi Kamir Kirian laughed gently. "But we won't talk of her in public, will we?"

"No," he answered sincerely. "But why is she of interest to them, and what is Father saying to them?"

"This is the Villa al-Kirian."

"Named for your mother's line." He nodded.

"But in recent years listed in the official rolls under your father's name. Do you understand?" She rocked back.

"For the protection provided by his family," he realized for the first time.

"If not protection, at least camouflage." She chuckled. "The Kirians have always been suspect, but I'm not sure which of the names is less offensive to al-Mansur, now. He grows more powerful as each month passes. Part of the concern, of course, is that he will stop the Dance."

"He couldn't," al-Kiran asserted, suddenly alarmed. "Could he?"

"He could." She nodded soberly. "But that's for ibn Shaprut and the allies. Your concern is to see that you are prepared to dance. In any event," she smiled reassuringly, "the maze is Kirian, from my mother's line, and so always will our home be known among those who support her work."

"Why is she important?"

"By her, the dance is in your bones and visions rise from your blood. Alpha ben Hebaron is not simply a scholar."

"He's a Sufi, isn't he?" Never before had he been so direct.

"He's a dancer." She glanced into his eyes. "He attempts to

draw energies from many levels in order to bring this world safely through its peril."

Al-Kiran pulled away, filled with the image of ben Hebaron sprawled on the ground. "What are you talking about?"

"What I know," she said. "What you are learning."

He suddenly remembered al-Mansur stepping onto the carpet just before Hakam II selected the dancers. At the edge, beyond Subh and the heir apparent, ibn Shaprut had turned to ben Hebaron, as if alarmed. He questioned his mother: "Is ibn Shaprut no longer the Caliph's principle adviser?"

"His power fades as al-Mansur's rises."

"Even you refer to the Chamberlain as 'the victorious'? Is he so powerful already?"

"Not yet." In the light of the oil lamp, concern covered her face. "But he will be unless something is done to protect the young prince and his mother."

"Al-Mansur is against the Dance, isn't he?"

"He seeks power through suppression of diversity."

"Then my father works with ibn Shaprut to resist the threat to the royal heir?"

"Al-Mansur, like the Blood Spiller, would take the throne from the Omayyads. We must do what we can to steady the world in its flight."

"Father always said the way to steady the world was through prayer, through inner peace, and that the political struggles were best left to the will of Allah."

"You have to ask your father about that," Mershi Kamir walked behind the bench and put her hands on his shoulders.

"But there are times, Kemi," she dug down with practiced fingers, "when the worlds interpenetrate. At such moments, the course can be changed. We prepare for that moment."

She leaned down and kissed the top of his head before reseating herself beside him. "The College of Eunuchs fear al-Mansur. He is cruel. They have concluded that if something happens to the Caliph, Subh will not be able to protect young Hisham."

"But what do the concerns of the College of Eunuchs and the Jewish prince have to do with Kristien and me dancing?"

"We hope to contribute to the development of certain qualities on this planet. Your father calls it 'Islam,' others call it 'charity' or 'right action.' Regardless of the words, ultimately, our purpose must be to save this world."

"The safety of the world is in submission to the will of Allah." Al-Kiran quoted the traditional instruction.

"Even the most learned of the Ulama disagree among themselves when interpreting the will of Allah." She spoke softly. "What is the divine will for you?"

"That Kristien and I dance."

The wind swirled in ghost streams across the dark sky as Mershi Kamir nodded then left him alone. Wondering when his father would return from the meeting with ben Hebaron and ibn Shaprut, he shivered. The temperature had dropped.

Deciding to approach the maze, he moved along the hedge toward the first gate. Bubbles danced in the pool at the base of the fountains, illuminated by the faint glow of the lamps.

"Only one moon cycle remains before the All Faith's Festival." Abu el-Ali's sonorous voice jerked al-Kiran from his contemplation. Pale light shone on his long beard. His eyes accented beneath heavy brows, he said: "Let us recall your beginnings within the labyrinth."

Inside the maze the wind stopped. "In the darkness," his mother spoke while leading them forward, "the Pleiades pierce the black skies with shafts of light."

Recognition rippled up and down al-Kiran's spine as, behind him, his father chanted responsively: "Venus and Mars, visible above the horizon, dance toward each other."

The sound of the fountains was absorbed in the outer corridors as Mershi Kamir shifted directions. Acknowledging each turn, she followed the Kirian emblem within the labyrinth.

Returning to the gate from which they had entered, she slipped through the shadow door and approached the center. Speaking softly, she said: "May the time we share here support you as you move between the worlds."

In the clearing,where al-Kiran had in the past spread his rug on the grass during private prayers, Abu el-Ali lit three candles placed on pedestals near the points of a triangle inscribed in a tile mosaic. Mershi Kamir poured water from a white pitcher into a trough stretched across the bottom of the pattern. Fires danced in the water. Six additional lines crossed the triangle, touching the rim of the circle.

"Al-Kiran Kamir Kirian . . ." She drew his attention. Standing at the point of the pyramid, dropping her robe, she was dressed as a priestess. Raising her arms, she said:

"Realize, son of the stars, planets, and earth mother — our child, teacher of the children who will follow us — this is the emblem of our family's hidden history. It is kept here in Cordoba, the city of many eyes, as a walking memory. It is called the 'Memory of Home.'"

Al-Kiran shuddered. A dream, a memory he had suppressed or a vision, rose through him. He was being pulled toward a mountain. Barren sheer cliffs spread below him in the distance. He reached to steady himself, his feet spread across a small streamlet. He was in a cave, facing the light flooding in from its mouth.

A bear, saliva dripping from his teeth, towered behind and above a cave priestess. The light shining around both of them, she moved toward him, her hair jet black, long, tangled and matted across her bare chest, her nipples bright red against dark skin.

Purple wings spread from a golden disk in the center of her forehead. She pointed downward. He kneeled. His own face peered up toward him from the streamlet running red along the cave floor. Rising to face her, her eyes, familiar yet terrifying, pierced into his own.

The bear reared behind her, like a huge shadow blocking the light. The cave filled with thunder. Blood-smell floated toward him from the depths of the cave.

"Come!" The priestess commanded, her voice steady. "I am Orwan Kamir Oshiwah. I have messages you must hear."

"You are my grandmother?" His voice choked on the words.

Holding her arms out, smelling of bear, she growled: "As with so much, your protectors protect you by half-truths."

Stepping closer, she thrust bloody hands against his chest. "The 'Memory of Home' . . . little one. My fingers in your heart, sweet providence!"

The priestess laughed, throwing her head back, exposing jagged teeth, her eyes blazing. The bear hovered over her. "These I have left." She held her hands before his face. One finger was gone. "With our flesh, child, we pay the Gods!"

"Al-Kiran," Mershi Kamir drew him back into the present. "follow me." She walked around the mosaic two and one-third times.

Stopping at mid-length along the line of the pool, she signed for him to stand opposite his father at points which, with her at the bottom, marked the obverse of the upward pointed pyramid inscribed in the tile circle.

"The embedded pattern, what is seen," she pointed, "marks the earth's energies rising. We now mark the invisible route by which the spirit descends to the waters. As the sun moves toward winter solstice, we follow the way of all life." She crossed her arms over her chest. "In each round of each year, death lies upon the visible world. But the promise of growth returns, reborn and vivified through the earth-womb.

"The pattern of the interpenetrating worlds is described by this tile mandala. It may not be shown while the dark prince walks the streets, lest its power be corrupted. These are among the mysteries of your mother line."

"And these," Abu el-Ali began after a long pause, "are among the mysteries of your father line. Though all men would be bulls, I have accepted no other wives. Though we could have many children, we have but one. Though we follow the Prophet, we have been students in other schools.

"You are born where the lines of our ancestors cross. We were prepared to receive you. Now we prepare to let you go.

"When Abraham left Ur for the Promised Land, many stayed behind to rebuild the city. When that proved impossible, the Mother accepted the seed, though she was already an elder teacher to the tribes.

"With her sisters and their children, she migrated to Balkh, then north across the Amu Darya. From their descendants arose the progenitors of the blue-eyed Omayyads and other lines which attempt, in the way of the world, to steady its flight.

"The emblem of the Kirians, this nine-fold pattern which you have walked since a child, descends to you through both your father and mother lines. It is the labyrinth of the stages of our initiation. We begin in the dark. We are born from and return to the cave. By these lines the wild gander inscribes the sky. By these stages, we find our way.

"Later tonight we will remove these tiles. We will close certain of the pathways to avoid intruders, should they come. You will carry what you have seen in your heart.

"Though it is our prayer that we see you often after the Festival of Faith, we understand that you will be upon a path, started in the 'Memory of Home' but evolving with the larger community. Tomorrow you will leave with the rabbi to undertake your final preparations. May he teach you well!"

Al-Kiran turned to his mother. She breathed deeply, then chanted:

"Mershi Kamir Kirian, I am.
By Beth-Sheba, Solomon and Christ,
the Prophet and the Bear . . . I pray —
as our son dies, as we all must,
in the way of reciprocal giving,
that he will also rise with the stars,
a true child of the Mother,
for the care of our peoples."

Her arms thrust upward, Mershi Kamir opened to the sky. Her legs spread beneath her, her blue cloak and green tunic caught the wind-breath rising from the water. Clapping her hands together above her head, she pointed to the Pole Star.

Bringing her hands down in a wide, gathering circle, she joined them, palms up, at her navel. Raising them to her heart, golden light burst forth. "In the silence," her eyes focused on al-Kiran, "rainbow warriors, the great ones of the splendid rays, move between darkness and light."

Leading them three and one-third rotations sun-wise back around the emblem, Abu el-Ali stopped. Father, child and mother were positioned at the corners of the inscribed pyramid, pointing from the earth base to the heavens. Al-Kiran was at the upper point, his parents at the opposite ends of the pool. Their images merged, carried by the flickering of the lights, in the movements of the waters.

Awed, reassured yet apprehensive, he felt their love as energy flowing up the lines of the pyramid to the apex where he knelt. The prayer of submission in his heart, he saw the will of Allah focusing through many lines of descent. As he gazed up, Abu el-Ali whispered:

"Our son, we mated as mother and father to you, child of our bodies and our home. Yet you existed before time and will exist after." Mershi Kamir, tears in her eyes, added:

"You are more than we have given. May the blessings we have go with you in love."

Al-Kiran was unable to sleep well that night. Tossing and turning as if haunted, he shot up in the dark, covered with sweat, thinking something had escaped from his dream. He heard the gate bang against the wall in the courtyard. Then he remembered.

A huge snake with wings and female breasts protruding above a throbbing penis had been leering at him.

A stallion preparing to mount a mare, the monster had approached. In the dream, he had been eager for ecstasy, for transformation — yet terrified.

The room was black. He wanted to wake his parents. An owl hovered in the air outside his window, surprisingly close. Calling: "Who? Who?"

"In what form," al-Kiran asked out loud, "did the angel appear to Mohammed?"

Following ablutions and prayers, al-Kiran folded and stacked enough clothes for the month of retreat with his teacher, then walked across the patio under the bright and reassuring sun. Clouds floated serenely in the blue sky.

The night dream, the confrontation with the dragon, had faded. He was glad to soak up the sun, have some time for lying in the garden, as he had so often as a boy.

No one had mentioned the ceremony, or the revelations, of the preceding night. He needed to pray and be quiet. They seemed to understand. Mershi Kamir left to visit friends; his father wouldn't be back until late morning.

He wanted to visit the maze once more before leaving for the Hermitage where they were to prepare for the dance. Walking through the garden to the tall hedge, he hummed a popular song about the beauty of Andalusian dancing girls.

He had reached the final verse before realizing that the melody and rhythms matched an ancient lament Alansha used to sing:

"For the prince prayed at the edge of the Mountain,
While the Lady in Black slept in the den,
The green crescent of the Prophet's Chariot
Thundering in the blue sky above them.

'Stop the world, stop the world', came the whisper.
The lady had risen from her sleep;
But the lad in his love of her beauty
Had leaped to his death in her deeps."

Remembering his father's reference to intruders, he stopped at the Lion Gate and scanned the walkways, peering beyond shadows thrown by the mid-morning sun. Everything seemed as it should be. Alansha was in the kitchen, busy with morning cooking. Her words rose out of silence:

"The child of the morning flew ever upward,
By the wings of the stallion made of gold.

From the Mount of the Ever-Faithful Mother
To the Heavens he was sold.

The values of emeralds and silver
Were hot sands in her parched throat
As she yearned for the cover of her lover
Who had drowned before she awoke."

Sun-rays angling across his face in the narrow lanes, his
heart aching, al-Kiran completed the song:

"As the child reached the sun in his glory
His black hair turned to gold.
His eyes caught the blue of the sunrise,
The blue of the ocean when it's cold.

And the dawn which had sprung from their union
Spilled red along the crags of the shore,
For the beauty of such consummation
Was too much for this world with its wars.

"There's no escape," he whispered. "Son of a mullah and
white witch," he laughed nervously. "Bound for the borders of
the universe." He repeated the lines of a fairy tale, thinking of his
mother and grandmother — "On a stick horse marching across
the sands." That was how it ended.

He stopped in the fifth gate, pondering the song which he
had overheard as he had entered the labyrinth. He could almost
feel Kristien calling to him. But 'almost,' he thought, 'almost is
never.'

Yet something in the words, in the images, in the rhythms,
played in his heart, stretched him. "I am al-Kiran Kamir Kirian,
son of the mullah and white witch. I am." The words faded as
he made a turn. Stopping to collect himself, focusing on the channels of the family seal, his breath caught in his throat.

A huge snake blocked the path. It was uncoiling about

half way to where the next gate should have been. He froze. The creature began to rise, wings emerging from its back, breasts . . .

His life flashed backwards behind his eyes. He knew this was the creature from his dream, perhaps a form of the angel who guarded the secrets.

"Karobla-Alborak." The name escaped from his throat. He knelt and whispered: "You carried the blessed Prophet from Moriah to the 7th Heaven. Will I ride you?"

The beast rose higher on her coil, her phallus throbbing as it had in his dream. But she didn't advance upon him. Her breath rancid and hot, eyes red, she hissed: "When you attempt to pass, son of the sacred Mother, we will have our ride."

The words were forming inside al-Kiran, the creature hovering about twenty paces ahead. "Where is the path to the other worlds?" he asked.

"You are walking it."

"Where is the gate?"

"Through the member which dances beneath your belly."

In spite of his fear, al-Kiran could feel his own male organ pulsing with blood, as it had in response to Kristien's touch in ben Hebaron's courtyard.

"Am I ready?" he asked.

"Only as you try me and survive."

"You are of my dream, Karobla."

"You saw me in your dream, al-Kiran."

"When will I be a snake-rider?"

"When the inner and the outer worlds are one!"

The creature spread her wings, filling the entire pathway, and started to advance toward him.

"Al-Kiran Kirian, I am . . ." He chanted while backing up, eyes on the creature. "Son of the mullah and . . ."

"Are you not coming, dear one?" The Karobla was hissing now, folding back down into her coil. "Are you not ready, little blackbird who would cover the sun?"

". . . white witch . . . I go to my teachers . . ." the boy responded, still stepping backwards. The creature returned to the size and shape of the snake initially coiled in the path, then raised her head once more, red eyes, tongue flicking toward him. "I await your dance, in the dark of the sun."

Shaken, he retreated along the outer perimeter to the Lion Gate and escape. He kneeled between the fountains, head to the grass, attempting to ground himself.

It was almost time to leave for the Hermitage. Alansha's voice floated across the garden: "Peace through Allah, by His most blessed Prophet, Mohammed."

A fist still clutching his heart, he sighed: "At least Alansha sings of hope." Her words hung in the silence:

"The violence of the sea meets the golden rays,
The wind catches the lad as he falls.
On the wings of an angel the child prays.
So goes the song of the laws."

A slight breeze rustled the rose scent. He could hear the street sounds and birds bickering in the olive grove across the back wall. Thoughts flooded his brain.

Marshalling his courage, he stood and breathed deeply. He had to reach the center of the labyrinth.

Unwrapping his indigo waist sash and winding it into a turban, he re-entered the emblem, hoping to avoid the Karobla, prepared to retreat rather than chance another encounter.

Half way along the path, between the tall hedges, where the Karobla might have been, a shadow flickered, seemed to rise, turn and recede in the opposite direction. Al-Kiran stepped forward, chanting:

"And the Prophet is a man.
By Gabriel came his song.
He rode the mule from the temple.
He brought the message to his people.
Submit to the will of Allah,
Or be gone!"

Hurrying forward he stepped through the shadow gate and entered the center. The mosaic emblem his parents had made in the labyrinth last night was gone. He walked to the center point, where he had practiced the exercises, knelt and recited a verse from the Hymn of Mohammed:

"The Prophet returned from the Heavens,
On the back of mighty Alborak He rode.
Messenger to the peoples of the desert,
Through the black winds and cold."

Unwrapping his turban, he placed it over the ground where the emblem of his family heritage had been. Standing in the center, he extended his arms toward the east, then crossed them over his chest, chanting:

"As the sun rises over Mecca,
The Prophet's message flows with the dawn."

Turning to the north, raising his arms, fingers, bringing energy down through his body and into the ground, he continued:

"From the higher skies and the mountains
Where the cold wind is a song."

Turning to the west, he extended his hands outward, palms down then up, closing his hands then releasing:

"Where the light is eaten by the bear,
but survives; the great teacher, death."

Facing south, crouching, his hands clasped under his testicles, then rising, pulling energy from the ground through his legs, his torso, shoulders, neck, lifting up to the sky, standing, he completed the invocation:

"Where the family is born, I am
Al-Kiran Kamir Kirian, carrier of the way."

Reassured, he lowered himself to the ground. A vision of the black dancer swirled and entreated him from the periphery of consciousness. A cold brick lodging at the pit of his stomach, he saw al-Mansur, regal and solid, step between himself and Kristien, soldiers running from the shadows, determined to lead her from the arena.

CHAPTER SEVEN

"LEAVING THE CITY"

He barely spoke during the meal, nor did his parents, nor did Alansha as she moved rhythmically about the long table.

Some new dimension, filled with silence, had descended upon them. He wanted to share what he had experienced in the dream, then in the labyrinth, and ask about the events of the night before, but couldn't find the words.

"You're going with the Rabbi today . . . " Alansha commented while bending over him to refill his plate, her Sudanese accent lilting, melodic, reminding him of her nursery songs and then the songs he had overheard, and the songs which had risen within him when he had entered the labyrinth.

Looking at her, his heart opened. She was warm and dark, her old skin soft, her big eyes over pugged nose reassuring, her smell dusky like her desert home, from which she had come as a slave-nurse — destined, she had later whispered to him, to be his mother's aid. He wanted to crawl into her arms, cry like he had as a small child, and let her rock him to sleep.

"He leaves in an hour," Abu el-Ali rose from the table, straightening his beard, his dark eyes moving from the women to al-Kiran. In silence, he followed his parents to his room, then, standing at the door, watched his mother wrap his clothes into a heavy wool blanket for his trip.

"Will it be so cold?" he asked.

She turned to him, a nine-pointed pendant, in the form of the walkways of the emblem in the maze, hanging from her neck. "You should be ready for whatever comes," she answered, her voice soft, adding: "We will miss you."

Holding her close, he wanted to say something but had no words. Pulling back, tears wound down her high cheekbones. "She's beautiful," he thought, then reached out uncertainly to touch her face. Small gold rings dangled from her ears.

Mershi Kamir leaned up on tip-toes, her lips slipping lightly over both his cheeks. Her hands in his hair, she pulled gently, lowering his head, whispering something in a language he could not understand, breathing out across and above his eyes. Lingering then backing away, her eyes deep through his own, she looked into his heart, joining him there.

"You have my blessing," she whispered. "Give my greetings to the Mistress Khayam."

Turning in the silence, she left the room.

"The Mistress Khayam?" He looked to his father. "Does Mother know the teachers at Taifa ibn Massara?"

"It is not for me to speak of the Mistress." Abu el-Ali picked up the Kirian prayer rug. Taking his bundle, al-Kiran followed him through the villa to the stables, then stopped.

"I didn't say good-bye to Alansha."

"There isn't time." Abu el-Ali extended his hand toward a shaggy donkey tethered to a post, her gray face stuck into the webbing of the hay net, contentedly feeding and, accepting al-Kiran's gear, tied it to the pack-saddle. "I'll speak to Alansha for you." The donkey turned to watch them, her eyes rimmed with black circles beneath huge ears.

"Why won't you speak of the Mistress?" al-Kiran asked.

Abu el-Ali, always self-contained and measured, seemed uncertain. He pointed to the street winding up from the old city, which would now lead to a new future of which al-Kiran had begun to dream and from which, at some deep level, he wanted to retreat. His eyes creased at the corners as he said: "Trust the Sheikh if the Mistress frightens you."

Al-Kiran waited under the tree near the dance area in the courtyard where Alpha ben Hebaron had so often barked out instructions for postures and steps. Carrying a knapsack over his shoulder and a staff in his hand, the rabbi opened the door and approached, moving like a man in his prime.

"You are ready then?" He scanned his student from the top of his head to leather boots.

"Yes, master," al-Kiran answered, a chill catching him in spite of his heavy robe and warm, baggy trousers.

"Then follow with the donkey, at a distance, until we're beyond the fields across the river."

Without waiting for an answer, he strapped his sack, much bigger than al-Kiran's, over the saddle, waved to his wife, and walked through the arch into the street, turning west through the old Jewish neighborhood, past the Synagogue.

Ben Hebaron seemed at ease, greeting acquaintances and visiting briefly with a group of rabbis, covertly signaling al-Kiran to wait, but not acknowledging him openly, then moving along the edge of the Central Plaza which spread from the great mosque, past the Alcazar of the Ancestors with its broad tree-lined walkways, and onto the cobblestone promenade above the banks of the Guadalquivir. Al-Kiran followed at a distance, uncertain why, but obeying his master.

Crossing the great Roman bridge, al-Kiran paused briefly, thinking of Marik while he gazed down at the line of royal barges moving slowly toward the docks, filled with goods and supplies from the Gulf of Cadiz and the Port of Lucifiri-Fani by way of Seville in the south-west and from Granada, by the river Genil, which joined the Guadalquivir in the south-east.

"What ever lies ahead," he told himself, "this is surely the greatest city in the world."

Other than outings with his parents to visit the Palace or his father's uncle's villa, just beyond the royal estates, this was the first time he had left the city. He and Marik had often fantasized about traveling the rivers, even working their way along as common laborers, visiting Granada and Seville, which formed a triangle in the heart of al-Andalus, with Cordoba at the apex, and then trekking across the Sierra Morena mountains, blue and majestic in the northwest above the Guadalquivir Basin, into the arid expanse of the high central plateau to Toledo and beyond, disconnected from the network of rivers which fed the South like arteries.

Approximately a mile beyond the royal estates, ben Hebaron turned along a narrow path through fields and orchards, leaving the river behind them, moving slowly toward the mountains while al-Kiran trudged along, the lead rope in his hand, the sun hot above them, glaring in the mid-day sky. Little bursts of dust rose around his boots.

He had grown bulkier and stronger since joining the group in the park near the kerm oak. "I am essentially a man now," he told himself, but was not wholly convinced. He wanted ben Hebaron to explain where they were going, what he might expect there, why they couldn't walk together.

Reflecting on the day before, when Kristien had danced toward him and he had reached for her, then fallen, he considered ben Hebaron's transformations from master to cripple to clown then back. He wanted to believe his failures led to growth. He wanted to prepare himself for the Great Dance toward the Black Princess who, warm with magic, had said she would find him "in the dark before the light."

Every once in a while a peasant, attached to one of the great farms through which they passed, waved from a field or led his own donkey past them, loaded with produce or timber, back toward the river which stretched in the distance behind them. They were climbing steadily toward the foothills.

Some fifty yards ahead, ben Hebaron leaned on his staff, then followed a path into a grove of ancient cork trees beneath which the shadows were so thick that al-Kiran lost sight of him. He tugged his donkey in an effort to catch up.

"Cordovan!" the rabbi stepped out from behind a tree. "Are you ready for this?"

"I hope so, master." Al-Kiran was anxious to speak. "But I have many fears," he admitted.

"So do we all." Ben Hebaron wiped his sleeve across his forehead. "If we meet anyone, let me do the talking."

Leading the donkey now, ben Hebaron turned to a path winding toward a meadow on the other side of the grove, al-Kiran following, wondering about the Hermitage ibn Massara, "which bears the name of the foolish mullah who was denounced for finding the scholar's ring in the changing light."

The Kirian prayer rug, which he had carefully unpacked and used during the afternoon prayers on the outskirts of the city, strapped to the side of the saddle, rose and fell with the donkey's gait. He had not been told what he would need and wondered whether he had sufficient provisions.

They moved through fig and olive orchards, interspersed with small grain fields and garden patches. Further along, the cultivation became less regular. The path crossed arid pastures and occasional meadows, dry and brown now with stiff grass where, earlier, it had been green and lush.

Ben Hebaron stopped before a stream. "The holy scriptures teach that wisdom begins in the fear of God. Allah is merciful, but difficult. You know the riddle:

> The sun comes out of night.
> The mother bears in pain.
> The child leaves its home.
> The old man needs a cane."

Leaning on his staff, dragging one leg, appearing to be crippled, he lurched ahead, grunting up the rise.

"Rabbi, you're strong as an ox. Kristien said that you are a champion wrestler." Al-Kiran was startled by his statement. He had never spoken to the Nubian about their teacher. He had meant to make a joke.

"So, Kemi," ben Hebaron switched his lameness to the other side, "she has already shared my secrets with you."

Now his left arm dangled uselessly down along his leg which, it appeared, he was just barely able to drag at all. "I am a great wrestler . . . a student of the subtle mysteries of the body. But look what it's done!"

"Master . . ." Al-Kiran's amusement turned to doubt.

Gaining the promontory, ben Hebaron stopped, turned abruptly back to the spread of the valley, and bellowed:

> "I have wrestled the eagle and the she bear.
> In my soul I am free,
> But the wounds in this body
> Will always be with me."

"I know that song. In fact," al-Kiran hesitated, "I've been

hearing verses which have new meanings. And . . . I have dreams which break into my ordinary life."

"I know." Sweeping his cane out over the fall of the land, ben Hebaron said: "Look with me for a moment."

Fig, almond, olive and citrus orchards spread before them. Workers were harvesting cork, their huge boiling pots sending steam into the skies. Beyond that, grain and cotton fields formed a quilt pattern through which the blue ribbon of the Guadalquivir wound its way. In the distance, merchant skiffs and dhows cruised to and from the city. The Medinat al-Zahar, the Mount of the Bride, constructed by Abd-er Rahman III for his favorite wife, where Hakam II held court, stood proudly on the rise on this side of the river.

Along the irrigation canals and over the aqueducts, long camel and mule caravans carried supplies to the 30,000 inhabitants of the royal palace. Across the Roman Bridge, throngs of citizens and visitors flowed into the central beehive of the old city.

"The great highways were built by the Romans." Ben Hebaron continued to gaze across the valley. "But Cordoba had been home to Greeks, Carthagans, Phoenicians and Iberians before the Romans arrived. We owe much to that city. There is much to fear where there is such abundance. We live at the edge of what is possible. We fear that at any moment the world will radically change and leave us desolate."

"Why have I been so lucky, rabbi?" Al-Kiran's heart swelled with the view, then collapsed in sadness. "Allah is merciful, yet many, even in al-Andalus, are suffering."

"Cordoba is called the 'Threshing Floor' because the harvest of humankind occurs here." Ben Hebaron held his arms out.

"'Blessed is the man whose delight is
like a tree planted by the rivers of water,
that bringeth forth fruit in his season.
The ungodly are not so: but are like the chaff
which the wind driveth away.'

"Kemi," he paused, "life is both kernel and chaff. Those who are driven by the harsh winds also serve."

Viewing Cordoba in the distance, al-Kiran imagined himself re-crossing the great bridge, entering the central city where cupolas and minarets glistened against the skyline.

"There is much to fear, and much to be gained." Ben Hebaron spoke quietly. "There will be a million humans in our city during the Festival of All Faiths."

Al-Kiran nodded, staggered by the thought.

"They will flow into our mosques and madrasahs, our synagogues and churches." His eyes swept across the vista. "Long ago, Cordoba was called Tardula, the 'City of Gold.' Tardula became the 'Threshing Floor.'"

Tapping his staff against the ground, he continued: "This is the land of the promise, of the incarnation of the dream. Under the guidance of the House of Omayyad, the rainbow array of diverse races, faiths, and cultures has been revealed in Cordoba. This harmonic must not be lost."

Turning from the majestic panorama, he looked caringly into al-Kiran's eyes. "Yet everything is at risk. Do you have the courage to face that and do what you can to protect what was nurtured here by our ancestors?"

"I think so." Al-Kiran shifted uncertainly, his gaze flowing back to the harmony of land, river, trees, city and sky. "My parents think so," he added. "But surely nothing very important can depend on me."

"You are a son of this sacred place. You can fail or you can fulfill the role you were born to serve."

"And if I fail?"

"That world would collapse."

"And so it is with each of us, is it not?" al-Kiran suggested timidly.

"It is so, Blackbird." Ben Hebaron laughed, then turned to the track into the mountains, leading the she-ass behind him. Al-Kiran followed, lost in his thoughts.

They made their way into the mountains. There were no

others travelers on the path. The rabbi had not spoken since their discussion looking out over the Guadalquivir Valley.

Following the donkey, al-Kiran recalled ben Hebaron's story about the crazy mullah and a passage in one of his father's books which said the 'Hermitage' ibn Massara was much older than the philosopher by that name, who had died there.

According to the author, the Visigoth kings, before their conversion from Arian to Roman Christianity, made contact with a group of "warrior monks" who had made a fortress high in the Sierra Morena mountains at the site of an oracular cave which had once been the center of a pre-Christian mystery school.

The Roman Christians insisted that Jesus was literally "god/man, co-equal and identical with Yahweh." The Visigoths had followed an earlier form of Christianity which saw itself as fulfilling the prophesies of the mystery schools, with Christ-Jesus as the supreme Master of the Age. The Roman Church had driven the heretics into hiding.

The "Hermitage" had been abandoned. But after Abd-er Rahman's conquest of the Peninsula, a Sufi tekke was established there. It was so inaccessible, however, that the author could not determine the nature of the activities of its initiates. Al-Kiran wondered what lay ahead.

Late in the afternoon ben Hebaron tethered the donkey. Pointing to a stand of cypress, some hundred yards up and to the east, on the top of the ridge, above the ravine through which they had been climbing, he said:

"Before going on to the Taifa, we will rest in that grove. Smell it?" He helped himself to a drink from the leather water pouch, then handed it over.

Breathing in, al-Kiran tasted the dry yet richly dark like earth turned over, air — loamy and evergreen, musky and piercingly clean through his nostrils, expanding his lungs — smell and texture were wholly different than in the city.

"This is a sanctuary of the Order we seek." He placed his arm around al-Kiran while moving forward. "The time of prayers approaches, but no muezzin's call will reach us here."

Dark-green cedars stood before taller and lighter tiers of

cypress, their feathery leaves rust and gold, dangling from dark branches stretched toward the sky. Wondering what type of "sanctuary" could be within the grove, al-Kiran moved to unpack his prayer rug, but the rabbi stepped in front of him.

"Al-Kiran Kamir Kirian, this is for those who have ears. Your father and your mother have charged me by the Order of Melchezedek and the succession of the Prophets, from Abraham through the most blessed Mohammed — to give you a new device for your prayers. Will you listen now?"

"Rabbi . . ." al-Kiran started backward, his eyes on his teacher's face. The fear which had haunted him since his first talks with Marik — regarding the dangers of study with a 'heretic' — flooded his mind. He had sworn he would not lose what he held most sacred. Words streamed from him:

"These prayers keep my soul within the will of Allah, the most merciful, as taught by the Blessed Prophet." Catching his breath, he noted that ben Hebaron was listening carefully. "I would practice such disciplines as you teach and my parents sanction — but not at the expense of the Shariah."

"Over that ridge . . ." his eyes moved from al-Kiran as he pointed, "beyond the next defile, lies al-Rusafa, built by Abd-er Rahman in memory of the Omayyad retreat where he was sheltered as a child, at a safe distance from the fury of rival Arab princes. Your prayers, Kemi," his voice smooth and unhurried, his arm around al-Kiran, leaving the prayer rug strapped to the saddle, he moved forward, "are the rudder which steers the ship while it crosses the seas.

"We are tossed back and forth." He paused. "Your striped robe over white tunic depicts the multiplicity of our outward lives and the unity of our inner life, our surrender to the divine impulse."

"The rug marks the space by which I orient to Mecca," al-Kiran insisted, "the Hajj which my heart takes that my body might follow."

"In this circle, there is no need for a rug. Bright Allah dances here with the Dark Mother."

Ben Hebaron took his arm and, allowing no resistance,

escorted him through bushes and scrub trees. Skeletons of wild-flower clusters bedecked the rocky soil in small clearings beneath the winter glare. They crossed a sand path which separated the outer cedars, thick and tangled, from an inner circle of cypresses, their long branches flapping in the wind like the wings of huge vultures. Two eagles circled above them, weaving through the sun-splashed clouds.

"As you know," the rabbi spoke casually, "Othman argued that the ancient gods and sacred sites should be honored, but bowed to the will of Allah when the Prophet demanded his head." He stopped to survey the tree-ring. "Eventually the six surviving companions of Mohammed elected Othman as Caliph. The Omayyads were to carry the revelation into a gentler time. Nonetheless, the fighting continued.

"Ultimately the descendants of Othman were massacred, and a second line of descent, the Shi'ite through Ali, stood alone to protect diversity, if it could. Of the house of Omayyad, only Abd-er Rahman had escaped. He came to this circle, ancient before time was marked — as do now the agents of Hakam II. Yet the present Caliph is more interested in his books than in the mysteries of the old order."

Ducking down, he passed beneath the branches of a cypress on the north, then stopped and cupped his hands beneath his solar plexus, bringing them slowly to his heart. They were standing before an ancient monolith carved with a Celtic sun-swirl surrounded by four crescents.

Al-Kiran's breath was shallow, his pulse accelerating. They were entering an archaic world, the atmosphere pungent, the silence deep. Moving with his teacher to the other side of the guardian stone, he saw nine menhirs standing before nine trees, forming an outer perimeter. A spring bubbled up and pooled in bedrock in the center of the clearing, around which crouched twelve additional stones, forming an inner circle, looking like humans at a ceremony.

A shadow, cast by the mountains to the west, moved across the glen. A dark hand, from the cypresses, reached toward the pool in the center. Ben Hebaron spoke:

"When Othman established the Omayyad succession, tolerance was at the center of the discipline. His armies marched forward, but the purpose was to stabilize the people.

"Your ancestors wore black when commemorating military victory, even in 'holy war.' Death and suffering do not excite you, regardless of the promise of the afterlife. The Omayyads love wine. They celebrate the flesh — the stimulation inherent in life, the pleasures of this world.

"Mohammed embodied the unity of love under the will of Allah. He avoided excess. He was ecstatic with an inner fire. He was equally warm in his consideration of clansman and outsider, male and female, rich and poor, free and slave.

"Your ancestors accepted the Messenger. But they are not steady in the way of the Prophet. The Omayyad are exhilarated by beauty. A love of excess pumps within their blood. Your blood, Kemi. Thank Allah, the Merciful, it is a love of beauty, not war . . . not doctrine."

He reached forward and lifted the hair from al-Kiran's neck, letting it flutter in the breeze. "Your peoples, and mine, rise out of the desert. We are from the same seed. We need the dark as well as the light. In some ways the light is more cruel than the dark." Pausing, he studied his student.

"Never forget that history is food . . . food for growth. But growth often brings suffering. The Prophet ate deeply and suffered. So did the Christian messiah. So did Moses and Abraham before them. They fed on history and they became a part of the history which feeds us."

He turned to the stone circle. "The fundamentalists finally breached Othman's palace. The fanatics assassinated one of the best hopes for stabilizing our peoples. The fire, which mixes light and dark, burns in your breast."

He shifted again, looking back into al-Kiran's eyes. "Recognize it. Control, but also nurture, your love of beauty. Never deny your natural appreciation of, and respect for, all life. We walk the sharp edge of a sword. Never lose courage. Let it be the other wing to your faith."

Pointing to the stones, he continued: "You will study, in due course, how Othman's widow thrust out her hands to protect the sire. The assassin chopped off her fingers with the scimitar meant to celebrate the moon. That was the price she paid in the work which we must do."

Gazing around the stones again, he waited for a response. Al-Kiran remained silent. He was re-living the dream of Orwan Kamir Oshiwah, his grandmother, in the cave.

After a few moments, ben Hebaron said: "It is the time for prayers." He was speaking softly, his voice personal and gentle now. "With the blessing of your parents, I introduce you to these ancient trees and stones. The winds of the wide seas can not reach you in this cove."

Chanting from the Koran, he moved forward, al-Kiran following him into the circle:

"La ilaha illa-llah: There is no reality
Apart from the resplendence of Allah.
La ilaha illa-llah: May the resplendence of Allah
Find a home in my heart. La ilaha illa-llah:
The sound of Allah's own remembrance,
Sings in my heart."

Since his first prayers at his father's side, al-Kiran had never intentionally disregarded the prostrations and prayers facing Mecca. Walking now among the stones, his movements coincided with the refrains of the great prayer. Instead of resistance, he felt the Messenger's love within his steps.

Dropping into contemplation, he sensed the rabbi moving around the inner circle then crouching at the foot of the pool. He barely noticed his master as the wings of the eagles spread above them, weaving a sign in the darkening clouds.

"Rabunni?" He approached from behind

"Yes, Kemi?"

"My heart is steadier here than I can remember."

"As is mine, Kirian." He patted the low slate stone in which the waters pooled. "This is a sanctuary between the worlds. As the Great Mosque in Cordoba opens to the side letting the sun shine through, this shrine has no ceiling. The only dome is the sky."

"And the wood here," al-Kiran broke in, "has never been cut. These are the living sentinels you spoke of.

Ben Hebaron nodded. "The living grove protects us. Do you also recognize the life in these boulders?"

"I sense a resonance."

"From the center of the earth."

Startled by an amethyst under-ripple in the pool, al-Kiran didn't respond. A red wave shot past them, from their left. They both looked up. The last splendor of the dying sun sprayed across the mountains, reflected off the clouds and into the pool, catching the rise of the air pockets exploding from the spring.

"And these waters," al-Kiran pointed, "are also alive."

"They are the firmament across which the Ain Soph breathes. Malkuth bears the children who, in the dance of the Elohim, brought forth our race.

"But," he patted al-Kiran's shoulder, "before I swoon back into Kabbalistic exegesis, let me compliment you. Here is the alchemical truth. You are feeling it directly."

Ben Hebaron chuckled and scratched his beard. "I'm an old scholar looking for the renaissance of learning. I'm also your friend and teacher." He smiled. "I would honor these moments. Yet something yearns for the debate, yearns to launch us into the world of abstractions."

"Rabunni," al-Kiran was flattered by the reference to friendship, "before I came to you, astronomy was just about planets and celestial spheres. Now, by your guidance, I seek to understand correspondence. My inner ear is excited by a music which sustains the universe. Your teachings put flesh on the skeleton of Allah. The scholars at the academy gave me the skeleton. You have shown me how life forms around it."

Shadows crossed the fountain in the middle of the grove. Nine larger monoliths stood like warriors in front of each of the cypresses forming the outer ring.

"Before these inner stones begin to dance," the rabbi grinned, "I have more practical messages to give you. While we walk toward the Hermitage, I will declare the history of the local princedoms. If we don't start now," he guided his student around the guardian stone and into the trees, "it will be morning before we arrive. I am a lover of the outdoors — but these bones yearn for a bed when I sleep."

Al-Kiran felt much lighter. The time within the trees, after the long hike into the mountains, had refreshed him. Following ben Hebaron, he thought about Kristien and yearned for her company. If the next month proved fruitful, they would fly at the eclipse of the sun. "Whatever that might mean." The words slipped out as they approached the donkey.

"Whatever that might mean?" Ben Hebaron chuckled. "While you think, nibble on this bread and cheese." He handed al-Kiran a packet. "We have now passed one round of the prayers without Mohammed's blue rug — the wine will keep."

A wave of apprehension hit al-Kiran.

"I do recognize your concern." Ben Hebaron glanced at him. "During the 337 years since the Prophet's death, the fermented grape has ruined many of the great princes.

"But, Kemi, there are mysteries in all that the Goddess has produced from the seed of the God, including wine, for good and for ill." He smiled, but al-Kiran felt as if a heavy weight had fallen from the sky, darkening now above them.

"Changing the formulae by which you have practiced your approach to Allah, breaks you from a faith which has served you. You realize, do you not," he paused while al-Kiran dropped his head, acknowledging but resisting his teacher's words, "that God's love is in this circle, and in your heart?" His finger, placed on al-Kiran's chest, felt like fire. "That the Ka'ba is in Mecca, but also here."

"Would you have me break the laws brought to my people by the Messenger of God?" Al-Kiran keep his eyes on the ground.

"Laws can become the bars on a prison window. They steady you at the beginning of your flight. They help to establish what is, in general, in a particular time and place, among a particular people, right and wrong. But there may be a time when, through the wisdom and love of the Divine Father and Mother, the laws by which the children were raised must become the platform from which they must leap."

"Or be pushed?" al-Kiran looked into his teacher's eyes.

"Or be pushed," ben Hebaron responded, his hand at the back of al-Kiran's neck, squeezing gently, then squaring him to the path they were to ascend together.

The last pink streamers melded into the darker blue and gray patchwork of the heavens above them. Trees were fewer and farther apart now. They were beyond the olive and fig orchards, so familiar in the valleys.

"Kemi," ben Hebaron broke the silence, "I referred to wine, the first miracle according to the Christian vintners. There is the wine of the fermented grape and there is the wine of the transformed spirit. Do you understand?"

"I do." But, trudging along beside him, al-Kiran knew that the Jew had no inhibition about wine of either sort. Based on the experience in the circle, he suspected that ultimately he would be expected to break each of the sacred pillars of Islam, and was determined to resist.

"Many Moslems in Cordoba drink wine," al-Kiran observed, tactically, "but it's forbidden by the Koran. The ecstasies of wine, as a symbol of spiritual flight in the Sufi poets, become for these Moslems an excuse for ignoring the Shariah, given by the most blessed Mohammed that we might serve Allah."

"And gain life everlasting in the divine gardens of another world," ben Hebaron added. "But is it not the will of Allah that we look to the circumstances addressed by the prophets? Is it not also Allah, whom we call Yahweh, who spoke through Jesus, whom Mohammed called the Savior?"

"There is only one God," al-Kiran agreed, "but you teach that His messengers have not always gotten his message right."

"Do you think that Jews and Christians, who have not followed the Shariah, are doomed?"

"They may have their own paths," al-Kiran answered thoughtfully, watching the ground. They wove upward across ever rougher terrain. "But for myself, I have received the

Prophet's message. It is the steady path by which I have been trained and the one I am determined to keep."

"It is wise that you see it as 'the steady path' by which you 'have been trained.'"

"Then why, Master, did you suggest . . ."

"That you must do that which violates your faith?"

Al-Kiran nodded.

"Because ultimately you must fly." He scanned the path ahead, then picked up his pace. They had been climbing since mid-day. He was much stronger than al-Kiran had suspected.

"I suggest that the Shariah of the Prophet provides a tent in the desert. The great disciplines protect the tribes against the sun and the cold, the heat of the mid-day and the overwhelming mystery of too much night."

Al-Kiran noted that it didn't follow that the tent wasn't necessary. He wasn't comfortable with what would follow.

"But just as the carpet isn't needed in the sacred grove, the tent is of no use to the traveler while he walks. Wine in the body can be spirit to the soul, even of a Moslem. Divine intoxication and drunkenness are parallel paths. You may travel one while avoiding the other."

They were rounding another rise where the path veered back to the north. Near a precipice overlooking a jagged defile, ben Hebaron tethered the mule.

"There are several points along this ancient way to which I wish to draw your attention." The wind surged up the ledge, flapping their robes. There was no moon, but the outline of the canyon stood out clearly under the night sky. The stars were shining with unusual intensity.

"That silver line," he pointed, "is the Kymerian Stream. From this point we can see that it is winding from those crags above us, to which we proceed. Beneath us it passes through the canyon beyond the Circle of Cypress, where we prayed. From the ledge beyond the circle, you can see the tip of the highest turret of al-Rusafa, beyond which the stream flows toward the sacred fountain of the central mosque in Cordoba.

"Now, Blackbird, turn north. Cast your eyes through the

black horns of those pinnacles." He paused while al-Kiran struggled to focus, then caught the flash of a gold beacon. "That, my student, is the Hermitage ibn Massara.

"The sanctuary between the worlds enfolds more than sky and earth. The emissaries of the Caliph's retreat often join the old dancers from ibn Massara among the cypress stones, encircling the clear waters."

"Master . . ." They were rounding a steep cliff. The drop into sheer darkness made al-Kiran nervous. "Can't we stop at the next clearing?"

"Grab the donkey's tail, if you must." Ben Hebaron marched forward, impervious to the danger.

Continuing to climb, al-Kiran became increasingly disoriented. The stars worked their way across the dark sky. A hoot owl fluttered within the shadow cast by a boulder above their path, reminding him of his struggle to distinguish dreams from the waking world. Ben Hebaron stopped suddenly and pointed: "The Taifa ibn Massara appears now."

Two figures stood approximately twenty feet in front of them. Al-Kiran could barely make out the shapes of two winged lions carved in the granite on either side of a natural tunnel which traveled upward into the further dark.

"Master," he whispered, astonished, "those are like the guardians to the maze in my family's garden."

"So they are." The rabbi patted him affectionately.

"Are they the lion and the lioness, after the Magian originals?"

"The Magians are based on those from which these also descend." Ben Hebaron held him by the shoulders now, looking into his face. "How do you feel?"

"Fine . . . Maybe a little tired . . . I am tired."

"Then you must rest before we go further."

Al-Kiran was losing consciousness. His eyes dropped. He heard himself chanting lines from his poem to Kristien.

In his dream, he pursued a black dancer, but remembered nothing further until he awoke the next morning in a cell — in the Hermitage ibn Massara.

CHAPTER EIGHT

"THE ZIRYAB, THE MISTRESS, AND THE SHEIKH"

"Ziryab's my name — 'Blackbird' — like you!" The person standing next to al-Kiran's bed and pulling at the heavy wool cover, came into focus slowly. Pure ebony, with beautiful eyes shining out of a face too big for the body, yet, somehow, just right, he tilted sideways. White teeth sparkled between large lips. A broad smile floated beneath a flat nose.

"Ziryab means blackbird, like Kemi," he repeated, apparently elated by the coincidence. "Or gold water, if you follow the Persians. Who knows?" he exclaimed. "They're too magical for me!" He was nearly shouting. Al-Kiran wanted to roll away, but Ziryab was tugging at him.

Sitting up, rubbing his own eyes, al-Kiran examined him. He was short, but his arms seemed very long — spread like wings, loose and cocked funny, his hands fluttering.

"Oh, Kemi, we'll have such fun, won't we?" The African stood on tip-toes, dancing in a circle. "It may be fool's gold or black water which flies. Who knows?" Crouching and rising, bobbing his head, he flapped his arms like a bird.

Al-Kiran stood-up, startled initially but amused now by Ziryab's clowning. "How old are you?"

"So old, Kemi," he spread his arms, emphasizing the space between, " — about your age." He continued his antics.

Cold now, al-Kiran hurried to pull on his trousers, tunic, and boots, gray with dust accumulated during the trek into the mountains. He wondered where ben Hebaron was and whether he had overslept. Had he missed the call to prayer?

A gust of nearly frigid air swirled into the room from the slit in the wall above them. The African — wearing only a light green cotton robe, striped with red lines, and nothing on his head, his hair kinky and drawn back into a plaited tail — took al-Kiran's heaviest robe from a peg on the wall and handed it to him, waiting patiently while he wrapped himself.

"Aren't you cold?" Al-Kiran shivered.

"Fire is cold, air is warm, it's all how you touch it," Ziryab answered. Looking closely now, al-Kiran couldn't be sure of his age. He had been acting like a boy. He moved like a young athlete, yet his black face, like old leather, was deeply creased. Crows feet stretched from his eyes.

A sun shaft beamed through the window, hitting the opposite stone wall. They were in a tower, the walls curving in a circle around them. Al-Kiran's gear was stacked neatly on a wooden bench, the only furnishing other than the bed and a lantern. His prayer rug was rolled up beneath the bench.

Someone else's clothes and a small African drum were piled at the other end of the bench. Apparently he and this Ziryab shared the room and had shared the bed.

"Where are you from?" al-Kiran asked, ready to search for ben Hebaron.

"From everywhere I'm not." His companion riddled back with a mischievous grin.

"Where exactly," al-Kiran smiled, disarmed, "before you came here?"

"Ah, Kemi. Your master said you would be fun." He hunkered over, in obeisance, reciting his pedigree: "I am Ziryab, the style maker, from the hills south of the great dessert. I am Ziryab, by descent from Haroun al-Rashid, who had his magic in Baghdad. I am Ziryab of the line of Abu al-Hasan. Captured and traded up from the forests of my ancestors by Yemenite corsairs, I became the grand master Abbas ibn Firnas, who made the stars appear in crystal goblets for the princess mother of Abd-er Rahman — and for you I can dance, then fly."

He crouched, flapping his arms, then spinning.

"A fine answer." Al-Kiran laughed. "I remember nothing since the rabbi ben Hebaron told me we were close to the Taifa. And," he added an afterthought, "what do you mean, my master said I would be fun? How do you know him?"

"You don't understand?" He twisted the question as if personally distressed. "This tekke moves but stays — has been here, may be gone tomorrow. Magister Alpha ben Hebaron, much revered, that old scoundrel, comes often."

"Scoundrel?" al-Kiran bit back, irritated, thinking he had caught the African in a slander and a lie. "He is my master! He couldn't have come. I would have known."

"He is here now," Ziryab responded reassuringly. "Down below. Don't be mad. He's visiting with the Sheikh." Pausing, he lowered his voice and whispered: "That old goat."

"What?" al-Kiran raised his voice angrily.

Ziryab rolled his eyes. Following his gaze, al-Kiran saw that the ceiling swirled to a cone-like point.

"But he may also be in Cordoba," he hunched his shoulders, "lecturing about rainbows or, in the synagogue, about old Tetragrammaton." His mouth fell into a pout. "Yod He Vau He knows I'm a dumb Chrestian — but," he pulled his lips into a toothy smile, "I teach what you know." Crossing his eyes, he stumbled around the room roguishly swinging his arms, conducting a sword fight with an invisible opponent.

"Chrestian?" al-Kiran asked, surprised, uncertain how to read the gestures, but interested.

"'Simpleton.' You know." He looked carefully at al-Kiran. "The title we use with the Romans. Better that than the lions and bears!" he exclaimed, his voice rising, holding his arms out, then dropping to a knee and bending backwards, bearing his chest in a gesture of martyrdom.

"Right?" he added, more seriously, when al-Kiran didn't respond. "Jewish/Christian/Mohammedan — but that's enough about the mysterious Alpha ben Hebaron." He bowed again, then lifted his robe and shook a bare foot, dangling at the end of a black muscular leg. "Tell me, who honors my bed?"

Puzzled but fascinated, al-Kiran said: "Blackbird, Riddler . . . I presume you know more than I do."

"A name for me now, is it?" Ziryab seemed pleased, then began whirling to his left, declaring: "Golden-haired . . . blue eyed . . . noble-blooded," emphasizing each combination of words as if uttering an oracle, his eyes on al-Kiran at each turn.

Stopping suddenly, arms out, then hooking in from the elbows, clawing into al-Kiran's shoulders, holding his face to his own, his breath musky with mint and raw turnips, he continued: "Arab-child . . . scarlet bobkin . . . sacred trees. Skull mountain holds blue water. Black fields — mother's song in death's kingdom. Children dance . . . blackbirds climbing . . . gold in the sky. Learn to fly."

Moving to the landing outside their door, laughing and shaking his hands, he swiveled back, head first, his body following like a puppet suspended from above, in a move which astonished and unnerved al-Kiran, and riddled in schoolboy play-song, his voice full of good humor:

> "We be magpies, ready and bold.
> Under broad skies, our home is the road.
> From the smith to the tent, to search we are sent
> For al-Kemi's gold in the heart
> of the black motherlode."

Clapping his hands together, coming close again, his breath warm, he whispered: "We're friends, al-Kemi. That's the thing," then disappeared down the stairwell, the words of another song trailing behind him.

Backing away, al-Kiran struggled to make sense of what had happened. He hoped he would be called soon to talk with ben Hebaron. He realized that he had slept through the muezzin's call. No inner drive had brought him to his feet for ablutions and prostrations, ritually repeating the name of God just before sunrise.

In the sacred circle, he had been broken away from the patterns which had sustained him to that point. Perhaps there was no muezzin here — no mosque or minaret at Taifa ibn Massara. Whatever moorings had secured him before, were gone.

The bed he sat on would normally hold several more sleepers — particularly as the cold season gathered and the solstice neared. But for the present, apparently, he and Ziryab were to have the chamber to themselves.

The drone of chanting and rhythmic clash of exercise weapons filtered through the slit in the stone wall above him. He climbed on the bench, hoping he might stretch to the opening and pull himself up — but the window was too high.

He wished that ben Hebaron, or Ziryab, would return with instructions and an explanation of what he was to do. Apparently he was on his own. He pulled a red sash out of his pack, wondering whether to wrap it about his forehead in a turban as was his right as a member of the Cordovan ruling class — but that, he decided, could be ostentatious.

Ziryab called the Hermitage a tekke — a Sufi working center. The night before, while he had gazed at the sentinels with ben Hebaron, he had felt a kind of electricity within his bones. He was feeling it again. Where was ben Hebaron? Why hadn't he explained more about this place?

He started across the landing and down the stairs. Wondering whom he might meet below, he composed a stanza:

"Al-Kemi, I am, Kamir Kirian, in a strange land,
Walking the way of the blackbird on a limb . . ."

The curve of the language pleased him. It acknowledged some of the crazy references suggested by his African room-mate. But poetry did little more than momentarily occupy his mind. In spite of his attempts at control, he was anxious.

The severe, stone staircase descended into the high-vaulted great hall in the middle of the keep. Several groups of men were huddled about, talking and gesturing among themselves. A fire was burning in an open pit, in the middle of the room, the smoke trailing upward.

There were no intricately carved trellises or beautifully elaborated mosaics, no marble columns and filigreed arches. The interior was simply a large stone room with torches ensconced about the walls, beneath high windows through which the smoke eventually escaped.

"Al-Kiran!" Ziryab came through the arch at the back of the great hall. "Over here. Aren't you hungry?" He was shouting across the din of the voices.

None of the adults, huddled in their circles, even turned to greet al-Kiran, or to hush Ziryab, who was comfortably rambunctious, child-like, of little concern to them.

Walking across the great hall, he noticed that many of the occupants were women. Like the men, they were dressed in large baggy trousers, with long shirts, tails extending beneath the knees, and bright cummerbunds. All wore soft leather boots into which their trousers were tucked. The men had on small compact turbans, like a mullah would wear. The women wore leather caps. Their hair hung loosely over their shoulders, falling onto patched, multicolored over-robes.

When al-Kiran reached the back arch leading to the cooking area, Ziryab waving him on, he was startled by a sudden gong. The men shouted: "Stop!" He froze. No one moved. Even 'the riddler" was frozen, his random gesture caught in still air, his arm suspended back toward al-Kiran. The rest of his body leaned into the next room, ready to leap.

"Begin!" the women intoned with one breath. Then everyone was moving again, as if there had been no interruption.

The African laughed at al-Kiran's shaken expression. "Don't worry, Kemi. That's not for us."

"But, Ziryab," puzzled, al-Kiran lowered his voice, "do none of these people even see us?"

"They do, Blackbird." The African looked into the Cordovan's face, smiling. "But it's the Mistress who has business with us, at least today."

"Where is my teacher?"

"In here." Ziryab placed his open palm on the center of al-Kiran's chest. Then more quietly: "In here, my friend."

The kitchen, much to his surprise, was splendid. Unlike the great hall, this room was warm and full of light.

Several men and women were busy at a huge stove built with heavy bricks. Beautiful mosaic tiles depicted plants and animals in a circle around gods and goddesses feasting together in an open field, against a bright blue background. Even in Cordoba, far from the iconoclasts of Baghdad and Damascus, he'd never seen such naturalistic art.

The adults turned toward them. The riddler stepped back

as a copper haired, hazel eyed, strikingly beautiful woman, in a ruby, silk gown stepped forward. Over her heart, she wore a nine-pointed pendant. Holding her arms out, she seemed to expect al-Kiran to come forward.

"Our guest has arrived, Ziryab." Her voice melodic and casual, her eyes flicked toward the African. "Have you, my faithful, given him water? Have you quenched his thirst?"

Ziryab bowed, arms crossed over his chest.

"Al-Kirian — al-Kemi . . ." Her smile drew him to her. "I am your Mistress here. Although you may resist, love comes for you. Love crushes you then sets you free."

She held him at arms length, examining him with approval, then turned him toward the small table in an alcove which opened onto a breathtaking vista. Mid-morning light poured through the window with reassuring warmth.

The table was spread with fruits, bread, and milk. A large ornate honey mug, in the form of a golden bee, sat to one side. He gazed out the alcove window, across an abyss toward the opposite cliff, then at the mosaic in the center of the ancient table, ribbed with cherry wood. Bright white, blood red, and black onyx tiles formed the pattern of the maze he had so often walked in the garden at home.

Fingers on his shoulders, she directed him to sit. The glow of perfume. Her lips sweeping his left ear, sending a chill through him, she purred: "Eat now. I awaken you. Don't try to understand."

Her fingers at his diaphragm, his umbilical and hips, she kissed his right ear. "All you know must die before you fly." Light glittered within his skull. He struggled for breath. "We prepare you."

Ziryab seated himself opposite al-Kiran.

Returning to the others, the Mistress instructed them in various chores while al-Kiran tried to focus on the food.

Ziryab was subdued, but ate steadily. Looking up, he said: "You've touched nothing, Kemi. The Mother . . ."

The breeze blew softly through the open windows. "Who is she?" al-Kiran whispered.

"The Mistress of the Kitchen. In her presence we are nourished."

"What of the pendant?"

"From the City of Balkh," Ziryab replied. "It is an old clan emblem — a ninefold impress seen in the ways of the bees. Do you see it here, as well, on our table?"

"It is the design, also," al-Kiran confided, "of a secret heritage, hidden in a garden-maze where I have walked."

"And that maze, Blackbird, is it guarded by lions?"

"It is."

"And is it free from intruders?"

"It has been."

"Then are we not safe here with the Mistress? Is this not the right place to learn the dance?"

At least an hour went by while the Mistress came in and out of the kitchen, giving orders to various assistants, absorbed in her own responsibilities which, Ziryab explained, included management of the tekke: "all the practical matters."

Sitting in the alcove, the breeze curling up from the canyon just outside the window, warmer now in the sun, they were left to their speculations. They watched a young Arab woman come in and deliver a message to the Mistress, who then sent two men out the back gate on some errand. Everything seemed to run smoothly under her command.

"When will I see ben Hebaron?" al-Kiran broke the reverie.

"Probably busy with the Sheikh." Ziryab picked his teeth with a long white fingernail. "Maybe about your dance."

"I can't understand why he hasn't called for me."

"The Tentmaker . . ."

"Mershi Khayam, the 'Tentmaker'" al-Kiran translated from the Persian. "That's what my mother called her."

". . . is in charge here." Ziryab nodded.

"How long have you known her?" Al-Kiran leaned forward.

"So long." Ziryab held his arms out, wrinkling his nose, but restrained compared to his antics in private.

"Be honest with me." Al-Kiran grasped the African's arm. "I have no idea what's going on."

Looking hurt, Ziryab took a small peach and four prunes from the bowl and placed them in a square, with the peach in the center, then picked up the peach, chewed dramatically, swallowed and held his mouth open to show it was empty. "You see," he pointed into his empty spot in the middle of the square, "the center remains even though I have eaten it."

"Not in this world," al-Kiran answered humorlessly.

"Oh but it does." Spitting the peach into his palm, unchewed and whole, he placed it in the center.

"How did you do that?" Al-Kiran was surprised.

Ziryab pointed around the kitchen. "We manipulate the surface to achieve the next step. We are talking about appearances." He glanced in the direction of the Mistress. "Sometimes," he widened his eyes, "I'm a Priest-King and she's my bride. She's a beauty, isn't she!" he exclaimed.

Seeing her now, directing her assistants at the great fire, the grace with which she moved, he imagined Ziryab disguised as her mate — but he pushed the thought away.

"How long have you been here, Ziryab?"

"Longer than you." He held his hands out. "Last night I thought you were dead. I'm the slave now and you're the dancer. Understand?"

"No. Slave to whom?"

"To the Mistress." His eyes watered as he watched her. She was dictating a note to a girl.

"I can't remember last night," al-Kiran mumbled.

"That old scoundrel." Ziryab sounded serious, but grinned disarmingly when al-Kiran started to react. "I mean your revered teacher, of course. It's just a nick-name, Kemi. Don't get so upset," he coaxed.

"Alpha ben Hebaron is one of the best men I've ever known," al-Kiran said, defensively.

"Sure, sure." Ziryab nodded. "But he did drop you in a heap before the Sheikh's divan."

"He was probably tired," al-Kiran tried to explain.

"If the Mistress hadn't ordered me to carry you to the tower, you might still be lying there." Ziryab held his hands up, sleeves falling to his elbows.

"I fainted." Al-Kiran ignored the gesture. "He must have carried me from the cliff below. Anyway," he let his irritation go, "what did he say?"

Ziryab leaned back. "Nothing."

"Ben Hebaron said nothing?" al-Kiran asked, puzzled.

"Nothing." Ziryab swung his oversized head, then seemed to suddenly remember. "Oh, yes, the rabbi, always gruff," he made a face, "shouted something at me while I lugged you toward the stairs."

"You haven't seen him since?"

"No." Ziryab flicked his hands down beside himself. "Nor had I seen the Mistress again until this morning."

"What did she say?" Al-Kiran was distressed and confused.

"You're to learn to fly after the owl. I'm the slave and you're the dancer. Kemi," he reached across fondly, "I am your friend." A burden lifted. "I do truly care."

Ziryab settled back. Gazing through the window, al-Kiran's mind swirled between topics without gaining a foothold.

Deciding to re-initiate the conversation, he leaned forward. "Aren't we to be given anything to do?"

"The morning has gone well enough — don't you think?" Ziryab brought his eyes up from the table, troubled. "I've seen her as the Witch of the Open Fires." He lowered his voice, shuddering. "She can change in an instant."

"Ziryab?" Suddenly reminded of his companion's prophecy about a dark wood and sacrifice, he leaned forward. "Remember my teacher . . ."

"Your teacher, Kemi, is in your heart."

"Yes, Magpie," he responded gently, deep sadness pressing him. He wanted to reassure the African, but didn't even know what the problem was. Filling his lungs with the bright pungency of the mountain air, he released his breath.

"Honestly, friend, where is ben Hebaron?"

Ziryab fiddled with the pattern on the table, as if he could not provide any answers.

Everyone except the Mistress had left. Approaching them in the alcove, she pointed across the defile to the opposite cliff. "Do you believe in omens?" she asked.

"I do, Mother." The African looked up to her like a child wanting to please. Al-Kiran resisted the impulse to call her "mother," although it wasn't an uncommon honorific. Nodding respectfully, he said:

"As the omen is predicted by Mohammed, the most blessed Prophet of Allah, the merciful; only then do I believe."

Her body against his as she pulled him gently upward, she said: "Then do you believe this?" At the bottom of the canyon he saw the silver ribbon of the Kymerian Stream, which must have been washing there since the beginning of days.

A line of trees stood at the foot of the granite wall rising on the other side of the gorge. Stretching her hand out, she pointed down, then pulled his attention upward to a dark hole, a cave mouth, which he could barely make out.

"Someday," she bent him gently forward across the dark stones of the window sill, "you will enter that chamber."

"It is a sheer wall," he shuddered. "I couldn't climb it."

"Then you must descend." She pointed to the top of the opposite cliff, then down to the opening. The wind from below billowed the silk folds of her gown.

He could see a circle of standing stones on the plateau beyond the opposite wall, but no path down the cliff.

"Nor that way either, Mistress."

"Then, Kirian, you must fly."

At that moment he was struck by a terror deep within his memory. The woman had pushed him. He had felt her hand along his spine, rising up along his neck, just beneath his skull as, simultaneously, her other hand plunged into his chest and pulled forward. She had lifted him up and out of the window.

While he fell his robe spread. Instead of the stripes and many colors which he remembered, it was sheer black. The wind pushed up under him. The Kymerian at the bottom of the ravine rose toward him, growing larger. Then he stabilized. He floated upward, across the divide.

Dank smoke filtered from the depth of the cave. Torch fires shimmered across a streamlet which rolled toward him, writhing like a snake. He bent down and cupped water to his mouth. It was red.

The stream was rising, insinuating itself about his ankles, gaining his knees. He backed to the mouth and bent over in the light. A white owl-face looked up from the water. His robe was covered with a black cape. He pushed back the hood and looked again. Kristien gazed at him as he fainted.

"Kemi, Kemi . . ." Ziryab was shaking him by the shoulders. He started up. He was lying on the tile floor in the kitchen. The Mistress was at his feet, her palms at his soles, gazing carefully along his body. They were still alone.

When their eyes met, the Mistress said: "What a problem we've had with you — and a Kirian, too." She shook her head then glared at him like a physical force boring into his heart. Falling back again, he heard Ziryab calling: "Kemi . . . Kemi . . . Spread your wings." But he couldn't move. He fell downward, spiraling into darkness, exhausted, his friend fading into the distance.

Sometime later, feeling soft lips on his forehead, smelling sweet breath, blood rushing into his penis, hard and throbbing, lying upward from his thighs, his pelvis lifting, buttocks flexed, pushing, a hand stroking his maleness, he saw Kristien bending over him, a rough tongue flicking down his neck, his shirt open, robe lying on either side, the cold of a pendant from her neck sliding across his bare chest. She was whispering: "Let it go. Let it go."

He exploded in white, thick ecstasy, moaning. On fire, he sunk back into warm darkness, folded in, moist and free. "Kemi . . . Kemi . . . " Ziryab was at his ear now, mint breathed, urgent, "wake-up. She has a message for you."

Struggling upward again, swimming toward consciousness, cold tile beneath his back, his robe folded over him, the African pulling at his ears, rubbing something about his temples, al-Kiran raised his head, hearing himself say: "What is it, Ziryab? I'm here," as if his friend had been looking for him in a dark room.

"She has a message for you," Ziryab responded, his eyes big. Tilting his head to the side, he pointed to the semi-circle of young women. Each was dressed in a silk robe and jewels. Houri-eyes peered out above veils. Each gown was a different color, virtually sheer. All the mysteries of the female body shown through a rainbow of suggestion. "Like the sacred harem at Medina," Ziryab whispered.

"Who are they?" al-Kiran asked, his throat dry, stunned.

"They're the Mistress's helpers, don't ask more," Ziryab whispered while helping him to sit up.

"Is he awake?" Mershi Khayam's voice came from behind the young women. They spread apart to let her through. A huge stew pot hung over the fire behind her.

Bending beside him, she scanned his body. "I'm sorry if I frightened you." She purred affectionately. "We'll try it again tommorow — okay?"

"Yes, Mother." Al-Kiran was surprised by his words.

"I do have some sad news for you." She scooted her legs under herself and bent forward. Suddenly angry, she barked: "Back, whores — all of you. Back to work! You too, slave!"

Jumping to his feet, Ziryab ran to the fire, and started stirring the contents in the kettle. The women fluttered away, scarves dangling, barefooted, each draping a hand over the African, like a totem, while they passed behind him and, in a line, went out the back gate.

Stroking him affectionately, a weird smile on her face, she whispered: "Now, little one, are you ready for this?"

Fear rising, he said: "What, Mistress?"

"Oh, sweetness, come now," she hushed. "It's just that your master had to leave."

"Ben Hebaron?"

"Yes." She looked upward. Following her eyes, he saw an eagle in the mosaic on the ceiling, a great snake dangling from its talons. "But I'll help you. Honestly, I will."

Rising, she pulled him after her. "My apron, please." She turned gracefully, indicating he should untie the clasps at her back. Raising her arms, she spun back to him, smiling. "And Ziryab will help." Then she turned and bowed to the men entering from the main hall.

"Kemi!" The African hissed from the caldron. "Get over here." Disoriented, he stumbled to the fire.

Sweat on his forehead, Ziryab pulled him closer as women

came through the door, looking older now, wearing aprons and working robes, leather boots. Ignoring Ziryab and al-Kiran, they hurried to stack bowls on a table near the stoves.

Ziryab pointed to the huge ladle. "Be ready to serve."

"What happened?" Al-Kiran whispered.

"You have a fear of heights."

Barely able to speak,he followed the African to the end of a long trestle table and watched while the women served the others. Some carried food into another room where, he assumed, the Sheikh and his senior students were taking their meal.

As soon as they were done, Ziryab left the dining hall. Then Mershi Khayam touched him on the back, leaned down and said: "Come to me when you can."

Dazed, he walked back through the great hall, which was empty now, then up the stairwell to the tower, and spread his rug. Reciting passages from the Koran and all of the songs and poems he could recall, he tried to occupy his mind.

About an hour later, frustrated with waiting for Ziryab and angry that ben Hebaron had left, he considered going to the Sheikh for help. Just then an old man appeared on the landing, cleared his throat, and announced that al-Kiran had been summoned to a private audience.

Tapestries depicting scenes from great wars, adventures, and festivals, hung from the walls. Oriental rugs displaying tribal patterns covered the floors. Next to the divan, on which the Sheikh sat cross-legged, wearing a purple turban and silk shirt over white trousers and calf-skin riding boots, a black antique table held a silver tea pot and cups.

Ab-Dar Il'ium, angular and dark skinned with black hair and eyes, his long mustache waxed straight in the manner of a desert chieftain, looked up from a letter.

Al-Kiran started to speak, but the old attendant silenced him with a sharp hand motion, then bent from the middle, fists closed and arms crossed over his chest, in a military salute. Stepping forward, he took the simmering pot to pour green tea for the master. Ab-Dar Il'ium flicked his hand, indicating that he didn't want any, and returned to his reading.

Then, without respecting any of the customary courtesies due to a guest, particularly one related to the royal family, he looked up again: "The rabbi said you are ready."

"Ready for what, master?" al-Kiran asked, respectfully.

"For instruction." He offered a silver cup.

"Thank you, master, but . . . "

"But . . ." The Sheikh interrupted. "A donkey's ass tells tales, but too much has been told, don't . . . you . . . think . . . An idiot, of course, but . . ." He paused, waiting.

"Who?" al-Kiran stuttered.

He grinned, not unkindly. "Any one who knows themselves. But we don't know exactly how the Mistress fits in. There will be a fight, no doubt, but you'll learn." Holding the tea cup, al-Kiran tried to understand what was being said. "Idiot is a term of honor, of course." The Sheikh glanced at the old man, then back to al-Kiran. "Stand on one foot, would you?"

Al-Kiran lifted one foot. Ab-Dar Il'ium looked him up and down, studying his physique, then leaned forward, taking the hot tea pot to fill al-Kiran's cup, but stopped just short, forcing him to extend his arm further; but as he did so the Sheikh looked away and pulled his arm back a bit, forcing al-Kiran to extend to his extreme, almost pulling him off balance.

"Hold there for a second, will you?" He signaled the old man forward and whispered something. They chuckled, seeming to have forgotten the boy stretched like a crane before them.

Replacing the tea pot on the brazier, he motioned to have his own cup filled, then leaned back. "Do you like tea?" he asked.

"Yes, master." Al-Kiran balanced before him, holding his empty cup out.

"With mint?"

His calf starting to ache, he answered: "Yes, master."

Blowing carefully across his cup, steam rising, taking a sip, the Sheikh commented: "We shall try to get you some." Nodding thoughtfully, he set his cup down. "The advanced techniques require a significant commitment. The Mistress is very busy."

Al-Kiran started to wobble, his arm heavy. The Sheikh added, very sternly: "So you will help her." He twisted his mustache. Pain shot up al-Kiran's leg into his back. "In any event, Kirian, you must learn to wait."

Unfolding his own legs, he stood and stretched, then took the cup from al-Kiran's hand. Leaning forward, he whispered: "Learn from that black rascal. Hear what he has . . . to . . . say."

Ab-Dar Il'ium turned, re-filled his own cup, and walked to the window. Lowering his foot gingerly to the floor, al-Kiran limped from the room, anxious to be alone.

He was left alone in the tower the rest of the afternoon. Confused and frustrated, he recalled a passage from one of his father's books: "Following the scriptural mandate to shatter all idols, the Sufis attempt to break the images which enslave men's minds."

The Sheikh had implied he was not to think, but rather to wait, and to work for the Mistress, and to listen to what Ziryab "'has to say.' Perhaps," he reasoned, "the African 'has to say' certain things."

The light stream through his window shifted upward while the temperature dropped. Spreading his rug, determined to find the rhythm which had rooted him in security and devotion, he prayed for Allah's protection and guidance.

CHAPTER NINE

"THE EMPTY HALL"

In the days which followed, the Cordovan ran errands and did chores under Mistress Khayam's directions and was generally exhausted. He and Ziryab ate their meals with the neophytes and attended the evening lectures by Sheikh ab-Dar Il'ium. Afterwards, he often walked with the African about the battlements of the Hermitage, but whenever he pressed for specific information, his friend turned all his questions back toward himself or feigned total ignorance.

Although the Mistress was kind, her only interest seemed to be in seeing that they got the work done which she assigned each morning. In that Ziryab seemed content, al-Kiran fell into the rhythm of their new routines.

The events of the first day faded from his memory. He was glad to be busy. The work was so physically draining that, with only a few exceptions, he fell into bed at night without questions and slept without dreams.

Sheikh ab-Dar Il'ium was wholly unconcerned with the traditional practices and made no distinctions between various hours or days. Initially, al-Kiran had attempted to pray in the afternoons, or whenever he found a moment alone; but gradually he had given up his former rituals.

One night, ten days after he had arrived, while walking with Ziryab along the parapet, al-Kiran asked why the taifa seemed more like a fortress than a religious retreat.

After peering into the dark, the African said: "Don't ask what I can't answer. Ask His Holiness if you must."

"The Sheikh is busy." Irritated rather than amused, al-Kiran held his arm. "I'm asking you."

Grimacing, Ziryab moved toward the light shining from the door to the Great Hall.

"Whom do you serve?" al-Kiran demanded.

Standing on tip-toe, Ziryab craned his neck, examining the

118

empty space. "I move the pieces in the tent which she has made." He feinted to the left then trotted off toward the kitchen. "And I have more work to do."

Even though al-Kiran believed that Ziryab knew much more that he was willing to share, he grew increasingly fond of him. He was also drawn to, although less sure about, "the tent maker." Always efficient in seeing that "her slaves" kept busy, she could be tyrannical and, at times, frightening. Yet to all appearances, Mershi Khayam was the steady hub around whom the kitchen revolved, and upon whom the entire tekke depended. She fed them well and made sure they got proper rest: "To balance off the intellectual work the Sheikh will surely give you soon enough."

But al-Kiran was anxious. "When will the exercises begin, Ziryab?" he asked. They were hauling in firewood, their last chore after the evening lecture. "I've been here two weeks, but have learned nothing of the dance."

"These are the exercises," the African responded. Dropping the wood on the stack near the largest stove, he spun quickly in a tight circle, his long arms floating outward, working at raising himself into the air.

"Don't push our luck, friend." He stopped. "This may be too fast for me. Shouldn't we learn together — black to white, wrong and right . . . you know?" Dropping to his knees, he cupped his hands in front of his mouth as if praying. A tear wove down the creases in his face. "Isn't this enough, Kemi? Aren't I enough?"

Feeling he had deeply wounded his friend, a pang hit al-Kiran. "But if I were just to do chores," he tried to explain, "I could have stayed in Cordoba."

"Oh, no, Kemi," Ziryab responded slowly, shaking his head. "You could never be a slave in Cordoba."

Pulling the African to his feet, al-Kiran hugged him sincerely. Ziryab wept, the smell of him fresh and strong, like a deep forest. Neither of them said anything further about the exercises.

The next morning a messenger delivered a note saying: "Al-Kiran and the Ziryab may undertake afternoon exercises in the Hall. <signed> Sheikh ab-Dar Il'ium."

As soon as they had cleaned-up following the noon meal, al-Kiran and Ziryab hurried into the Hall where, under the Sheikh's direction in the mornings, they had often seen the dancers practice complex combinations of movements and stops, breathing exercises, and whirling to certain rhythms.

Walking about in the room, they stopped occasionally to limber up. Al-Kiran asked: "Do you think the Sheikh has begun a new class?"

Ziryab twirled on his toes, seeming to dangle in the air, more playful than he had been for several days, then shrugged.

"This is serious." Al-Kiran insisted.

"Well," Ziryab hesitated, "I've never seen anyone in here, from the noon-meal until sun-set, except the cleaning slaves." Al-Kiran frowned. Taking his arms, Ziryab added: "We'll do what we can." He smiled, pleadingly. "But whether the blackbird dances or falls depends on whether you can rise to her, through the energy at your root, without exploding. Let it rise, Kemi. She'll call you. Then hold back."

At that moment Mershi Khayam entered from the hallway. Snapping to attention, Ziryab turned toward her. She wore a cap, a dancer's robe, and soft leather boots. She carried two additional robes over her arms.

Al-Kiran's breath caught. He had often found himself gazing at her astonished by how she dressed like a young queen while administering the kitchen. He had never seen her in anything but fine gowns. Then he saw himself lying on the cold tiles in the kitchen, back from some dream or vision of yearning.

She glanced at him coyly, put her finger to her lips, then pointed to the dais where the Sheikh normally stood. Motioning them to sit where they were, near the center of the room, she pulled on one and then the other extra robe, striped and patched in the manner of the wandering dervishes. Again signaling them to remain silent and stationary, her face radiant, she raised her arms parallel to her shoulders, and began a slow whirl in a counter-sun direction. Maintaining the inner revolutions — she began moving in an outward arching sun circle, then spiral.

Al-Kiran was amazed by the speed of her turns on the inner

axis and the rapidity with which the outer circle, in the opposite direction, increased. Within seconds she had encompassed the entire hall, swirling past them and the dais without a mis-step, her eyes closed during the entire performance. For a brief moment she hovered above the dais, then she was on it, whirling.

"Blackbirds . . . seek . . . the . . . owl," she intoned from the dais, her words punctuating the spin of her body, the outward and inner revolutions, in opposite directions, growing slower, her voice suggestively sensual.

She seemed suspended, for an instant, each time she faced al-Kiran. He was filled with desire for whatever magic she controlled, her body beautiful and athletic beneath the whirling robes, silk pants tight to shapely legs — until she was totally frozen, looking out over the hall through closed eye-lids, the robes, the skirts of which had formed an array which spread from her waist, fluttering down upon each other.

"The Goddess sends greetings." Her voice was matter-of-fact now. "Come forward."

Approaching her, al-Kiran struggled to suppress the fantasies her dance had aroused in him. Languidly, sensuously, she removed one robe and then the next, folding them carefully to one side on the dais. She leaned forward. The Kirian Pendant dangled between her breasts — her skin moist with her breathing.

He tried to calm himself, but his body disobeyed his mind. Her eyes smiled at him. Ceremoniously, she straightened, took off her cap and leaning forward again, extended it toward al-Kiran, then set it on the dais.

He stood before her, his breath rapid, flesh raised in bumps, maleness hard between his legs, trying to deny his experience of her, breathing in her scent, searching for verses from the Koran or anything to distract himself from her eyes, which pierced into him, demanding something.

She stood before them, her legs spread. Al-Kiran gazed at her, his mouth open, throat dry, struggling to suppress his desire. Her movements, then her smile, her eyes bathing him with the soft flickering of breath, of whispers, her hips rotating slowly, suggestively, her musky smell — called to him. Frightened, he was sure she had intended it.

"Mistress . . ." he whispered, remembering ben Hebaron saying: "Never deny the Mother — Matrona-Shekhina-Elohim — who dances with the phallus of the God." In the Great Hall of the Dancers, the Mistress was matriarch and seductress. He glanced quickly at Ziryab, beside him now, nudging him not to speak, bowing reverently.

"These robes will be yours," her voice, even and directive, startled al-Kiran, "for the practices. But," she sighed and rubbed her sleeve along her forehead, "there is a lot of work to do." Pausing, she studied the hall. "Ziryab, get the buckets. Kemi, bring the brushes."

As the African sprang to his feet and ran out the side door toward the stream, al-Kiran addressed her respectfully: "Mistress, are you to be our teacher?"

Throwing her head back, a husky laugh echoed about the Hall. "Of course, Kirian, I would love to teach you, but . . ." extending her arms, still on the dais, she whirled again, her skirt spreading like a Gypsy girl's in the market, "although I have a dance for you, I defer to the Sheikh's decisions."

Stepping down, her hand on his shoulder, her tightening fingers reminded him of being hurled from her window. "Today," she glanced toward the ceiling, "he said your lesson would be 'the cleaning of the stones.'" She started for the door. "Everything in it's time."

"Mistress," he hurried to her side, "is the movement you just demonstrated the one I need to master?"

Throwing her head back and laughing wildly, the sound amplified against the stone walls, she cackled, frightening him, reminding him that she could change in an instant, could become the Witch of the Open Fires — and of something she had done or said the first day, when he had fainted.

"Oh, Kemi," she soothed, "we have the Sheikh to contend with, but I do hope you learn something from my steps." She gave him an affectionate hug. "His rules, you know — just like your needs. All men are frightened. Love rises to kill their smaller selves. I take you to the edge. Don't leap, yet. We tease what is blind and asleep in you so that when she calls from the storm you will die in love and awaken."

"Someday, Mistress . . ." Struck by the memory of the cave mouth across the defile outside the alcove and the cave in his dreams, he hesitated.

"Someday, yes." She placed her hands over the top of his head, not touching, but he felt great warmth pulsing from them. "Your mother cares for you, more than you know."

"My mother?" he asked, tears aching in his chest.

"Yes, Kemi," she touched her lips to his forehead then turned him away, "your mother, your grandmother, myself, and the slave-priestess."

"You know her?" He tried to turn back, but she held him. Voice erotic, she whispered:

"Just wait, Kirian. We're doing all that we can."

Popping her hands against his stomach, knocking the breath out of him so he bent forward, shocked, she spun him back to face her. "The men say to wash the stones. Watch out for the Ziryab, though." She leaned forward confidentially. "He defies the rules." Softening, playfully, she added:

"My dance was for you. Don't . . . think . . . Just find what your body knows. Let your mind ride that." Ziryab reappeared carrying two buckets overflowing with water. She pushed al-Kiran back. "And get the brushes for my slave."

She turned abruptly and left the Hall.

When he returned with brushes and brooms, the African was already splashing water over the stones. Taking a brush from al-Kiran's hand, he started scrubbing vigorously.

"What did you think of all that?" al-Kiran asked. He was excited and wanted to know what Ziryab had seen. And he wanted to trust the Mistress, to whom his mother had sent greetings. But he mistrusted his own perceptions of her. He thought she had said "watch out for the Ziryab," but he didn't know what she had meant. She evoked sexual responses which he wanted to deny, but couldn't.

Looking up from his scrubbing, Ziryab said: "She said not to think."

"What else?" He checked the room to make certain they were alone, determined to tell him his experiences.

The African straightened his back. "That we may not touch the robes until the floor and the walls— to your height, arms stretched, and on toes — are done. And that the Sheikh said this is the next step." With that, he began scrubbing as if there wasn't a moment to spare.

They had just finished the walls. It was nearly supper time. The hard physical work had been good for al-Kiran. While he had moved from stone to stone, his mind had stopped racing. He was tired and achy, but pleased.

The lights streaming through the high windows had shifted upward, no longer hitting the exercise floor. Still on his knees, he watched Ziryab stand and mop sweat from his brow.

At first al-Kiran had been frustrated by his friend's attitude and refusal to talk. Yet Ziryab had taken so seriously to the work, as an exercise, that he had fallen into the rhythm. Neither had spoken for some time.

At that moment, the Mistress reappeared. Dressed in the motley of dancers in the Sheikh's morning classes, her trousers tucked into high leather boots — somehow elegant, she stood examining their work. "Blackbirds followed the owl. That's good!" Her voice was strong and proud.

Waving her hand toward the east, pointing in a line above the windows, where the sun's rays now reflected against the wall revealing a magnificent mosaic frieze which encircled the Hall, along which stylized Arabic phrases from the Koran could barely be read, she said: "But see how scuffed with soot our scriptures are."

Walking slowly across the room, her hips swaying between long steps, she leaped lightly onto the dais and, pointing down to the robes which they had not touched during the long afternoon, said: "Maybe soon, I hope, dear ones."

She smiled mischievously at al-Kiran, like a courtesan. "You are assigned to clean the scriptures." Shaking her head, and squatting down swiftly and exquisitely, her legs bent at the knees, she gathered the robes and caps, adding: "Sometimes I wonder whether males really care what is cleansed."

Folding one leg over the other, she spun upward. A robe hanging over each arm, she glided to the floor then whirled about the room. At the door, spinning back toward them, she called: "See to your chores, Blackbirds."

CHAPTER TEN

"THE LETTER AND THE DREAM OF HISTORY"

Later that night, alone in the tower, al-Kiran discovered a letter stuck between copies of passages from the Koran in the flat leather sheath which he had brought from home. It was written in elegant Arabic script. His hands trembled.

"Dear Kemi,

The Mistress Khayam insists that you not be told the circumstances of my leaving you until you discover them for yourself. Her claim to you is unique and her power immense. Therefore, in order to avoid her wrath and to make certain none of the aids to al-Mansur discover the contents, destroy this letter immediately."

Like a rock had fallen on his chest, al-Kiran struggled for breath. Uncomprehendingly, he took up the letter again.

We, who have had the care of your development to this point, agreed to the terms under which I am required to leave you at ibn Massara. We concluded that only the Mistress and the Ziryab can give you the additional experiences you need in order to free your body from the prison of what you believe you have mastered with your intellect, so that body and intellect can be re-united at the climax of the Dance. But, as a precaution, we arranged to have this letter hidden in such a way that when your own force is ready to 'discover your circumstances' — according to the letter of Mershi Khayam's law — these words will be available to you. The Sheikh will insure that you discover it in private.

I would have liked to explain more earlier, particularly regarding the Nubian; but you would not have understood. It is not personal design but rather necessity which makes so much of what you receive from us obscure. We have given you planks which ultimately you must assemble into a bridge.

126

This is an extremely difficult time for you. Part of you is dying, and must. These are extraordinary circumstances. If we could have gone slower, we would have. But the stakes are so high and the time so short that we felt we had no choice. The nearness of the Dance requires that the pace be accelerated.

My efforts to demonstrate the limitations of intellect have been gentle compared to the techniques practiced by the Mistress. There is risk. But if we did not have confidence that you will survive and grow, we would never have left you.

We aim for the sacred marriage between the masculine and feminine energies, out of which union a miracle can arise — within yourself and between yourself and the Nubian Priestess, between the creativity of the Goddess and the stable strength of the Organized Faith. The Omayyad Caliphs have preserved that marriage in al-Andalus, but al-Mansur would have it otherwise. We only have one month before the Festival begins.

I can not suggest how you might best conduct yourself, nor what the Mistress might do. Your sense of abandonment, upon my leaving, will be painful. Even knowing that what I say in this letter may confirm your opinion that you have been betrayed, I hope it will be of some help to you. I do believe that, through your pain, a deeper essence will be distilled which will in turn become the energy body through which you will fly.

We all recognize the necessity of this experience for you; but, frankly, ibn Shaprut, ab-Dar Il'ium and I are not comfortable giving absolute control to the Mistress. Therefore the Sheikh will intervene if necessary. But we dare not interfere except in an emergency because we are not masters of the energies Mershi Khayam manipulates and our attempts at assistance could ruin her efforts, perhaps with disastrous consequences for you personally and for our determination to stop al-Mansur.

The Mistress is an ally whom we profoundly respect. She agrees with the goal. But her relationship to history and the allegiance we men have formed against al-Mansur is of less consequence to her than to us. Like your mother and grandmother, and the princess-slave, Mershi Khayam is of a more ancient Order. Her primary interest is to make you whole and ultimately free you of the chains of history. She may want you for herself, devoted, as the Ziryab is. But remember, he is a sorcerer and magician with loyalty only to those of his own choosing. He and the Mistress are of the body, wholly personal, and abhor abstractions. But, as your father has taught you, that is not our relationship to history. We work for the preservation of the splendor of this world. And this world, Cordoba, needs us now.

Mershi Khayam has agreed to awaken in you a knowledge and power which is profoundly personal and can not be taught rationally. We trust her, but not completely. Nor does she fully trust us. We do, however, revere her. And as you will discover for yourself, one does not purposefully provoke her. Nevertheless, we will not give you up to her other than on the terms negotiated between us. You may choose your own course later. But first you are pledged to the All Faith's Festival and the Public Miracle prophesied by Mohammed which, if it occurs, will promote the continuation of the Omayyad Tradition and halt al-Mansur, whom it is critical we not underestimate. He has his allies, Kemi. Our plans must remain secret. Therefore, in order to insure that none of his agents — nor even Mershi Khayam or the Ziryab — find this letter, do destroy it immediately."

His head spinning, al-Kiran lay the letter on the bed and tip-toed to the landing, afraid that even now Ziryab or the Mistress may be coming. He couldn't believe that either of them would betray him or the effort to save al-Andalus. He could not comprehend or accept what the rabbi was saying. Suddenly chilled, he realized that ben Hebaron, for all his apparently good motives, may not have understood at all what Mershi Khayam was or intended or how things actually had developed with her and in the Tekke in general. Yet, he could see now that the Sheikh might have been playing a type of game consistent with what ben Hebaron described. Shaking his head, exasperated, he picked the letter up again.

"This is my attempt to summarize exactly what we see as being at stake and how, if we are successful, the threat to history might be overcome. Al-Mansur gains power over his Majesty in ways which are dangerous to the Kingdom. With the birth of a son, Hisham, Hakam II is satisfied with the succession and places his attention on other matters; but we foresee that the Caliph will not survive another nine years.

Certain Christian ascetics seem determined to demonstrate their faith by blaspheming Allah. They polarize the Moslem judges. At the same time, the Berber chieftains believe that the Omayyad support for diversity is a threat to Islam. Al-Mansur is playing one faction against the other in order to consolidate his own power.

Using the fear of a Christian invasion from the North, al-Mansur preaches that Islamic unity, through suppression of heresies, is necessary to the preservation of the Kingdom. With subtle genius, he twists the truth. Under his direction, intolerance, racial hatred, and religious strife are on the rise.

Upon Hakam's death, al-Mansur will attempt to become Vizier for the Heir. He would control al-Andalus with sword and flame. This world, where we are pilgrims, would slip back into night. We can not stand idly by.

As the sun fades now to it's darkest point, do not be discouraged. Even though you may seem to be making no progress, there is much of which you are not conscious. Out of the darkest hour comes the light. Much of al-Andalus will be gathered for the Festival. The vast majority will be of good heart, excited with expectation, devoted to the chants and rituals, emotionally supporting the dancers. These energies must be used also.

You have begun seeing into the spiritual worlds, crowded with the potentialities of what may be realized here on earth. Your native powers frighten you, but those visions open channels to a wider sense of your self and your role in the world. By blood and physical talent, you are the chosen male to attempt the prophetic dance. Kristien, uniquely trained, is the female.

At solar noon there will be an eclipse and two dancers will fly. That is the essence of the prophecy. At that moment the inner and outer worlds will coincide. Consider a formula, which applies to your time in Taifa ibn Massara and your lessons with the Mistress: 'Al-majazu quantaratu'l-Haquqat.' The Phantasmal is the Bridge to the Real. No power can separate you from God, except you allow it. Although you may be thrown from the cliff, the angels will catch you, if you but reach for them.

Through your dreams and visions — and moments when you think you are mad — new pathways are being driven to the secrets in your blood. What part of you knows, another has forgotten. The angels and the monsters are presenting you with parts of yourself through which you may know other dimensions which overlap your own. I will watch for you along those other planes.

When creatures from your inner world appear in this world, or you don't understand what is happening, simply observe without judging. You are not ready to discriminate. Remember in those times to chant and rehearse the rapid stomping that I taught you. Panic can not control your mind while you control your body. If it persists beyond your endurance, petition the Sheikh. But remember, each event comes to you for a reason. Learn what you can from each encounter.

Regarding the Cordovan Caliphate, it is our hope that the energies of the dance will bring you and Kristien to the further attention of Hakam II. We build upon that which passed between you and His Majesty at the summer solstice and foresee that Kristien will be joined to the harem at Medinat al-Zahra, where she may help Subh in the struggle against al-Mansur for control of the Heir.

There will be a moment when all is dark, and all is open. Look then, Kemi, into the crowd around the Caliph. Enfold your young cousin in the wings spread from your heart. All will evolve from that moment.

Allah is as close as your jugular vein. I will do what I can to guard you, lest you fall. What comes of this the future will tell. Our only duty, as you know, is to do what we can to steady the flight of the world.

Alpha ben Hebaron"

Folding the letter, al-Kiran struggled against the command that it be destroyed. He desperately wanted to study it in detail. At that moment, Ziryab entered the chamber. Startled, al-Kiran stuffed it under the mattress. Ignoring him, apparently distressed, Ziryab went immediately to bed.

Sitting on the bench, al-Kiran tried to decide what to do. Two weeks had passed since his arrival. He and Ziryab were simply errand boys, barely tolerated by the neophytes, ignored by everyone of any importance except the Mistress. Yet he knew a huge responsibility would be resting on his performance at the Dance of Created Lights.

They had been allowed to attend the evening lectures by the

Sheikh, which were filled with complex diagrams, similar to those given by ben Hebaron in the park. But al-Kiran could no longer see any sense in them.

Although Ziryab insisted that the chores they performed were practical exercises, and al-Kiran knew his body had become stronger, his stamina greater, he was deeply distressed that he had received no actual training. When possible, he had watched the dervishes in the mornings and, once, Mershi Khayam's exquisite exhibition — but she had implied that the Sheikh would not permit her to give him formal instruction.

The letter raised many more questions than it answered.

As the days passed, al-Kiran moved further into darkness. He believed the Sheikh and his followers were engaged in work which was extremely important, but he was restless with his role. He couldn't understand what the Mistress intended, or what he was to learn. She had only brought out their robes that one time. She hadn't danced again. She did say, however, that he and Ziryab were doing well. "Ahead of schedule, in fact."

Al-Kiran could not bring himself to destroy the letter. He had, on a few occasions taken it out and studied it, carefully hiding it afterwards in the sheath. He was unnerved. Neither the letter nor the scriptures helped. Yet he could not bring himself to go to the Sheikh, who was not to intervene except in an emergency. He wanted to believe that his lessons with the Mistress were what ben Hebaron intended. But he felt he was dying. Yet at some other level, he was stronger and growing.

As the days followed, he gave up trying to understand and simply worked ahead, trying to do his part. But a cold fear, powered by guilt, gnawed at him. Who could be trusted? What would happen if al-Mansur, through his agents, discovered the letter? What if the Mistress did? Why was he unable to obey Alpha ben Hebaron's explicit instruction that it be destroyed?

On his eighteenth day, al-Kiran ventured to speak: "Mistress," she stood over them in the alcove where they were scrubbing, "are we not to do specific exercises, like the others?"

"I don't know." She bent forward. "I can ask ab-Dar Il'ium, if you wish."

"Me, too, Mother." Ziryab swirled playfully in a puddle.

"You know how busy the Sheikh is. If only ben Hebaron, that old rascal, were here." Sighing extravagantly, she put her hand to her forehead. "Old ben Hebaron would surely know what to do. Wouldn't he, Kemi?"

Al-Kiran was inclined to agree, but when he started to speak, she swirled, her scarlet gown flowing out from her fine slippered feet, and walked brusquely toward the ladies of the kitchen. Turning back suddenly, fist out, her voice sharp and piercing, she screamed: "Have you followed my steps? If not, you will fall like blackbird-dung from the owl."

Apparently in a rage, she stamped forward then squatted and whispered: "Don't ask what you can't understand, Kemi." Starting to rise, she moaned grotesquely. Unable to unlock her knees, she revolved so her back was to them, railing: "No more of those questions or I'll have his African ass."

The women assistants, dressed now in rainbow gowns, like on the first day, rushed forward. Lifting her gently, they carried her from the room.

As soon as the Mistress was out of hearing range, Ziryab returned to scrubbing the floors. Al-Kiran stared after the women moving in a procession toward the Great Hall.

"What happened?" he asked, his heart pounding.

Ziryab looked up from the water he had splashed onto the stones. "She got angry."

"I could see that, stupid," al-Kiran said, then regretted his tone. "What really happened?"

Apparently hurt, Ziryab looked into his eyes. "I may sound like a magpie, Kirian, but I've learned a few things."

"I'm sorry, Ziryab. Just tell me the truth, please."

"Don't chatter at me, al-Kiran." He craned his neck to make certain no one else was present. "If you want to fly, watch the stage as well as the dancer." Then he spun in the water, scrubbing furiously at the stones.

"What are you doing?" Al-Kiran reached out to stop him.

"I'm following what the Mistress says, but from my dimension."

"And what is that, Ziryab?"

"From the ground-up, on my knees." Looking sad, his big eyes on al-Kiran like those of a devoted dog, he added: "Be busy now, Kemi. I'm serious."

That night, while they climbed the stairs to the sleeping chamber, al-Kiran told Ziryab that he would not ask the Mistress any more questions. "If I do, I have the feeling she'll take it out on you. She scares me."

"This is a dangerous place. You never know when she'll change." Ziryab stopped and put his palm against al-Kiran's chest before continuing: "Just keep busy. Watch for the lessons and be ready. Do what she says."

Late the next afternoon, after cleaning the night pans, he and Ziryab returned to the kitchen for further instruction.

"Mershi, Great Mother," the African bowed respectfully, "when may we go to the Hall of the Dancers?"

"When you're not busy with other chores." She returned to her own work, dismissing them.

The next morning, while al-Kiran hurried to clear the dishes in the dining hall, the Mistress called him to the side. "Understand, Kemi, your friend means well; but you're too busy in the mornings to go to the Hall and," she whispered, "ab-Dar Il'ium doesn't approve of the Ziryab. In fact," she giggled, "he isn't sure about me."

Holding him at arms length, she examined his chest then down to his crotch. "For now," she purred, "just be patient." As she pulled him back to herself, his head was spinning. He couldn't understand. He wanted to run away.

Turning him around, her hands on his shoulders, he nearly panicked when she seemed to lift him from behind. He was hovering over the abyss. The cave mouth half way up the opposite cliff, gaped before him. Her fingers stretched his shoulder blades, filling him with pain.

"Wings here, shouldn't there be?" she chuckled, then, releasing her grip, laughing, sent him toward the kitchen. "Go help your friend."

"If we hurry, Kemi," the African called out excitedly, "maybe we can watch the dancers this morning."

Al-Kiran joined him without saying a word. When they had stacked the last load of bowls and plates on the tables near the wash tubs, expecting the women attendants to take over, Mershi Khayam entered from the hall and clapped her hands.

"Women," her voice boomed, "the great Sheikh, his Holiness ab-Dar Il'ium, blessed be his name . . ." She spread her arms upward in humility and gratitude, then knelt and touched her forehead to the stone floor.

The women hushed while she straightened to address them, her mouth open, searching for words, then grinned garishly. "His Holiness has at last announced that you, even you, my humble serving ladies," her voice rose in excitement, "may join the men in the dance."

She cupped her hands above her head and shouted: "Thanks be to Allah and his most masculine prophets that . . . we . . . are . . . so . . . blessed." At which, chattering happily among themselves, all the ladies normally in charge of washing the kitchenware, pulled off their work robes, under which they wore silk gowns. Looking younger and prettier now, they hurried toward the Hall of the Dancers.

When the last had disappeared beyond the door, the Mistress hissed at Ziryab: "Get busy. I told you what to do."

"I will, Mother." Ziryab was shaking.

"You and Kemi clean the kitchen!" She hurried toward the door, still very angry. "And make sure everything is ready."

Ziryab worked furiously at cleaning the kitchen and preparing for the noon meal. Pushing to keep up, al-Kiran felt the edge of exhaustion. When the cooks returned, in their work robes again, several hours later, all was ready.

That afternoon, when they finished removing everything from the tables in the dining hall, Mershi Khayam left the kitchen without a further word. The women attendants seemed delighted to be back at their normal stations.

Ziryab, rubbing his hands along his robe, said: "Now we can go to the Hall and practice."

As was always the case, the Great Hall was vacant during the afternoons. Stretching his back, Ziryab began humming an old tune. Circling al-Kiran, he inspected him. Then, throwing his gaze around the room, he said:

"There must be a pattern in the lessons she has given us. Did you see how she breathed, Kemi?"

It was as if no time had passed since the day Mershi Khayam had whirled through the room and hovered over the dais. While al-Kiran stood in the center trying to remember the Mistress's movements, Ziryab presented an inner revolution, in the opposite direction, each time he passed.

"Was she breathing through her forehead?" Ziryab questioned, moving faster now, his eyes shut, his feet crossing each time he twirled inward while simultaneously following the invisible track of the outer revolution.

"Yes . . . But there was something else, too."

"Through the solar plexus, right?"

"Yes. There was some force from the solar plexus."

The African stopped, and came over to him. "Do this with me." Taking his hands, Ziryab faced him, then pushed out to one side so they spun in opposite directions, then faced each other again. "Let's try that while we walk the perimeter, practicing the spin and the pacing."

Al-Kiran appreciated his friend's eagerness to pursue the exercises. Ziryab was immensely talented at physical mimicry. But, he remembered Mershi Khayam had said, he only means well.

"Nevertheless," he whispered, "he is my teacher."

"What?" Ziryab paused, puzzled.

"You're my teacher," al-Kiran said, seriously.

"No, Kemi." Ziryab pointed to al-Kiran's heart. "That's the only teacher."

"But the Sheikh explained that 'learning how to learn' is the most important lesson," al-Kiran referred to the previous night's lecture. "You're helping me to learn how to learn."

"No, Kemi," Ziryab stepped closer. "I'm teaching you to forget the prison of what you know."

Then he pushed off against al-Kiran's shoulder, so they turned in opposite directions. Trying to pace themselves, they moved around the outside of the room, beneath the ribbon of scriptures inscribed high in the stone walls which the Mistress had insisted, at virtually every free moment, they continue to scrub, pointing out that they had not yet made much impact.

Thereafter, they always had to clean the dining hall and kitchen after the morning meal, making sure everything was ready before the female attendants returned from their lessons with "the Master," as they now referred to Abd-er Il'ium, in hushed tones, when the Mistress was out of the room.

In the afternoons, Mershi Khayam always seemed too busy with other matters to give them additional chores, so Ziryab and al-Kiran practiced almost every day in the Great Hall.

The African could do amazing things with his body, mixing steps and postures. But al-Kiran felt clumsy and inept. He also felt certain that, like himself, the African could not anticipate what the Mistress would do next. And, like himself, he suspected that Ziryab was uncertain what his relationship to her might be.

Left alone late one evening, he re-read the letter, particularly the section on the diminution of the light and the formula: "The phantasmal is the Bridge to the Real. No power can separate you from God, except . . ." but it still didn't help. He wanted to destroy the letter, but he had nothing else to cling to.

During the afternoons, he and Ziryab faced each other, breathing together, spinning in opposite directions and circling the Hall — but never reaching the next stage.

Once, as they sat in the center of the Hall, al-Kiran tried to explain ben Hebaron's suggestions regarding the Kabbalah, the Tree of Life and the Tree of the Knowledge of Good and Evil, and the limitless darkness from which the light-seed explodes. Ziryab listened carefully. Then, frowning, he stood up, spun quickly, and left the Hall.

Al-Kiran had no idea whether what they were doing, or what he had thought he had learned, meant anything at all.

On his twenty-fourth day, while the Sheikh delivered his

evening lecture, al-Kiran and Ziryab sat at the back of the room, cross-legged, surrounded by other students.

Al-Kiran was trying to concentrate, but his mind kept flowing back to the Kerm Oak, and the morning on which he had first seen Kristien, the Nubian Princess, whom he yearned to touch.

Suddenly, intruding from another world, he heard: ". . . a certain operation is critical to the survival of al-Andalus."

Ab-dar Il'ium, looking directly at him, was twisting his mustache. Chills ran up and down al-Kiran's back.

"The Khwaggan Masters resist al-Mansur as he attempts to control the Palace." Holding his hand up for silence, his voice barely audible: "The enneagram awakens the fire, sending crows into startled flight." Pausing: "The lessons I speak are of the eclipse. Go now for the night."

While most of the students got to their feet, their words buzzing about the room, Ziryab leaned over and touched al-Kiran's arm. "For the Mother I go, to do her bidding." Shaking his hands, he spurted upward, and did a step they had practiced that afternoon. "Wait here, Kirian."

Looking up, he saw that he was alone except for the Sheikh. There was complete silence now. Head down again, he struggled to resist the desire to run to his room.

At that moment, Ziryab frantically pulled him to his feet, shouting: "Kemi . . . You must come!"

His heart pounding, he raced up the stairs. Turning the last corner, Ziryab, gasping for air, pointed up at their window, high in the stone wall above the bench. "What is that?"

Trying to escape, Ziryab ran into al-Kiran, still frozen in the door. Moonlight cast shadows across the chamber walls. The fire from the lamp swelled suddenly, then died. The tail of a snake disappeared upward, the rest of its body already outside along the wall or in the air.

Then he heard the flutter of huge wings, followed by the squawks of lesser birds. A feminine voice: "He has it. He's mine!" preceded utter silence.

"Al-Kiran," the African spoke first, having regained some composure, "was that the creature from your dream?"

"What did you see?" Al-Kiran scanned the chamber, suddenly aware that his possessions were thrown across the floor, but Ziryab's things remained stacked on the bench.

"I don't know." Ziryab backed onto the landing. "I was lighting the lamp. Something jumped from the bed." His broad nose wrinkled back into his face as he looked up, sniffing. Shrugging, he flicked his fingers as if shaking something off.

"Don't magpie me, Ziryab," al-Kiran insisted, familiar with his frequent, although usually playful, dissimulations. "What did you see?"

"Nothing." Looking directly into al-Kiran's eyes, he whispered: "And in that nothingness, your future and mine."

Angry and anxious to search for the letter, al-Kiran said: "Run your errand then and leave me alone."

"Will the creature return?" Ziryab bent forward, arms over his stomach, but cocking his head back to keep on guard.

"That's my concern."

Sniffing toward the window and rolling his eyes around the chamber, bowing with arms wide, he backed toward the door, mimicking the subservience of syncopates at royal courts, chanting:

"Ready you are by the dance of the star
And the fowl who passes by the sea.
Were it you, were it me, remains to be seen.
But we dance, and we bow at the foot of the dream.

"So I go at your command." He backed across the landing, shaking his hands in a final flourish.

Lighting the lamp, al-Kiran rummaged through his things, telling himself that he must have moved the letter, but knowing that wasn't so. Shadows cast by the lamp, the breeze curving down from the window, unnerved him. It was cold.

He snuffed the wick. Not much of the heat from the fires below reached into the tower. He practiced the warming exercise, through breath control, which one of the dancers had taught him one day while Ziryab was away, saying that he was not to tell the

African about the technique, implying that the Sheikh had said it was just for him.

The exercise helped him to center. He put on the fox-skin cap which his mother had sent, then wrapped himself in a heavy robe. His body-heat started to return.

He pulled on the boots which had appeared the day after he and Ziryab had scrubbed the stones in the Great Hall. They were not the same as the dancer's boots the Mistress had left on the dais, but the African, delighted, had said the boots were from her. "She's pleased with our progress!"

In an ecstatic burst, Ziryab had flipped over backwards, laughing, and had then said, very seriously: "The scripture needed to be cleaned. Kemi. She said it had been neglected by the men." Coming closer, as if excited and sharing a revelation, he had said: "You should scour each word, since you are the student. Give them to me, scrubbed as clean as the stones in the exercise Hall. That's what she meant."

Al-Kiran had attempted to redirect his attention to the traditional prayers. But since his time in the cypress circle with ben Hebaron, his ability to sense and identify with the rainbow bridge to Mecca had steadily diminished.

Unrolling the Kirian prayer rug and facing Mecca, chanting refrains from the Koran and counting his beads as his father had taught him, he repeated the opening stanza forty times. Finally his mind merged with his breathing, his body relaxed, and confidence returned with the memory of the bridge hovering before him, the belief that his parents, or ben Hebaron, or someone would catch him if he fell.

If the Karobla returned, he would be ready. But nothing further happened that night, except for a dream:

He was in the great Mosque of Cordoba. While the mullahs chanted from the holy Koran, he kneeled, reaching in mind and spirit toward Mecca, seeking the wings of the Prophet's message. His body moved in unison with the array of worshippers. The prayer of the community flooded his heart.

He could see the great courtyard through hundreds of open arches along the side of the mosque. Light streamed into the sanctum, across the backs of the faithful, prostrate in the rhythm of their prayers, foreheads to their carpets.

Outside, in the great plaza, a swarm of lute players, jugglers, acrobats, puppeteers, magicians, and storytellers washed about in slow rhythmic swirls. But the only sound was of the orchestra of birds in the adjacent park.

Realizing that he was dreaming, al-Kiran walked through the aisles of the devoted. This was the Friday service, the holy day, sacred to Venus, approved by the Mothers of the Black Stone of the Ka'ba in Mecca.

By noon, over 100,000 of the faithful would gather. Caliph Hakam II would come down from the Medinat al-Zahra, dressed in white, a bright green sash around his waist. His young son would walk beside him, followed by courtiers, scholars, poets, eunuchs, and favorite companions. The great Caliph, perhaps the last of the Omayyad line, would lead his people in prayer.

Then he saw the city from above. Cobblestone lanes wound between walled buildings leading toward the Great Mosque. Arches led into cafes and homes. Beautiful blue pots hung from the balconies, filled with flowers. Brilliant green vines trellised down white-washed walls. The city was a living organism.

As the sun rose toward mid-heaven, he saw himself moving forward through the arcades and marble columns of the sanctuary. He merged with the rhythmic succession of filigreed arches, arabesques, and exquisite tile murals inlaid with quotations from the Koran. He stood with the faithful, lost in contemplation of the Prophet and his Message. He saw himself among them, although they couldn't see him.

He approached his father. Abu el-Ali turned from his prayers and embraced him, then faded back into the rhythm of the congregation. In the next arcade his mother kissed his forehead, then returned to her companions.

Hakam II was reciting sections of the Koran. His voice carried the message from the Mihrab to the people. Throughout the entire Mosque and into the streets of Cordoba, the shell-shaped amplifier, at the extreme wall of the last extension of the holy building, projected the message.

Turning toward the Mihrab, al-Kiran felt the words of the
scripture, from the heart of Hakam II, channeled from the invisible to the visible world. Within the geometry of the shrine, he
saw the evolution of all worlds — the invisible and secret face
of God, from which all else issued.

He moved toward the Caliph. Hakam's eyes sparkled with
inner vision. The music of the Prophet's message sustained the
Faithful and pounded within al-Kiran's heart:

"With each breath may we take refuge
in the Living Truth alone,
released from coarse arrogance and subtle pride.

May every thought and action be intended
in the Supremely Holy Name Allah,
as direct expression
of boundless Divine Compassion
and Most Tender Love.

May the exaltation of endless praise
arising spontaneously as
the life of endless beings
flow consciously toward
the Single Source of Being,
Source of the intricate
evolution of endless worlds.

May we be guided through every experience
along the Direct Path of Love
that leads from the Human Heart
into the Most Sublime Source of Love."

The Caliph and the congregation and the dreamer were of
one voice, one body. During each pause the faithful chanted:

"la ilaha illa-llah
la ilaha illa-llah Muhammad rasulu-llah
la ilaha illa-llah Muhammad rasulu-llah"

Weaving through endless arcades, spiraling slowly along alabaster beehives, al-Kiran floated on the waves rising from the worshippers, absorbed in the Message, toward Mecca, the holy city. Through Hakam II's recitation from the Mihrab, the entire congregation breathed together. The refrains gathered then projected, between the specific promises, the purpose which sustained the community in the simplicity and splendor of divine love.

Al-Kiran's heart leaped, then stopped. Al-Mansur, dressed in black, stepped forward, unrolled the Caliph's white turban, raised a double-edged and flaming scimitar, sword of Islam, symbol of the bleeding moon, in wrath, ready to sever the head from the body of the people. Subh and the Heir Apparent raced forward in slow and painful motion, their screams lost in the prayers, in the drone of the chant of the Faithful, in the sacred recitations, in the rhythm of their devotions.

Alpha ben Hebaron and Mershi Khayam stepped forward from opposite sides of the Caliph, in the Mihrab, in the holy of holies, sheltered in the cave from which the voice of Gabriel, by the Prophet of Allah, the Compassionate, issued to the congregation of the Faithful. Glaring at each other, they ignored al-Mansur, blood flowing from his mouth, rage in his eyes, the scimitar whirling above his head. Distracted by their argument, which rose in a smoke-cloud to meet a shadow flowing from the open arches across the heads of the congregation, al-Mansur hesitated. Al-Kiran tried to scream, to warn them, to protect the royal family and his teachers, to struggle with al-Mansur and hold him back.

Having no substance or power, he watched in horror as Subh and Hisham collapsed before the beheaded Caliph. Ben Hebaron and the Mistress continued to argue with each other. Laughing wildly, moving independently of the trance which held the Faithful, al-Mansur rolled the white turban about his own head and raised the scimitar again, turned to the Heir Apparent, still just a boy, and prepared to strike.

As the scimitar hovered in the air, the shadow hissed and extended into wings flapping slowly, absorbing fire from al-

Mansur's sword. Turning within the Mosque, it passed across the congregation and wheeled over the milling but silent thousands in the courtyard.

His consciousness flowing beneath the shadow, al-Kiran moved through the markets, plazas, and parks — then up the winding lanes, and into the gate of the Kirian villa, passing through the familiar halls and kitchen of his family home and out into the patio — then between the lions and into the labyrinth, the sacred impress of his ancestors.

Suddenly everything was silent and still. He sat cross-legged, back straight, on his blue rug. He was in the center of the emblem, the Memory of Home. It was midnight. The pole star was pulsing above his head. He was facing East.

Ben Hebaron's voice floated across the hedge. The rabbi was walking in the garden, outside the maze.

"The boy is my student, Mershi. I would have him back."

The Mistress responded: "He is; but he is also mine."

Al-Kiran woke with a start. A shaft of light shone through the high window, glancing against the opposite wall. A sun swirl was inscribed in the stone blocks of their chamber.

"Ziryab, wake-up." He shook the African. Ziryab pushed him away and rolled back toward the wall, muttering.

Giving up, he climbed onto his bench for a closer look. But the light shifted and the design faded into the random scribbling of the surface of the stones. Wrapping himself in his heaviest robe, he remembered that his letter from ben Hebaron had disappeared. Then he remembered the dream.

"Kirian!"

He spun around to face the landing. Mershi Khayam, in a velvet gown, maroon sash at her waist, stood in the door, her copper hair flowing loosely about her neck, eyes fiery green.

"Blackbirds!" She pointed, her voice demanding, angry. Rolling swiftly to the side of the bed, Ziryab stood at attention, breathing rapidly, facing the Mistress's raised hand. Restraining herself, she sneered: "While you sleep the moon bleeds!" A controlled fury, she descended the stairs.

Rushing to get dressed, they followed her toward the Great

Hall where, the dancers already at work, she paused, scowling, then commanded: "Follow me! Be quick!" — before moving directly into the swirl of the dervishes, her gown resplendent in contrast to their patched robes.

The clank of training weapons sounded like drums from the courtyard. Ab-Dar Il'ium, dark and strong in plain wool, stood on the dais studying the movements of his dancers.

"Stop!" The Sheikh's voice shot through the Hall then hung in the silence. Even the rhythms and yells from the courtyard were suspended in mid-air. Ziryab's black hand, reaching for al-Kiran, froze at the command.

"Move!" The Mistress's voice cut the silence while she spun in slow motion through the human statutes. Her arms spread, her fingers pointing to the Sheikh and his devotees, she whirled around, taking them all in, laughing, railing:

"Fly, or I'll pluck and cook you for the feast."

Ziryab surged forward trying to regain his momentum, but stumbled into al-Kiran, knocking him into one of the dancers. "Kirian." The voice, pleading, full of concern, came from behind his ear. Disoriented, he struggled. Ziryab was pulling him upward. "Spin, Kemi!"

He forced himself forward, the Mistress ahead of them, the world reeling, the African pushing him in the pattern they had practiced, shouting: "Fly, Kemi, through the forest of stone dancers. Quickly!"

An eternity of silence descended upon them in slow motion, freezing the space. He spun, sliding through ice currents, behind Ziryab, in the fire-trail of the Mistress — panting, filled with panic. As the African pulled him into the passageway to the kitchen, through the opposite door, like a hammer the Sheikh's voice shattered the ice: "Stop!"

The clang of the weapons in the outer courtyard beginning again, the dancers spinning out of their postures, the entire assembly took up where it had left off as if Mershi Khayam's voice had not echoed against the stone walls of the Hall of the Dancers: "You're all dung for the fires in my kitchens!"

Her attendants hurrying from their positions near the cooking stoves, furious, eyes blazing, she grabbed Ziryab's hair, yanking his head backwards. His mouth jerked open. "I trusted you," she hissed.

Ziryab trembled inconsolably, pleading that he had done his best, asking forgiveness.

Suddenly, from behind, al-Kiran thought he heard the Sheikh. The Mistress turned as ab-Dar Il'ium strode through the ornamented arch. "Your Lordship," her expression was gracious now, "may I have a word?"

"Of course, Great One." The Sheikh responded.

"This slave has betrayed a certain errand. He has lost a certain letter. Is there a punishment fit for the crime?" Ziryab lay prostrate at her feet, silent and waiting.

Ab-Dar Il'ium glanced at al-Kiran before saying: "The decision is yours, Mershi."

"My kitten." She pulled Ziryab up. "To the stacks then." He scrambled toward the outer door. "And you!" She pointed at al-Kiran as if asking about his punishment.

Then, like waking him from a dream, she burst into laughter. He stumbled then raced out the door to the back of the garden where Ziryab was gathering wood from the pile.

"What letter?" he tried to talk and catch his breath at the same time. His arms full, Ziryab responded harshly:

"The letter of her law! I forgot the wood last night."

"Because of one chore?" Al-Kiran asked, incredulously.

Ziryab continued working in silence.

"But I had a letter. Was that the letter?"

Transferring his logs into al-Kiran's arms and returning to the pile, Ziryab said: "Your letter is none of my business, Kemi," his voice softer now. Then, his back to al-Kiran: "I am the blameworthy, friend. Hurry or the blame will spread."

"But Mershi Khayam has forgiven us." He tried to laugh. "It was a game, somehow, wasn't it?"

"A game?" His face wrinkled, his eyes heavy with years of which al-Kiran had only the dimmest inkling, he whispered: "Yes, my friend, a game I must play. So far, I survive."

When they re-entered the kitchen, the Mistress called politely, pointing to the floor at her feet.

He started to unload the logs, but Ziryab urged him to drop them. The attendants fluttered to their stations while he approached their Mistress. "The work I give you has a purpose." Sadness filled her voice. "Ziryab, who protected you, will pay."

Ab-Dar Il'ium and a guest stood visiting beneath the arch. Taking al-Kiran by the arm, she turned and bowed toward them, whispering: "Do as I say."

Signaling al-Kiran to approach, speaking to his guest, the Sheikh said: "He reminds me of Abd-er Rahman III."

"I've heard that the House of Omayyad throws a peculiar line," the stranger commented, his accent that of a Damascan courier; yet he was light-skinned and dressed as a Christian.

"Some are blond and blue-eyed," ab-Dar Il'ium responded. "And those are among the elect of a great house,"

"It's their fondness for northern women," Mershi Khayam added, bowing slightly.

"Ah," the guest acknowledged thoughtfully, "and his Highness Hakam II has such a concubine, does he not?"

"Yes." The Sheikh reached forward and, holding al-Kiran's face, inspected him. "They call her Subh, but among her own people she was Aurora, for the Dawn Lights."

"And how does she fare?" the guest asked casually.

"She is the mother of Hisham." He released al-Kiran and turned to the Mistress. "The only child of the direct line."

"This child," she put her hand on his shoulder, "came here to study for the Dance. I've done what I could."

"Kemi," the Sheikh addressed him directly, "we regret that the Honorable Alpha ben Hebaron . . . "

"He ran off." Mershi Khayam interrupted, her hand tightening, temper rising. "This boy is under my tutelage now!"

Al-Kiran knelt, frightened and confused.

"Mershi," ab-Dar Il'ium responded gently, "he has been the boy's teacher, and we must honor that." Turning to the stranger, he continued: "The rabbi was to be here this month, but was called away. We will appreciate anything you can do."

The monk bowed slightly. "I will work with him today."

"Today?" She flashed. "I had other exercises in mind."

"It must be today, Mershi." Ab-dar Il'ium asserted, gently. "I will need our guest for my students tomorrow."

"Do you have a letter?" Her voice biting, she placed her hands on her hips like she could not be easily moved. "All letters should be to me. I am his teacher here."

"Yes, certainly, Mistress," ab-Dar Il'ium acknowledged, "but it says here," he unfolded the letter and glanced at it, "that if anyone arrives from Fleury, in the rabbi's absence, the boy should spend time with him."

She reached for the letter, but he refolded it. "So, Great One," he used the honorific again, "I have no choice." He nodded to the stranger. "This is Mesire At-Talibin, of the Monastery at Fleury, from which place great teachers will change the flight of the world."

Pushing al-Kiran forward, she acquiesced: "I present my apprentice, al-Kiran Kamir Kirian."

"This will take some time, you understand?"

"Yes, of course." She backed away. "He is yours . . . but . . ." she began spinning, a word spoken each time her eyes flashed past them: "it . . . will . . . be . . . hard . . . on . . . Ziryab."

CHAPTER ELEVEN

"DESCENT TO THE CENTER"

Mesire At-Talibin guided al-Kiran into the Great Hall, past dancers moving in elaborate exercises, then out into the courtyard. Circling to the back of the fortress, they entered the gate house built into the great stone walls. Signaling him to remain silent, the monk hoisted a portion of the wood floor, revealing a tunnel carved into the mountain below.

Pulling the cover shut behind them, he struck flint to a torch, crouched and moved downward, the light dancing in streamlets against walls covered with chrome and ochre beasts, until they entered a cavern. On the ceiling a blue shaman, his phallus erect, approached a bear.

Pushing forward, touching cold stone on the right, the light disappearing into a void to their left, the sound of rushing water deep within the mountain below, they shimmied along the rocks until, at last, they came to another passageway.

Exhausted, al-Kiran stumbled. At-Talibin held his torch up. Fresh air rushed toward them. Light waves pulsed through brown-green limbs waving across a cave mouth. The stale breath of the bowels from which they emerged flowed toward sheer light.

"Al-Kemi, of the blackbirds, is it? Or the bats?" The monk chuckled, snuffed the torch, and moved through the cypress branches onto the ledge. Disoriented, al-Kiran glanced across the precipice toward the cave to which Mershi Khayam had hurled him. Afraid he would fall, he inched backward.

Seated, closing his eyes, he felt the claws constricting his heart slowly release, his breath returning. His mind snatched memory: the combatants at their exercises, the Sheikh with his dancers in the Great Hall, and then the Mistress, in a rage. Shaking his head he insisted that Ziryab was safe.

"Do you know about Fleury?" The monk glanced at him then walked to the cliff-edge and gazed out into the expanse.

"A Christian monastery?" He shifted his attention.

"Bridge builders." At-Talibin nodded. "We wish to drink from a cup housed in al-Andalus." His back to the cold brilliance of the sky, he pushed back his cowl, revealing the clean shaven face of a young warrior. Suddenly blinded by the sun, al-Kiran lowered his eyes.

"You have done well, Kemi," ben Hebaron's voice spun through his head. Panicked, he turned to the cave mouth. The dark wings of a cloud covered the sun. A shadow flowed upward over the ledge in a cold wave.

"Where are the lions?" At-Talibin asked.

"Don't you see them?" another voice — soft, caring, strangely familiar . . .

Bewildered, the sun bright again, flooding around the dark figures hovering over him, he turned back, his heart racing, trying to focus through the glare. Then, in a moment which felt like lightening, but smelled of the park where Alpha ben Hebaron gave his lessons, he realized the man standing beside At-Talibin, arms out, a gray-iron beard cropped short to his face, was his teacher.

"Rabunni," he sobbed, unable to control his words: "I saw the lions . . . like at the gate . . . to the Memory of Home . . . then I fainted . . . I was in the tekke . . . "

Fragments choked in his throat. He tried to speak: "I lost the letter . . . Ziryab was punished . . . the Mistress . . . I didn't . . . Forgive me." He was losing consciousness. Ben Hebaron was pressing on his temples, holding his face upward.

"Keep your eyes open, Blackbird. Do you see the cave?"

"Yes, master."

"See the lions. This is the way to ibn Massara. Remember this gate. At-Talibin brought you out because we thought it best. He must return now."

Al-Kiran started to speak.

The rabbi hushed him. "Not until we reach the sanctuary. Don't try to explain. Watch the gates and remember the path."

In the silence, ben Hebaron led al-Kiran along the ledge beneath Taifa ibn Massara. Reaching a tethered mule, he took a leather pouch from the cradle, saying: "A quick drink now, then hold your tongue until we reach the cypress spring." Setting a careful pace downward, leading the mule around the tight turns, the rabbi hummed a melody. Words floated through al-Kiran's memory of a song sung by Yemenite dancers in the market following summer solstice:

"The blackbird flies beneath the wings of the owl.
The truth lies at the teats of a sow.
She ruled the heaven before the lions of the south
Sprinkled the leaven in the unsalted mouth."

About an hour later, still in the forenoon, proceeding in single file, ben Hebaron rounded an outcropping and pointed downward, over the ledge, before pushing on.

Looking into the gorge, al-Kiran gazed at the Kymerian Stream. Locust trees stood naked and stark along the banks in the distance. He ached for an explanation of his suffering.

During the weeks at the tekke, the new moon had grown steadily against the night skies and al-Kiran had begun to feel that he was learning — even without his master. But when the moon had passed full and begun to decline everything had gone wrong: the letter had been stolen, the Mistress had been enraged, Ziryab had fallen to her wrath.

Why had the stranger taken him through the tunnels beneath the Taifa ibn Massara? Who was At-Talibin?

He had received praise from the Mistress. Although she was terrifying at times, she had cared for him. Sorceress or not, she was mother-like and had tried to teach him. And Ziryab had assured him that he needed no other teachers.

One night, while they had leaned against the parapet behind the hermitage, Ziryab had said: "The Tentmaker provides the foundation for our dance — but you must marry the Master to the Mistress in your heart."

"I'm a novice!" Al-Kiran remembered being angry. "I can't do it on my own." Ziryab had responded plaintively:

"She sighed in her dream, al-Kemi,
And rolled to the lord in her bed.
Warm in her pillows she seemed
Back from the haunted dead.

While she had reached for her lover,
He claimed his sword, not the dove.
Mohammed would march with his soldiers
At war with himself and her love.

In her love she moved toward the Messenger.
She flew from her sheets as a song.
For he was her rightful lover
Or life in the silk was all wrong.

She stretched to embrace the Prophet.
But he leaped in a sweat from her bed.
He beat on his chest with a mallet
Then bowed to his lover and said:

When from the battle I return, dear Moriah,
When with the soldiers I march by,
Remember the flowers of spring time,
Put them on my grave as I die."

A sadness in his face, Ziryab had pointed wistfully across
the canyon. "Do you see it?"
"What?"
"The Cave of the Mother." Tears forming in his eyes, he had
sung another verse:

"She awaited his embrace in the sun set.
She danced in the dark waves of the night.
Like the houri in the garden of Mohammed,
She danced alone in the cave out of sight."

Uncomfortable in the silence which had washed around them, al-Kiran remembered asking: "What's it about?"

"About how you must return to the cave." Ziryab had taken his shoulders and, looking into his eyes, said: "It's simple. Which death do you prefer? Die now? Or die at the end of your life, having never really lived? Look to yourself, Kirian. Al-Mansur will have his way if you don't."

"What do you mean?" al-Kiran had asked, alarmed. "Do you refer to the Royal Chamberlain?"

"I only know what I hear." Ziryab had held him and turned slowly under the moon. "But if you wish to meet your lover, die now. Let go of the Master who would lead you to wars which never end."

Ziryab had then gazed down across the gorge, toward the opposite wall. Al-Kiran had followed his eyes. The Mistress had told him that if he could not climb up or down that face, he must learn to fly. He knew that was what he had come for; that was why she had thrown him from the alcove into the abyss, but his fear was too great.

"Die consciously, Kemi. Choose your death," Ziryab had whispered. Then, his voice full of longing, a sadness flowing from his heart, he had completed the song:

"The Lady waits alone for her lover.
An owl, she flies through the skies.
The warrior leaves her to suffer
While he, in search of his master, dies."

They had said nothing further that night, nor had Ziryab returned to that theme during the succeeding days. Now, as he followed Alpha ben Hebaron down the trail, winding along the face of the cliff beneath Taifa ibn Massara, he realized he might never see his friend again.

Ben Hebaron waved al-Kiran to his side. Taking a bundle from the cradle, he said: "Wrap yourself against the wind."

"Rabbi," al-Kiran faltered, "I have so many questions."

"Be wary, Kirian," he responded sternly, his gray eyes

almost black. "Keep silent until we reach the cypress grove. The path narrows before the final descent."

Al-Kiran fell in line, following the mule, as ben Hebaron struck forward and down into the gorge. Some hundred paces further, he turned back and shouted something, but the wind, sweeping up from the bottom, catching his robe and billowing within his sleeves, carried his words away.

Then again: "Blackbird," he boomed. "Watch the gates!"

Al-Kiran attempted to note landmarks as they wound forward and down.

Suddenly a wind-blast hit his face, catching his cloak, stretching it behind him, and pulling him toward the edge. The cave mouth opposite the Mistress's alcove flashed through his mind. He tried to scream, but had no voice.

Whirling around, his eyes fierce, ben Hebaron glared at him, then beyond, out into the abyss at his back. While al-Kiran was struggling to regain his balance, his heart pounding in his chest, the blanket he had worn around his shoulders fluttered down toward the canyon floor.

Then, without a word, he turned and pressed forward. Following more carefully now, al-Kiran hummed a song:

"The violence of the sea meets the golden rays,
The wind catches the lad as he falls.
On the wings of an angel the child prays.
So goes the song of the laws."

But he wasn't sure an angel would catch him if he fell.

Rounding a bluff, they passed under a huge boulder jutting out into the air above them. He tried to focus. The sun was bright, almost a glare, in the cold sky. Leaving the cliff face, ben Hebaron led through a side-canyon, then down a stream bed and into a hollow sheltered from the wind.

Tall grasses and winter weeds, frozen after their last bursts of life, stood in ragged clumps about the clearing. Driftwood bunched into random stacks near the center. Scrub trees and bushes, like those which had dotted the landscape where they had descended inland from the cliff, stood at the edge of the hollow, black-ribbed and leafless in the wind. A fox darted from their left and behind them.

"Was this where the sacred circle had been?" Al-Kiran started to panic. He tried to focus his eyes. Steadying his breath, he looked for the cypress and ancient monoliths.

Ben Hebaron signaled to remain still, then turned and led him out of the clearing and along the stream-bed which narrowed and disappeared, across a mesa, past boulders and occasional scrub trees, tangled in their exposure, then stopping before a huge standing-stone, turned back to him. To the left the ground grew rougher, slanting upward through a wasteland toward a granite wall. To the right a trail, the first they had seen since leaving the cliff-face, led down toward a copse of trees.

Remembering the instructions, al-Kiran scanned the stone carefully. A Celtic sun swirl, just above the rabbi's cap, was carved into the granite surface. A cloud passed overhead.

In the distance on the right toward the trees, a path, well marked with smooth stones, formed broad stair steps. Ben Hebaron glanced at him, then nodded and turned the opposite direction, moving upward across the trackless land.

About a half-hour later they reached the granite bluff. The rabbi, leading the mule, pushed forward, picking his way up the cliff. Stumbling behind, al-Kiran was unable to think clearly. Hunger fought with the cold sun, the renewed fury of the biting wind. Then they were on a ledge. Ben Hebaron raised his arms. Two eagles circled in the stillness of the blue sky.

Lowering his arms slowly, he looked carefully at al-Kiran and then downward and to the east. In the distance, on a promontory jutting out of the cliff below them, the lush green of a cedar grove hovered in the air. Within the cedars, like elder brothers, taller, their green tinctured with red, the tops of ancient cypress trees waved in the wind.

Stunned, al-Kiran wanted to slap himself awake. The grove seemed to be suspended in mid-air. He knew that an underground stream fed the trees, but couldn't imagine how. In the far distance, at the bottom of the canyon, he could barely see the silver ribbon of a river.

Remembering his experiences on their way up, he started to ask a question; but ben Hebaron thrust his hand across his mouth, forcing him to keep silent, then led forward again, descending some fifty feet, to a point where it was impossible to stay on the cliff-face, before cutting through a gorge, at the other end of which al-Kiran could see the sacred grove.

Tethering the mule behind some bushes, he took a bundle from the pack, unrolled a monk's habit and placed it around al-Kiran. Pointing at the center between al-Kiran's brows, he made a symbol with his hands, then down to his heart, making another sign, then to his groin, where he clapped, sending a sharp retort through the hollow, startling the mule.

Stepping back, he whispered: "The waters replenish us." Working with his hands, he pulled energy from al-Kiran's mid-section to the top of his head, then down through the snake root at the base of his spine and into his feet.

CHAPTER TWELVE

"THE SACRED GROVE"

Ben Hebaron moved toward the trees, leaving the mule behind. Feeling better now, al-Kiran concentrated as they wound into the thick and tangled cedars at the edge of the grove. The rocks became pebbles in their path, then sand.

Suddenly the path widened into a perfectly smooth moat of fine gray sand circling between the outer cedar ring and the cypress trees in the center. Al-Kiran took a deep breath.

Turning to him, ben Hebaron whispered: "Leviathan's mouth. The old whale carried Jonah. The lips of the mother's womb," then walked across the sand to the nearest cypress — its long feathery leaves floating gently in the wind.

Searching for the nine menhirs, the guardian stones, all al-Kiran could see was the cypress ring curving in both directions, forming an inner wall. His heart thumping with excitement, he followed as ben Hebaron slipped behind the cypress, then turned, his back against a huge monolith. "This is the north, Blackbird. Do you remember this gate?"

"I do, master." The words cracked in his throat. He noted a sun-swirl circled by four crescent moons carved in the face of the stone. He had not spoken since the blast near the cliff edge, when he had tried to scream.

"Then we are ready." Pushing back his cowl, ben Hebaron moved around the menhir, keeping it to his left, then wound in and out through the other stones, each in front of a huge cypress. Stopping at the north, he said: "While we walk, alternate your nasal breathing, as I have taught you. Observe carefully. We open the paths between the Guardians."

Moving from the ninth to the eighth stone, he cut across to the fifth, back to the seventh, over to the first, and so on — staying outside of the twelve smaller stones which formed an inner circle around the sacred spring. Returning to the north gate, al-

Kiran realized that he had no apprehension of an encounter with the Karobla he had met in his dream, then in the Kirian Seal — who had, he suspected, stolen into his chamber at ibn Massara.

Although he had been only vaguely aware of it the first time, each menhir had a definite persona, some as birds, others humans. Some looked like warriors. Each expressed a primordial energy pattern. Each was alive — but moving in a slower or different time than that inhabited by humans. The 9th, 6th, and 3rd gates, forming the overlapping inner triangle, appeared as a crone, a mother, and a virgin.

Facing the inner circle, ben Hebaron raised his arms and looked upward. The sun was a golden eye in the dome of heaven. "These, my student, are the twelve. In the center sits the dove." Then he chanted:

"La ilah illa 'llah — La ilah illa 'llah
May the blessings of the Father and the Mother
Be realized in the Child."

At that moment, a thunder crack burst above them. Lightning exploded and crossed back again, directly overhead, slicing the blue-gray sky, rolling up into large black funnels before exploding again. Al-Kiran dropped to his knees.

"What was that, Rabunni?" he shuddered.

"It's the Old One, Blackbird, looking for his mate." Then, turning him back to the inner stones: "And this is the nest of the Mother he seeks."

Suddenly, out of nowhere, Kristien appeared, circling in and out of the guardian stones, then through the inner circle, her black skin shimmering with light. Rainbow wings extended across a cape spreading from her shoulders. Her arms, moving in quiet patterns, seemed to raise her between earth and sky.

Circling the inner stones three times, she gained momentum then leaped the sacred spring, and landed gently, exuding a gorgeous, girlish joy.

Grinning, eyes sparkling, she walked forward, bowed, then eagerly hugging him, said: "Where have you been, al-Kiran?"

Leaning up on tip toe, she kissed the center above his eyes causing lightning to shoot to his feet and back.

An amethyst rain burst above his head, showering down
through each of his centers, growing hotter at each stage. He
remembered what the Karobla had promised in the Kirian
labyrinth. Urgently, he pressed against her.

"Wait!" She smiled, her voice melodic, teasing, then turned
and stood beside him. Pointing at the supine monolith in the center of the circle of twelve stones, into which a spring rose of it's
own force, ben Hebaron chanted:

"The thirteenth is the foundation
stone of your dreams. The one
cast away, always remains — laughing —
female and male — the ancient, invisible
base, even as the world fades.
From this center the terebinth bears
and the kerm-oak is made."

Following Kristien, al-Kiran went forward and knelt at the
spring. Eyes shut, he drank. Rising, he gazed at his face peering
back from between the worlds. Both worlds, male and female,
danced in the water.

Ben Hebaron approached with a blue prayer rug, sending a
rush of relief through al-Kiran. He had worried it was lost at the
Hermitage. But when the rabbi flipped it up to settle on the stiff
winter grass, he jumped backwards in alarm.

In the center, where the familiar tribal patterns should have
been, the Kirian seal had been woven. From upper left to lower
right, wings flowed between a golden chalice and a black bee out-
lined in silver. A counterbalancing world tree crossed the rug in
the opposite direction. A dove, or white raven, soared upward on
either side.

The sun, just beyond high noon, poured down into the circle. Despite the nearness of the winter solstice, he felt warm now.
Ben Hebaron moved to the central stone where he cupped water,
then sprinkled it at the four corners of the prayer rug, saying:

"This is the spring of life. We meet here to do what we can to stabilize the world."

Stretching his arms out, his gray cloak fell open revealing his striped robe. The Seal of Solomon, a cross, and a crescent hung across his barrel chest.

"As taught by the Messiah of the Christians: find the fire in the water; die and be reborn. Rabbi Alpha ben Hebaron, I am." He grinned mischievously, then sang:

> "Merchant and miscreant, the devil with sin,
> a saint as old Lucifer, star-child, must have been,
> at first calling, forlorn, wanting to pray,
> but then forced by 'His Worship,' Satan to play."

Placing hard-rolls and a wine-skin before them, he lay his cloak on the grass and sat down, his back to the spring. "We're safe here." He winked at al-Kiran. "Enjoy yourself."

Removing and spreading his own cloak, hesitating slightly, he sat down facing his teacher. Kristien walked through the stones then returned to sit next to him.

"Students, listen now," ben Hebaron exhorted them. "We have each other. We have bread and wine. This is the feast the divine parents have given us. Celebrate and be glad."

"You old scoundrel!" Kristien smiled playfully, shocking al-Kiran by her response. Ben Hebaron grinned. Putting her hand gently on al-Kiran's arm, she asked: "Do you drink wine?"

Looking from the Nubian to the Jew, he thought of the Shariah, of his responsibilities as an Arab, of Mohammed, Blessed Prophet of Islam — of his prayers to Allah.

By his own references, the rabbi had acknowledged, or even honored, Iblis-Lucifer, called Satan, seeming to confirm Ziryab's accusations. Yet ben Hebaron had returned for him, was his bridge to the dance, his teacher, approved by his parents . . . the man they, and he, trusted with his training.

Beneath the glowing sun, he resolved to accept whatever might come. "Obviously," he glanced at Kristien, "our master plans to break the last of my disciplines."

"Are you troubled, Kemi?" ben Hebaron asked.

"Yes. But I won't stop now."

"Then let us pray." The spring flowing into the pool behind him, in the center of the cypress and stone circles, Alpha ben Hebaron held his hands out, and recited:

"La ilaha il-lah-lah!
There is no God but Allah
Who by the bread of the earth
And the fruit of the vine
Brings forth the father, the mother,
And the child.
There is no other Source but the Ultimate,
Neither masculine, nor feminine,
Beyond and within all distinctions.

"Eat and be merry, for today we celebrate. From the Most Subtle through Gabriel to Mohammed; from Moriah by Alborak to the 9th heaven; from Ain Soph through the Tree in the Garden to Malkuth, by the Dance of the Created Lights — we are here to praise all that is, all that has been, all that will be."

Breaking the bread and pouring wine into it, he indicated that they should do the same. Raising it, he said:

"This is the body and blood of the Messiah
Promised from the beginning of days,
Yet to come, has come among us already.
This is the body and blood of the Mother
Impregnated by sacred love,
Transformed by conscious sacrifice.
As we drop our disciplines
We stand naked before divinity.
Sweep us, oh Parents, into
Your loving embrace.
What you have created,
We will celebrate consciously,
Knowing that we also are consumed

To die before we die —
Conscious food for the world
In its flight."

Raising bread toward the sky, flesh sopped with blood, they saluted the eagles gliding above them, circling the sun. Following the rabbi, al-Kiran bit and chewed the bread. It was bitter, then warm in his stomach.

"Be conscious of the gifts, Kemi," ben Hebaron said. "These are the flesh and blood of the mother."

"Hooo." The call of an owl floated from the cedars

"Who?" Ben Hebaron jumped up. Turning in a circle, he slapped his diaphragm. "I said," his voice boomed, "the Kirian by Omayyad descent, and the Nubian princess!"

A flutter of rooks, startled by the rabbi's declaration, rose into the sky. His laughter, like a roar of a lion above their excited chatter, drowned them back into silence. Then he sat again, prepared to enjoy his meal.

Taking a large bite and chewing slowly, al-Kiran realized that he had been famished. He remembered that, after singing of the lady in her cave alone, Ziryab had recommended dying consciously, now, rather than waiting for the end of life.

But he hadn't understood. Since the full moon, he had been unable to hold thoughts or examine them. Had his parents really authorized the breaking of the Shariah, everything which had been sacred — the very basis for his life?

He was drinking wine with a rabbi and a dancing girl who, if the political suggestions in ben Hebaron's letter were true, would eventually join the Caliph's household. The rabbi was trying to stop al-Mansur. Perhaps the Nubian was being groomed to tease pleasures into the body of Hakam II. It was well known that certain of the Academies in Medina were specifically devoted to the perfection of sexual techniques.

Deep in his own reflections, he said: "The bread of Allah has sustained me this far." Ben Hebaron motioned him to continue. Relaxed by the wine, he thought out loud: "When we left this grove on the way to ibn Massara, you said that just as a tent isn't needed when one is walking, a prayer rug isn't needed when one is in a sacred circle. Today, you made a point of spreading the prayer rug as a carpet for our meal."

He soaked another piece of bread and took a bite before speaking: "You said, 'Wine in the body can be spirit to the soul — even of a Moslem.' And that, 'Divine intoxication and drunkenness are parallel paths.' But you added, 'May you travel the one and avoid the other.'" He paused. "But under your sponsorship, this wine is affecting more than my soul."

"It is warming your stomach as well." The rabbi laughed. "Is there any harm in that?"

"But I dare not lose my senses."

"And so," Kristien broke in, "you learn," she tossed her hair back along her shoulders, "when to quit."

"Intoxication, when filled with the spirit, can be good." Ben Hebaron picked it up. "Inebriation, when the balance is lost, delays our work. We are not here to deaden our senses, nor our minds, nor our hearts. In both our languages the root of 'sacrament' is 'consciousness of the divine.' Wine can be a sacrament if used as a vehicle to greater consciousness."

"According to the traditionalists, wine is Luciferic," al-Kiran protested mildly.

"Like all emanations, Lucifer's origin is in the divine source." Ben Hebaron waited while al-Kiran chewed carefully, considering his statement. "Lucifer, like Ahriman, has his divine impulse, his purpose. But neither the impulse toward spirit, nor the resistance in favor of pure matter, has form, nor expression, except through our responses. We hover between the extremes."

Patting the ground beside him, he continued: "The grape, and all life, exists due to the combination of both forces. The grape, raw or fermented, is a source of nourishment. You can drown in it or you can drink lightly and be refreshed."

"I could have refrained." Al-Kiran felt argumentative.

Kristien leaned forward, her voice inviting: "At the Palace, to not drink would be rude."

"To not drink," al-Kiran replied assertively, "would be to set the proper example."

"These mysteries descend from Adam, Seth, Enoch, Noah, and Abraham," the rabbi intervened, "and each of the great Mothers, the Magnificent Ones, from whose flesh and blood both Arabs and Jews trace their lineage. Jesus created wine from water. The Blessed Messenger called him the Savior. Each of us must decide how to respond. But, Blackbird," he smiled now, "don't fear heresy — rather," he held his hands out, "search for truth." Then, standing and pacing, he continued:

"Following Cain's murder of Abel, Cain was cursed for 7 and 77 generations. The true seed was to descend through Seth, who replaced the dead brother." He glanced at al-Kiran to make sure he was listening. "Yet the dwellers in tents descend from Jabal-Cain; the musicians from Jubal-Cain; and the builders of temples and mosques from Tubal-Cain. While the mothers labored, these men laid the foundations of civilization and fought to control all things.

"The curse has been lifted but the divine marriage has yet to occur. It is time." He squatted down. "Before this world can pass away, we must acknowledge the pain which we have caused ourselves and accept the gifts which have been constantly available."

Resisting the implication, al-Kiran said: "Can we not accept that wine is dangerous — that it should be avoided?"

"You have accepted the Prophet's point on that, Kemi." Ben Hebaron dropped his voice, almost whispering. "Now is the time to accept another teaching." Then standing again:

"The danger is in exerting too much control — refusing to drink altogether or drinking to excess — both are instances of trying to dominate — both see the power in the wine rather than in the person who approaches it."

"But I don't know the line between myself" al-Kiran patted his chest, "and the danger of which the Prophet spoke."

Kristien leaned forward. "The danger lies in drawing that line, Kemi." Her voice was soothing. "That line causes a war between ourselves and the magic which lives around us. Is that not true, Master?"

"From the dance of the Father's seed in the womb of the

Mother, all that lives comes forth." Ben Hebaron turned to her. "But the human power of naming affects the field in which our experiences occur. What we name 'evil,' including the fermented fruit of the vine, is experienced as such.

"Some, fascinated with its power, lose themselves in wine. Others, equally fascinated with its power, shun it. Both paths are dangerous due to fascination with and misapprehension of power. Both approaches create demons which generate warriors. In turn, the warriors generate wars.

"Until we recognize that the outer world and the inner world reflect each other, and that the line between may be passed in gentleness, acceptance, and care, we are at risk."

Kristien got up and stretched. Sitting again, she asked: "What should we expect at the Festival of All Faiths?"

The rabbi laughed. "Do you always leap ahead?" He looked at her a moment, then back to al-Kiran.

"We have drunk of the fermented grape, but we are not drunk. Our bread is sopped in the wine-blood of sacrifice. It is warm in our stomachs. We are refreshed."

Taking the three wine-bags, he placed them at equal points around the stone into which the spring bubbled.

Scratching his beard, pacing, and measuring his words, he said: "Al-Andalus, united under the Omayyad Caliphs, looks forward to the Dance of Created Lights on each ninth year anniversary. The vision of the most blessed Prophet has encouraged a Festival which celebrates all faiths.

"Our preparations are devoted to the realization of Mohammed's vision, objectively — in this world. When the moon turns from her darkness in order to be reborn, chased by the sun in his western flight, from the moment of daybreak . . ." He broke off, then turned to al-Kiran.

"This morning at sunrise, as I have the story, you and the Ziryab were fast asleep while," he waved his finger in a scolding motion, "the princess and I marched these stones."

Caught off guard, al-Kiran responded: "The Mistress was furious." Ben Hebaron stepped closer and whispered:

"'Wrath' is 'the impassioned movement of the soul.' Remember that as you face the Hound of Heaven."

"Ziryab called her the Witch of the Open Fires." He repressed an image of the letter.

"So she is." Ben Hebaron nodded.

Angry, al-Kiran said: "You didn't stay with me."

Ben Hebaron knelt on one knee. "The All Faiths Festival coincides with the ancient rites. It renews the hope that al-Andalus may not only be preserved, but may spread as a new world order. We had no choice but to push your development."

"Who decided?" Kristien interrupted. "I should have been allowed to work with him."

"I will explain; but it requires your patience and understanding, Kristien. There are barriers which must be passed, even here." Eyes heavy, he gazed at her. "I pray that the dance will bear fruit for both of you and for al-Andalus and the world." He paused, before continuing:

"Our objective is to bring Kemi to the point where his soul takes over and the veil between the inner and the outer temple is broken. We prepare the way for him and for you. You two are the chosen dancers."

"I am no novice," Kristien asserted.

Nodding, he said: "There is no language adequate to what I want to convey. We are forced to attach messages to the wings of blackbirds chasing the owl of objective knowledge. Blackbirds are neither precise nor predictable. They harass the owl, yet, followed carefully, tell us where she has gone. They betray her presence. You then have to interpret the message and save the owl which originates in my heart."

His eyes asked for their understanding. "Even though you haven't known what the training is or how it is being applied, you have accepted me as you teacher and I have accepted you as my students. We translate that relationship into words at great risk to the work which we are to do. Yet there is nothing in life which is free of risk."

Glancing down at the carpet, he continued: "The primary

world is objective, immediate, and whole. The words I must use are derivative, creatures of a subjective and linear world in which one event seems to follow another. The words are not adequate, but may provide a boost to carry you toward the heart. They ride the impulses which flow between us." Squatting on his haunches, insistent, he added:

"You must follow the reflected light until you have found the primary light, that which is so real that you can touch it." He paused. "My purpose is to transfer to you the power I have gained to fly after the owl of objective knowledge, but if you hear only my words, you have missed the message."

Al-Kiran strained forward, wanting to understand.

"By our words we can harm those whom we love. But the risk must be taken." He looked at Kristien. "We must work for the protection and betterment of the world."

"Who are we working with?" she asked, still impatient.

When he didn't respond, she added: "We accept that your words convey messages, and that these messages point from a derivative to a primary world. That is the first gate?"

"Yes."

"And that you are relying on us to accept the rooks as the carriers of messages, not the messages themselves. That is the second gate, is it not?"

"You must find the message in the flight of your own heart." Fixing her with his gaze, he added: "As you two go to your further work, even beyond the dance, and in your turn try to convey these truths to others who search for objective truth, always insist that your students honor both gates."

"Then master," her mouth glistened between the soft fullness of her lips, "those being the conditions, what are your suggestions regarding the dance?" Rising to her knees, she stretched upward, then tucked her legs under her gown, the cloth flowing in lines along her thighs.

Al-Kiran swiveled closer to her. He wanted to put his nose into her hair and lose himself in her mysteries.

Behind their master, the spring swirled in the pool. The sun splashed gold in the spray. He said: "The work is to unite the community of created lights in a new harmonic."

Al-Kiran, now alert, responded to the depth in his master's eyes, the mixture of struggle, sadness, and joy there. Kristien took his hand.

"In four days, when we gather for the festival, you two will be opposite each other."

"But . . ." al-Kiran interrupted, no longer able to contain himself, "where has Kristien been? And," he looked at her, "where do you come from? Why haven't I been able to ask?"

CHAPTER THIRTEEN

"Kristien's Story"

M ay I?" Kristien looked to the rabbi, then shifted to face al-Kiran, her hand on his knee. "We have talked through our bodies not words. In our hearts we know each other."

As silence washed around him, al-Kiran felt he couldn't look at her. Lowering his eyes to the carpet, so different, yet the same as the one from which he had sent his prayers to Mecca, he could see ben Hebaron watching from the other side. "Though I honor Alpha ben Hebaron," Kristien nodded her respect, "my lineage descends from the Queen of Heaven and her twin, the Dark Mother." Spreading her arms, sunlight twinkled at the golden rings in her ears and about her neck. "The rabbi called me. But I came because I chose it. He forbid I tell you. I chose that as well. Now I speak." She grinned.

Her gown hung loose at her shoulders, open to the rise of her breasts. Knees bent beneath her, back straight, hands on her hips, she smiled coquettishly. Cocking her head to the side and glancing at him through the corner of her eyes, pleased, she prepared to recite her history. Aware of the urge beneath his belly, a flutter at his diaphragm, his eyes soaked her in while sensuous, and playful, she began:

"Born in the Sudan near Wad Medani, I was initiated at the first moon of the great cycle which courses through this body." She brushed her hands down across her front, holding them at her womb. "I came to Cordoba to dance with you. Ben Hebaron," she eyed him, "tried to keep his secrets . . . but I danced for you from the first day, while he bantered with his students about history.

"In Alexandria, the Goddess, my sponsor, is Black Isis. To my people, She is Oshiwah." Kristien held her arms out, hands flicking invisible cymbals, her shoulders swaying, smiling. "To some she is the Magdalen, to others the Black Madonna. She is both the Lover and the Mother. She is called the three-fold and the nine-fold feminine."

"To my people She is Shekhinah." Ben Hebaron stood up. "She is known by many names, Kemi. Her power shakes the priesthoods who have fought to establish a foothold in this world. Kristien," he focused on her, "I kept no secrets which I could have revealed."

Ignoring ben Hebaron, she continued: "Outwardly we practiced Islam, but inwardly we followed the sacred mother whose son was sacrificed, whose lover was lost. We cultivated the techniques of reassembling Osiris." She smiled coyly. "Do you know which part of Osiris was missing?"

His head swimming, al-Kiran couldn't think. Ben Hebaron supplied the answer: "The winged phallus."

"The God's penis had been deadened; a club for domination, without pleasure." She paused briefly.

"Having completed my training, I returned to the temple at Wad Medani, hoping my heart would be enflamed so my womb might be quickened." Her hand tightened on al-Kiran's knee. Catching his breath, he said:

"You wanted children?"

"As a vessel of the Goddess, I yearn for a child. I initiated aspirants, but never found, in Wad Medani, my heart's partner." She ran her hand up al-Kiran's back, caressing him. "Then, one night, the Mistress of our Temple told me I was needed; that I must go where two Arian monks would take me. We left the next day by camel train.

"In Byzantium, I learned of Cordoba and the crisis which approaches. I was told that adepts of the Omayyad alliance were waiting for 'a slave princess.' I had not been consulted. But Oshiwah appeared in my dreams, saying: 'Do their bidding. My fire will cleanse, then save, the city.'"

Al-Kiran turned away, the image of the cave priestess, his grandmother, vivid in his mind.

"From Byzantium we went to Carthage, where we stayed with Jewish merchants and I met Moses ben Hanoch, who was grieving over the loss of his wife. A month later, arriving in al-Andalus, I was disguised as the victim of a corsair raid, consigned to the slave market, then gifted to the Royal Uncle. "Ben

Hebaron," she flashed her eyes at him, "I learned later, had arranged that." He nodded.

"Arriving on the same ship as myself, Moses ben Hanoch assured me that the masquerade was a ruse to place me where I might be of service, and that a certain rabbi would protect me. Ben Hanoch went directly to the synagogue where he succeeded the Babylonian rabbis as the judge of all questions Jewish. He," she emphasized, "is a wonderful and kind man.

"But our teacher didn't bother to meet me." Her temper rising, she pointed at ben Hebaron, and scowled. Head high, a fierce power and authority pulsing along the vein at her throat, she glared at the rabbi. "Virgin consecrated — I am no slave to be told what I will do."

"Virgin consecrated?" al-Kiran muttered, uncertain what the title meant, affected by the wine, acutely sensitive to and drawn by her presence.

"The Sacred Harlot," ben Hebaron explained. "Like the Magdalen of the Arian Christians. We play roles which are necessary to the work. Forgive me, Kristien."

"I do," she nodded regally, "but I was irritated." She turned back to al-Kiran. "My body is a vessel for the remaking of the God. Were it not for Oshiwah's instruction, I would have rejected the stratagem. It was my right to do so and, ben Hebaron," her voice softened, "you should have explained about the Royal Uncle and what I was needed for."

"What did happen?" al-Kiran asked, trying to understand.

Turning back to him, she continued: "During my first audience with the Uncle, having been powdered and groomed by his immaculate eunuchs, and suspecting that I was to open myself to him, bringing his member to attention, a courier arrived with a letter from ben Hebaron."

"What did it say?" Al-Kiran tried to envision the scene.

"The Royal Uncle read it to me. It stated," she assumed an officious tone: "'The Rabbi Alpha ben Hebaron has decided he will accept the Nubian slave as his student.' Can you imagine?" She put her hands out as if baffled. "What our teacher lacks in subtlety, he makes up for in self-assurance." She laughed, ben Hebaron joining her.

"The royal uncle is a good man; but all I knew was that he recommended I accept. Certain that you," she pointed at ben Hebaron, "must be the rabbi ben Hanoch referred to, I accepted, thinking," she grinned, her face back, shining in the sun, "does this rabbi know who I am?"

Ben Hebaron responded with a grizzly grin. Her eyes never left his face. As his eyes met hers, he said, gently and sincerely: "I am sorry, Kristien of Nubia," then stood. "The Arian brothers assured me you were here for the purposes of our alliance. Each day was fraught with hope and danger. I had no opportunity to become your confidant; nor did I know exactly what your techniques might be, though I was assured you were Mistress of many charms."

He paused before going on. "My audacity came from the conviction I must, without delay, bring you into my group and expose al-Kiran to you without either of you yet knowing what might evolve. At that point, many issues remained unsettled."

Al-Kiran, not comprehending the play between them, pulled away from her and walked to the pool to splash his face. As he reseated himself, Kristien took his hand then continued:

"I knew at once that the rabbi didn't comprehend my disciplines, nor perhaps even my status. From the first day, he made it clear he and I wouldn't talk directly."

"As with the Mistress, Kemi," ben Hebaron broke in, "I recognized her authority, but only knew I must let matters develop without interfering."

The rooks rose from the trees, squawking among themselves, then settled. Ben Hebaron stood as if concerned.

Her arm around al-Kiran's waist, Kristien said: "Tell Kemi about our separation."

"Kristien was to go to an Arian monastery, south of the city," ben Hebaron kept his eyes on the carpet. "She is fully aware of the mysteries of her body. Whereas your intellectual training has been excellent and, as an athlete you have great skills and control . . ."

"We start with the fire," Kristien placed her hand on his thigh, "which will unite our bodies."

"Although I am uncertain how to behave," the rabbi cleared

his throat, "I do know you are Mistress of his destiny and, Priestess," he looked carefully at Kristien, "he is Master of yours."

"I understand." Shifting, she guided al-Kiran so his shoulders and head lay in her lap.

Ben Hebaron paused before continuing: "Consulting with ibn Shaprut, and Moses ben Hanoch — whom I have followed in all this — it was decided that the two of you should be temporarily separated."

Al-Kiran was lost in the touch of her hand across his forehead, the feel of her lap beneath his head.

"Are you listening?" he drew al-Kiran's attention back to himself, then began pacing.

"The Arian brothers recommended that Kristien stay at their monastery. I trusted their judgment. You, Kemi, were to be established at Taifa ibn Massara, where you were to be introduced to a knowledge which can not be rationalized."

"Why couldn't you have explained you were leaving?" He leaned up on his elbow, Kristien's hand on his shoulder.

"As explained in the letter," ben Hebaron's eyes probed him, "the Mistress demanded it."

"Or at least wake me?" al-Kiran continued, distressed.

"You were exhausted and," he plucked at his beard, "you were in trance. You had accepted the abandonment of your prayers in this sacred grove, which was not lightly done. That, combined with the outrageous behavior you would experience under the tutelage of the Mistress Khayam . . ."

The anger which he had suppressed shot through al-Kiran's body. "What about the messages from your heart?"

Crossing his arms over his chest, ben Hebaron said: "My actions in leaving you were as full of pain, as incomplete, as frightening to me — because I did fear that you might be harmed — as any words which I might have spoken."

Kristien bent to his ear and whispered: "He loves you, Kemi. We all do what we must."

His head in her lap, he accepted the silence washing through her to himself. Anger drained from his body. Aware of the earth beneath them, the stone sentinels, the cypress and cedar circle, and that they were floating, sheltered and protected in a sacred sanctuary, he saw the promise of the Dance, the mysteries of the Prophet's vision of an eclipse, of dancers flying, the preservation of tolerance and splendor, of grace and beauty.

"I," ben Hebaron spoke, "had to leave you in her care because I could take you no further and, as you know," he paused, "I decided to hazard a letter. In the wrong hands, that information could have the wrong effect. Yet it felt right, and I risked it." Al-Kiran sat-up, dreading his next question: "How did you lose it?"

"What letter?" Kristien asked.

"The Karobla . . ." al-Kiran didn't know how to start.

"Alborak, the white mule, carried Mohammed to the highest heaven." Ben Hebaron spoke quietly but precisely. "The Karobla carries you to the depths of yourself. But how could such a creature destroy a letter in this world?"

"I don't know."

"Can you tell us about it?" Soothingly, Kristien pushed her palm up against his back.

"Ziryab thought he saw her. When I came running, a black thing, like the tail of the Karobla . . ." He broke off, troubled by the inadequacy of words, suddenly unsure what had happened. Dreams flooded into his mind. Another series of owl calls came from the trees — then a screech as several clouds collided and darkened the sun.

Kristien lay her head on his shoulder.

"Could the Ziryab have taken it?" ben Hebaron suggested. "Struggle, Kemi, to think clearly. As your body awakens, slices of what happened can come back to you."

"No!" Al-Kiran wanted to shout. "Ziryab was the only one who helped me . . . except for the Mistress." He stopped himself. Pushing aside images of Mershi Khayam raging at both of them, and the fact that she always became furious when he talked about the rabbi, he started again: "Something, from between the worlds, slipped into our room."

"Yes." Ben Hebaron nodded.

"That was last night — before the dream. Were you really there? With the Mistress?"

"Go on," the rabbi encouraged him.

Uncertain, al-Kiran hesitated. "I went to the Great Mosque. You and the Lady Khayam were arguing. Al-Mansur beheaded the Caliph then attacked young Hisham." He looked down again, hoping for an explanation. So much of what he thought he knew, he didn't understand at all. He remembered the Karobla in the labyrinth, then in the tower.

Turning in the circle, ben Hebaron scanned the cypress sentinels behind each monolith. Watching him, al-Kiran was acutely aware that they were hovering on a ledge over a great chasm. Turning back to them, the rabbi spoke carefully:

"You must understand that, from the other planes, I can only see patterns; but," his eyes met al-Kiran's, "I did see that the Ziryab, at some cost to himself, took the letter."

"What about the Karobla?" al-Kiran asked, astonished, unable to sort the pieces into place.

"Your creature, Kemi, went to defend your treasure. Your emotion, regarding the letter, had become an obsession for her as well. We think, though we can't know, that the Ziryab must have recognized that you could no longer stand the strain. Perhaps, in delivering it to the Sheikh, he was doing the Mistress's will."

"She was enraged." Al-Kiran tried to re-envision the scene. "When she started to beat Ziryab, the Sheikh intervened. Then she laughed. But Ziryab was dead serious. She said, if I didn't come back it would be hard on him."

"She is using her anger to stoke the fire. Don't worry about your friend, Kemi." Kristien patted his shoulder. "The wrath of the Mistress won't burn him."

"What about the rug?" al-Kiran was too confused to think clearly.

"It is the twin to the one you learned to pray on, beside your father." Ben Hebaron paused, then began pacing. "Your birth-rug showed the patterns by which the Arab tribes have sought to climb to Allah. Through the Prophet, those who were lost in the desert found strength, discipline, and identity.

"The rug before you was woven by your mother's brothers, also in anticipation of your birth — but not to be given to you until you were ready. This one bears the No'Koonja Naqsch of the honey makers, the emblem which is hidden in the maze in your family's garden. The sign of the owl, with the white-ravens, is associated with the ancient totem of your mother's line. The ravens are, at least potentially, doves."

His hands worked across the patterns spread between them. "Your mother said I would know when you were to receive it." Bending forward, he placed his hands on al-Kiran's head, then shoulders. "The men now, through me, recognize you as a man."

Kristien turned toward the Ninth Gate. Breaking contact with his teacher, al-Kiran followed her eyes. "Master . . ." She walked toward the pool, drawing them to follow her. "Why would the men weave the owl, the pattern of the mothers?" Her voice rose in accusation: "By what right, rabbi!"

"The pattern constantly changes with the children. The goal is always to find the balance." Raising al-Kiran by the arm, ben Hebaron stepped back quickly.

"Yes, certainly, Magister Rabbi!" Kristien fired at him then twirled left, landing in a low squat, knees spread.

"Priestess of Oshiwah," ben Hebaron bent his head forward, "you and the Kirian will fly." Scanning the tops of the menhirs, he pointed to the rug. "Please, sit now." As she complied, he walked forward to stand before her.

"You are black as the night from which a dove flies; fresh as the morning; as hauntingly lovely as the full moon passing over the sun. You will ride him. He climbs into you." Then, to al-Kiran, pointing for him to sit with her:

"Your eyes, sharp as the blue skies, must face the dark hidden in your blood. Make a fire in the princess, that the priestess in her may make you a king. Dance in the flames cast by the midnight sun."

CHAPTER FOURTEEN

"The Silence Beneath the Grove"

The sun had progressed further to the west, but it was still warm and bright in the Cypress Grove. Ben Hebaron seated himself opposite them, his back to the pool. Al-Kiran gazed at Kristien, innocent and soft now, reminding him of the first day when she had joined the group in the park near the kerm-oak.

"'The Phantasmal is the Bridge to the Real.'" Ben Hebaron broke the silence. "What did you learn?"

"I memorized the formula, Rabunni." The words followed a memory, seeming to come from someone other than himself. "But I understood only that I was being carried forward."

"What you think you understand is that which you must challenge first." He emphasized each word, his eyes boring into al-Kiran. Kristien scooted away, the tone, the magic between them changing now.

"Rapture is a bridge by which one may join the real, or," he paused, "from which one may fall."

"Or by which one may learn to fly," Kristien asserted.

"This world is the bridge." Ben Hebaron pointed at the carpet, then the circle, then the sky. "From this bridge you can see the unreal, which you are leaving, and the unreal, to which you proceed. Only the bridge is real.

"I follow my heart," Kristien responded, her eyes down.

"So you do," he spoke firmly. "You prepare so that the Kemi may pass over the bridge, with you, to the permanent. But there is no where to go. You tease at what may be, forgetting that your strength and his are not yet matched."

"I do what my body yearns to do," she whispered, her dark eyes on ben Hebaron, her hands folded in her lap.

"The phantasmal consists of our imagery of the past and the future. See through it to the present."

Reaching across, he placed a hand on al-Kiran's shoulder. "She pushes you. It is my job, just now, to pull you back." Turning to Kristien, he added: "Mershi Khayam is of the Tentmakers, as are those who sent you to us. She is Mistress of the Fires. The past and the future curve back into the Real. The Real is where we must stand, hoping we will not fall.

"You are Priestess of Oshiwah, adept, and honored among us." He touched her face, stopping a tear. "But the Mistress of ibn Massara rules by both hands. She is whole and extraordinary. She builds bridges where most dare not follow."

"And I may not be sufficient," she lowered her head.

"You are honored among us, the key to the dance."

Her legs unfolding, Kristien circled behind them.

Uncertain what had happened, al-Kiran turned back to ben Hebaron. Trying to grasp anything, he said: "In my dream, you were demanding I be returned. Was that Real?"

"We are pulling you in and out. Distraction has its uses. Try to see this in slices. Then release. At that moment, it was Real. By the crows you perceived, and now recall, I did argue with the Mistress." He paused while Kristien returned.

"In the present, we can compare memories and by those build bridges and discover objective truths, but it wouldn't be that moment, it would be this moment. With each breath a new world is born. Your world and mine just barely overlap."

Ben Hebaron stood and walked to the pool. An envelope of silence settled upon the circle.

The mule, tethered to a bush up the path above the grove, brayed. Thinking of the Karobla, al-Kiran recalled three verses Ziryab had recited one night while they walked the parapets:

"The stallion burst his tethers.
His veins were open sky.
Our bodies have no feathers.
We're borne, but we must fly.

They fight upon the sacred hill.
They spin until they break.
Our parents love until they fill
The mountain and the lake.

Just as the courser rises,
We swim within their fears.
The mother earth in crisis,
Opens her womb in tears."

Isolated, perched on the ledge over the precipice, ibn Massara, invisible above them, the City, in the distance below them, al-Kiran shuddered. Reseating himself, ben Hebaron said: "You understand that the 'Kirian' name is important?" The words floated toward him with no significance. Kristien touched his shoulder.

"Yes." He tried to focus.

"The Lady Khayam is also of the Kirian line. Her claim to you, during this time, was more urgent than mine."

Al-Kiran felt like a boulder had fallen on him.

Kristien rubbed across his shoulders, along the back of his neck. Ben Hebaron continued: "These mysteries can not be taught. They can only be sprung upon the student. I don't begrudge the Mistress her right to be rid of me."

"But, how could you know that she would not harm me? There were times when . . ." He broke off. Kristien stroked him, her fingers and palms sensuous, yet demanding. His mind struggled to pursue the rabbi's comments, to relate them to his own concerns, but his body's attention was on Kristien.

Suddenly seeing himself from the eye of the eagle which circled over them, it seemed that the cypress circle was a laboratory — that he was the subject of an experiment. He was being toyed with. He couldn't accept the Nubian's affection while following the complexity of his master's revelations, yet her hands on his body, breath on his neck, the smell of her near him . . .

"Is this a dream?" He recognized the voice as his own, then Kristien's voice: "Dream, or not, listen." Then ben Hebaron's voice broke in: "Breathe. Center yourself. You are almost ready." Conciliatory, yet urgent, he was leaning forward. "But do not go beyond the powers you are, at real risk, accumulating within your bodies."

Kristien released her breath. She got up and went to ben Hebaron. "I am sorry, Master." She hugged him. Tears flowed across the dark mystery of her face. He was like a rugged pillar in the clearing. She was like all that makes life delightful, eager, brave, yet wounded, fragile.

The sun danced through the trees, among the stones, splashing in delicate rainbow sprays along the surface of the spring rising into the pool behind them. Al-Kiran watched as stanzas, from an ancient hymn Ziryab had insisted he learn, flowed through his heart:

> "Gen-Isis sought her husband.
> He was buried in a tree.
> Her tears upon the barren land
> Set all the children free.
>
> At first they had such gentle dreams,
> They slept within the seed.
> Then moon flew forth on raven wings,
> And taught the world to bleed.
>
> A slave, she bore the marriage rite
> And danced upon his tomb.
> She searched the night for living light,
> To bear within her womb.
>
> She bore the wedding sanctions.
> She lay beneath his doom.
> She filled his many mansions
> From her majestic loom."

He watched Kristien embrace, then seem to merge with, Alpha ben Hebaron. He remembered asking Ziryab how the hymn might reveal anything of his own relationship with the Nubian slave. Ziryab had responded with another verse:

> "The stars are demon angels.
> The blades are green with doom.
> The flowers are forged by devils.
> From fire and storm they bloom."

In the silence, Ziryab had turned to him and said: "You don't understand yet. But you will." Then he had launched into a strange riddle, chanting against the dark:

"Behind the moon, when the sun is black,
The crow goes down to the mysterious fact
That the soul grows as the earth glows
Through the whirl of their journeying.

The ice in his blood boils as she treats
The throb in his club yearning to meet
The shadow of her dark nurturing.

Remember the pledge which first you encountered
Within the hedge where first you found her:
In your home, all alone, with your studies.

The mule who was dead became a snake instead
To beget the child of your union. From the home
'Al-Kiran Kamir Kirian — I will know you.'"

"As you say . . ." The voice jolted him back to the present. Ben Hebaron kissed Kristien on both cheeks. She sat next to the pool, as he seated himself opposite al-Kiran. "Like the Ziryab, I defied the letter of her law. I'm not sure what she will do next."

"Her law? The Mistress's?" al-Kiran asked.

"Only slightly." The rabbi nodded. "We assume she knew about the letter I left for you."

"Through Ziryab?"

"Or through you. Either way, her law was that we not reveal your circumstances until you discovered them for yourself."

Al-Kiran nodded. "I should have destroyed it."

"Disastrous, perhaps, had al-Mansur found it. But not likely with the Ziryab watching you. No," he paused, "we were playing against the tension Mershi Khayam set. She said, 'until you discovered it.' We just made it available."

"It said you or ab-Dar Il'ium would intervene if . . ."

"Necessary," ben Hebaron completed the statement. "While Kristien and I camped on the way, I sensed that Mershi Khayam might have plans for you which were different than ours . . . that she was determined that you stay with her."

"Did you actually talk to her, in the dream?"

"In a sense we met within your heart. You provided the bridge. Your dream was spread out from the Taifa to the Mosque to the labyrinth in the garden at your parents' home."

"Was I at the Mosque? Did I really see the Caliph?"

Ben Hebaron sighed. "The brief answer is: not in the world you inhabit during your waking state. The Mistress and I were both conscious of your dream, and its general nature, and of your attention to us, but I did not sense that His Majesty was conscious of being in your dream."

"But al-Mansur saw you."

Ben Hebaron glanced toward the guardian stone in the north before responding, his voice lowered: "That was between him and the Mistress."

"He backed off when you and the Mistress approached."

"He was aware of me?"

"He seemed to be."

"Let it go."

"But you said the Mistress was aware . . ."

"Stay with your own purpose." The rabbi glanced at Kristien. "Let her draw you toward flight."

After a moment, he leaned forward, apparently lost in thought, and traced the Grail figure in the upper corner of the carpet with his finger. Breaking the silence, Al-Kiran said:

"Who came for me this morning?" He saw himself in the kitchen, Mershi Khayam violently pulling Ziryab's head back.

Ben Hebaron stood. "At-Talibin came to me with a message from ab-Dar Il'ium. I was to bring you out of the tekke without you becoming conscious that it was over."

"Why?"

"Maybe Kristien knows?"

"If he had known," she rose from the pool and approached, "she would have known. She may have made it more difficult."

Nodding, ben Hebaron pointed for her to sit next to al-Kiran, then continued: "The Sheikh suggested that a direct confrontation with the Mistress should be avoided. Our first concern must be with the Caliphate in Cordoba. Al-Mansur must be stopped. The Northerner and I thought our little ruse would . . ."

The mule, up the path above them, whinnied. Slapping his side, ben Hebaron stood and chanted while rotating in place:

"And the sun danced with Hermes as
Venus sailed the skies
For the lion of the mountain has
his own disguise
So the children of the stallion, fed
by the mad bear's teat
Can forage in the desert on
royal, sacred meat."

Stopping, he raised his voice: "Old tales refer to ancient tribes. Token and totem are confounded. But we figure," he laughed, "one trick deserves and balances another."

Pulling his beard, ben Hebaron scanned the circle. Shifting forward, his voice lowered, he explained: "Mershi Khayam makes tents. She evokes specific states and experiences in her students — but she does not keep the students brought to her by others."

He studied al-Kiran before continuing: "She may create a tent so complex that one is tempted to stay. She plays dangerous tricks. Hers was that I should leave. Ours that you should."

"I had no idea what was going on." A nerve twitched along his neck as he thought of Ziryab.

Ben Hebaron seemed pleased. "Then At-Talibin did well. I do wonder how he fared on returning to the Taifa."

Kristien backed away. Al-Kiran turned to her, wondering what the rabbi was looking at. A white-faced owl perched on top of the Ninth Gate. It's call floated over Kristien.

"Who, indeed?" ben Hebaron asked. The creature stretched.

Its eyes still on them, it settled on a high limb in the sentinel cypress. As they watched, it disappeared.

Clapping softly, he drew their attention. "When she comes here, they say, it is not the Mistress personally. An animal double, a familiar, works with her."

He didn't laugh, and there was no responsive rush from the rooks. Motioning that they should stand and wait, he checked each of the inner stones, in a quick sunwise circle, then walked to the pool and splashed himself before signaling them forward. While they bent to drink, he recited:

"What ever goes with the owl and the crows,
We herders of sheep in the dessert
Just watch, entranced, and wonder:
Does she know us? Does she care?"

Pointing them back to their robes, spread on the other side of the Kirian prayer rug, he said: "And so, students, we continue." But his iron-gray eyes belied the casualness of his smile.

Hand in hand with Kristien, al-Kiran could think of nothing but the warmth of her touch, the pulse along her wrist, her nearness. Looking at al-Kiran, ben Hebaron said:

"What in another time and place must evolve over months must now leap into your world in one afternoon. She elicits a unity in you between mind and body, but one which your age and training will resist, though your heart screams to go forward. Give yourself, Kemi, that she may fully awaken you. After tonight, you will not see each other until the dance."

Glancing at Kristien, he added: "There are no eyes here other than those which approve and honor the magic of your love. Build now on the rhythm of life," then walked the outer perimeter of the stone circle, beneath the cypress trees, their branches stretching like arms over him, adding, his words seeming to come from the distance: "You are alone and safe here while I walk the circle from outside. I will clap three times before I return."

Apprehensive, yet eager, al-Kiran followed Kristien's hands as she guided him to lay back, his hair spread against the soft gown covering her lap, her legs crossed beneath his neck, her thighs holding his head, the woman of her filling the sky while her fingers circled slowly across his chest, opening his robe, then searching beneath.

Breathing crystal air down along his neck, she bent over him, her breasts in his face, her tongue playing across his skin. His nipples hardened in response. His maleness throbbing, he dreamed of entering her, being lost forever in her moist, warm care; then, struggling to pull away, the tip of her tongue behind his ear, he swiveled to sit straight.

In the silence, Kristien rolled her head down into al-Kiran's lap, his legs crossed beneath her face, her mouth coaxing him into one pointed flame surging against the purring in her throat. His head back, his heart aching, he felt her as pure animal, beautiful, innocent, dangerous power.

His fingers lost in the black plaits of her soft hair, he looked down. Nuzzling at his inner thighs, her hand exploring beneath his spine, she pulled him through his clothes up to the touch of her tongue. The shaft of him ached against her. She rolled, smiling, face up. Her hair in his exposed lap, she held him against herself. Lifting his buttocks beneath her, he throbbed against the side of her head, wanting to rupture. Her mouth opened, her eyes closed, her hips raised.

Bending forward, he fumbled to unlatch and spread the folds of her gown, moving against the warm creases of her skin, her thighs shuddering open, the nest covering soft lips. Pink within black, engorged, she quivered to his touch, moist like her mouth, warm, his finger finding where his maleness must go.

Swelling firmer, trembling, he lifted away, gently laying her head on the rug. His tongue between her breasts, across the salt of her stomach, down toward the sweetness of the mother cave, eclipsed in her mystery — his back to the sun, her mouth up, her thighs spreading, catching him, her lips settling around him, pulling him into her — he plunged forward, head first, into the soft thunder of her darkness.

"The Mistress blesses us," she whispered, her legs circling his head as she rolled back on top, her gown covering him like a tent perfumed with musk, the sweet scent of her. His tongue stretched into her, his nose and chest breathing her in, his phallus outside, in the cold air, her fingers around his sack, the stones aching. A small man, homunculus, stood straight from his groin in the sun.

"The rabbi blesses us, as well." She hovered above him in the dark. Thumping him back against himself, the fire going cold, she bent to him again, her flanks rising from his mouth, his tongue and throat aching with the taste of her. She covered him again, sucking, licking between his thighs, pulling him up into the sun, aching as she spread, his tongue in the bristle of her hair, in the darkness, her fingers tightening around him, then caressing him like a baby.

She was humming, as a mother would, tucking him back in, pulling her leg away, her inner thigh soft, her skin eternity. Sliding around, she brought him back up and lay her head in his lap. Placing his hand between her legs, she moved it across her stomach to one and then the other of her breasts breathing beneath his touch, her flesh warm. Her hips rocking up, her lips pursed pleadingly, she draped her gown over his hand, the buds of her nipples erect between his fingers as she whispered: "When the sun disappears behind the moon, your maleness in my womb, I will give my life to you."

Rolling her face into his lap again, she pulled him up and into her mouth. His every cell screaming to explode into her, she squeezed tight, but gently, holding him erect.

Suspended, he fainted. Lost in darkness, he floated across the cliff, beyond the circle of trees, the stones, the pool in the center, the white of the Kymerian Stream in the distance an ecstatic ribbon coursing through his body. Wanting to give himself to her, he was stopped, painfully held at the tip of his phallus, throbbing at the edge of rapture and release then curling back down into himself.

An owl, it's face a white mask, called and spread huge wings above the Ninth Gate. "Yes," Kristien hushed, her voice somewhere between herself and the Mistress's, patting him into calm. Raising her head, her eyes up, indigo then dark-amber, the pink of her tongue moist between her lips, she looked into his heart then lowered again to kiss his organ, limp now but all consciousness, yearning to explode in her.

Mouth soft about him, then licking, her tongue rough like a cat's, brushing, purring as she looked up, her eyes smiling, she whispered: "Not now, Kirian. Wait in the mid-night sun. Come to me then. Resist now," she grinned, "as the rabbi requested."

The owl rose, long wings fading into blue sky. The white face disappeared in the glare of the sun. Pulling her gown around herself, Kristien stood and glided bare-footed to the gray rim of the supine monolith in which the spring pooled from deep within the dark of the mountain against which they hovered, her body the object of it's energies — then returned and held al-Kiran's hand in her own.

Three claps broke the silence from outside the grove. A moment later, Alpha ben Hebaron emerged from behind the trees, bowed and touched water to his face, then, facing them, said:

"The Mother and Father dance between you. Learn to ride the fire-rapture of their love. Use it for good;" he let the words sink in, "otherwise, it will destroy you." He paused, studying them. "I wish you the joy I share with my mate. It is hard, I know, to keep the balance."

Kristien settled her head against al-Kiran's shoulder. Nodding his approval, ben Hebaron continued: "I want to give you what I can before our time in this circle ends. This is my teaching." His eyes moved slowly from Kristien to al-Kiran. "Hold each other here." He pointed to his heart. "By memory of and reverence for your experience, you may pass to each other, meeting on this bridge, during the dance. Even after that, through this memory, in your hearts, you will be able to touch — even though you are separated by continents."

Breathing as one, they attended to their teacher's every word. Pointing at al-Kiran, he continued: "You knew how to dance before you were born. The energy in your heart will carry you toward Kristien. Yearning for the union of earth and sky, you will be carried into and beyond the eclipse."

"What of the steps we practiced?" al-Kiran asked.

"The fire at your belly, the drive in your loins, the words in your throat, the visions behind your eyes, the snake in your spine, the infinite reaches beyond your crown, the energy of the Kirian seal . . ." he leaned forward and placed his palm on al-Kiran's head, "all shall join in strength and anguish, love and pain. By these you will be transformed."

Looking with deep care at Kristien, he placed his other palm on her head. "This beautiful earth is the heart of our planetary system. By your passionate energies, we move beyond our petty concerns and join the great dance."

Then looking back at al-Kiran: "You need not remember the exercises. Your heart has been chained to a higher love. In Kristien it has found the object which will take it across the bridge to the world of objective flight.

"Kristien, Princess and Priestess of Nubia," he addressed her with deep tenderness, "there is nothing I can teach you. But remember, the Kemi carries the fire by which you also will be reborn. Shut not your gates. Accept and nurture him as he, in turn, fills you with his love. He is the fire which glows in spite of the darkness. He will seek you out. His is the tree which will bloom in the desert. You are the womb which will accept him into your waters."

His face gentle, his eyes warm and moist, he added: "You two are the hope of the world."

Lines of energy coursed between al-Kiran and Kristien. Fire streamed from the earth, through the owl and white raven carpet upon which they sat, passing about the stones, across the pool, and spiraling into the sky.

"This sacred place is a generator for this energy." Ben Hebaron turned in a circle. "Each of the monoliths magnifies currents which rise through the hollow of the central stone. The cypress is the tree of transformation. The cedars of the outer circle guard this place. The Kymerian waters underlie the stage upon which the actions of this world are played out.

"The extremes are the tips of the wings of the owl of our knowledge of the love in our hearts. By the expression of love, you shall fly. And thus the flight of the children, of the sacred line of the Prophets of Allah, shall occur in the world of objective fact."

Turning toward the spring, ben Hebaron knelt. His eyes sparkling, cupping water in his palms, he approached them. Taking Kristien's head in his hands, cool with the waters, and bending her backwards slightly, he kissed her forehead.

Returning to the spring, he repeated the ritual, kissing al-Kiran as a hush fell into the grove.

A cloud passed across the sun. Shadows had begun to creep forward from the cypress in the west. The menhirs seemed to tilt, spreading a deeper dark from the roots where each connected with the sacred earth.

"Al-Kemi and Kristien," ben Hebaron's spoke softly, "we return to Cordoba tonight." He leaned forward and took one of their hands in each of his own. "The next three days are yours. Enjoy your old routines and companions. Accept the strength of what has sustained you so far. Thank those who have helped you — and prepare to say good-bye."

Touching their hands to his lips, then his forehead, he said: "There are no new steps to be learned. Nothing further is required," then stepped onto the Kirian rug, raising them to their knees. Leaning against him in the silence, each touched his legs while he looked up to the sky and recited:

"There is a forest where the wild crows go.
There is a glen in the woods where they rest.
There is a spring in the heart where the owls glow,
Where the song is the heart at its best."

The sun suddenly broke through the clouds, shooting a tunnel of light across the clearing, angling directly into the pool behind their teacher. Throwing his arms outward, he radiated and received its energies. His head rolled forward slowly. Looking down at them, his features faded. The white mask, of the owl creature, peered through his face.

Pulling themselves upward, al-Kiran and Kristien wrapped themselves about his body — a tree anchoring them at the foot of the sacred pool beneath the endless sky. Enfolded in his arms, their arms around him, he whispered:

"May the love of the one soul rest within you.
May you grow wings and fly.
May you join in the union,
The marriage of earth and sky."

Hundreds of ravens rose in the air. The sun glazing their wings in light, they swirled together, then melded into wings extended beneath the white owl face. A rainbow snake body between the wings, the creature spiraled, hovering in the blue sky, then rising toward Taifa ibn Massara.

"The rainbow bridge will carry you," their teacher whispered. Turning slowly, an arm around each of their waists, his strength steady and reassuring, he guided them from the circle toward the mule braying in the distance.

CHAPTER FIFTEEN

"Homecoming"

Kristien barely spoke during their long trek down the mountain. At first, still excited, al-Kiran had wanted desperately to whisper something to the Nubian. But she had folded herself ever more deeply into the shadows. Following behind the mule, he had settled into the steady work of his body. Night descended before they crossed the Roman bridge and entered the outskirts of Cordoba.

Treading steadily toward the Arian Abbey where Kristien was to stay, the rabbi nodding from time to time to various acquaintances, they passed the Royal Gardens and the great plaza, then through the empty markets and the wine district, full of night-celebrants, into the old Roman and Visigothic neighborhood, home now to many Arab aristocrats.

The mule's hooves, scuffing against the cobblestones, mixed with voices floating through lantern lights reflected in glowing pools across the walls from gardens where parties were underway. Al-Kiran tightened the cowl around his face against the chill, whisking in sudden bursts along the street. He noticed that Kristien, her eyes down, was shivering. He wanted to reach across to her.

"Stand, stranger." The Captain of a group of Berber soldiers stepped in front of them, his hand out, surly and self-important. "State your business."

"Alpha ben Hebaron of Cordoba." Ben Hebaron spoke directly but non-confrontationally.

"And who is she?" He pointed to Kristien.

"Kristien of the Household of al-Ladian, Uncle to Hakam II. I am her instructor."

Drawing Kristien's hood back and pulling her robe open, the Berber examined her rudely, glanced at ben Hebaron and then spit in disgust. The soldiers crowded up behind him.

"As I understand al-Mansur," he spoke malevolently, "this is the danger which approaches. A Jew accompanies the Uncle's concubine. No doubt she professed Islam while practicing idolatry; but who can guess at the Omayyad taste?" The men laughed harshly. "Perhaps we should castrate the rabbi so the 'Princess,'" he accented the word sarcastically, "might be better kept for the true service."

Shocked and alarmed, al-Kiran searched for a way to deflect the soldiers. "Gentlemen," he stepped forward, speaking with authority, "I am son of Abu el-Ali. By the request of the Royal Uncle and appointment of the Caliph, this Nubian is my partner for the Dance and this rabbi is our teacher. Leave us or regret any insult you might give."

Smirking, but apparently unwilling to chance the displeasure of the royal family, the Captain backed away. While the soldiers disappeared into an alley, Kristien re-wrapped her robe and lowered her head. "What of these soldiers, Rabbi?" she whispered. "How real is the danger?"

Nodding approvingly at al-Kiran, he moved forward before answering: "They are too fresh from the desert wars to understand the diversity of light."

"But even here in Cordoba?" al-Kiran asked, still trembling, not wanting to believe what had happened.

"So long as Hakam rules, we are protected, provided we move carefully. After that," he paused, "history will tell."

The words tight in his throat, al-Kiran said: "Won't the Royal Uncle protect the heir?"

"Like His Majesty, al-Ladian assumes all will go well so long as he is himself of good heart. It's not so simple."

"What of young Hisham's mother?" Kristien asked.

"She is Christian Basque."

"Al-Mansur?" al-Kiran asked.

"Plots abound," ben Hebaron responded. "The Chamberlain attacks. But there is also hope, here." Handing the lead rope to al-Kiran, he turned toward a group of approaching pilgrims who, arm in arm, were adjusting their gait to their song. "Listen."

"The Prince of the East sought the Golden Fleece.
The Argonauts sailed as the winds hailed
The glow of the sun about the moon —
The dark moon over the sun.

Green flows of the earth soul —
The Golden crown in the blue sky found.
The dancers know that the answers grow
From the rainbow gardens of Cordoba."

They moved back into the street, then fell silent again.

Al-Kiran thought of the old Christian church, the time when
Kristien had stopped him on his way to ben Hebaron's, outside
its courtyard — her touch like fire on his chest. He wondered
about the Arian brothers with whom she had traveled from the
Sudan through Byzantium, then Carthage, on their way to Cordoba for some purpose of which she had not been told.

Turning a corner, they entered a quieter neighborhood. The
street wound between white walls attached to smaller houses.
The city was older here, the street narrower. The residents,
mostly Iberians and descendants of the Christians who had settled in Cordoba during the time of the Visigoths, had learned,
even under the Omayyads, to be discreet.

Arab by blood and connected to the Royal House, al-Kiran
had grown up believing all residents and guests in Cordoba were
secure. But he recognized now the precautions practiced by those
descended from alien faiths.

"Why must these people, whose ancestors built Cordoba,
hide their lights?" Kristien shivered while she spoke.

"The Jews, even with Hasdai ibn Shaprut at the Caliph's
side, are similarly cautious," ben Hebaron commented.

"But why must it be?" al-Kiran asked.

The shadows of the church and monastery, where Kristien's
companions awaited her, were just visible beyond the distant
trees. Pushing his cowl back, the rabbi scanned the Plaza of
Angels, saying: "Kristien would know the song of the desert."

"There are many," she responded. Her eyes on al-Kiran, she pushed his hood back, then her own. It was her first touch since they had left the cypress grove.

His hand on her shoulder, ben Hebaron said: "The Black Madonna of your lineage preserves the seed for the Magdalen. Though we fear, as is wise, the mysteries of the dance between God and Goddess, we honor and seek to protect you." He turned her toward the gate. "We complete the sacred songs."

Tethering the mule, a fist in his heart, al-Kiran hurried to catch up. As they moved forward, Kristien was reciting:

> "Gen-Isis sought Osiris.
> He was buried in a tree.
> His parts were spread about us,
> Then scattered in the sea."

She walked beside the rabbi but seemed to be in trance. Al-Kiran followed immediately behind them, but it was as though she had breathed another world into herself. She was already distant from him, her consciousness wholly on what awaited her. Sighing with a shudder, she chanted:

> "Upon a throne she nurtured,
> Her breasts gave living sap.
> The God of Light was butchered,
> Then laid across her lap."

Looking into their teacher's eyes, her voice a whisper, she asked: "How, Rabunni, is our mission to be fulfilled?"

Holding her briefly, then running his hands gently over her head, ben Hebaron responded:

> "The druid hawks were suckled,
> By breasts along the beach.
> To Isis they were buckled,
> Then broken free to teach."

Kristien, on tip-toes, kissed the rabbi lightly on each cheek. Stepping back, her eyes shadows, she bowed quickly to al-Kiran before running through the gate toward the Arian brother framed in the light at the door to the church.

"These druids, master? Who are they?" al-Kiran asked, unable to grasp the significance of the exchanges he had just heard. The escape from ibn Massara, the hours in the sacred grove, the long walk in silence, the ancient chants and riddles, had left his mind numb, his thoughts desolate, his heart sad and confused.

"Initiates of the North and West — the singers of the sacred oaks. But for now, Blackbird," he moved his hand along al-Kiran's back, turning him away from the Arian monastery, "the Priestess greets the good brothers who brought her to Cordoba and prepares to say good-bye.

"Pray, Kemi, as we have been taught," he added, his words heavy as they moved back through the plaza, "that from the darkest night the new light is born."

"And that from the blackest fire, Rabunni . . . " Al-Kiran hesitated, feeling strength but also concern from his teacher. Suddenly he knew that ben Hebaron needed them as much as they needed him, and that he was uncertain what the outcome of their efforts would be. Steadying himself, he completed the ancient formula: " . . . the Phoenix rises."

Kristien's silence and withdrawal while returning to Cordoba had left al-Kiran perplexed. His sudden realization that he would not see her again until the dance, left him weak and exhausted in spite of his excited anticipation and hope.

After their brief exchange in the Plaza of Angels, he tried to ask questions, but ben Hebaron said to follow at a distance. Leading the mule up the winding pathways, he tied the animal to an olive tree and checked both directions before directing al-Kiran through the gate toward his parents.

It was nearly midnight. Mershi Kamir ran forward and hugged him affectionately. Alpha ben Hebaron bowed to her then to Abu el-Ali, who waited under the oil lamp in the archway, his eyes sharp and steady, his long black beard streaked with white, a string of beads hanging from his right hand.

"I will return on solstice morning," the rabbi spoke formally, then started to back away.

Releasing her son, Mershi Kamir said: "The Ziryab was here." Al-Kiran's heart stopped.

Apparently startled, ben Hebaron asked: "Has al-Mansur made a move?"

"The danger rises." Abu el-Ali nodded seriously.

Her arm around his waist, Mershi Kamir turned al-Kiran through the door, leaving Abu el-Ali with ben Hebaron outside. As they moved down the hall he heard his father say: "Protect the Princess, and . . ." then Alansha's voice floating toward them from the kitchen:

"He played in the sun before the moon dance.
He walked in the shade, the breeze in his hair.
He had wrestled with the men for the golden lance.
He won it for his love at the fair."

Recognizing "The Return of the Lance," he was eager to see the woman who had sung to him of dragons and contests, heroes and maidens determined to serve each other in love. Withered with age, yet soft and vital, salt-tears of happiness streaming down her face, Alansha folded him to herself. As his mother spread her arms around them both, he relaxed into the swaying of the women who had raised him.

Eager for his father to return, in spite of the warning he had heard, confidence swelled in his breast — the faith that his love for the Nubian would be sufficient for the dance, the flight, the eclipse, the dark-fire . . . whatever Allah might bring by the Prophecy of Mohammed, the Blessed Messenger, to Cordoba and al-Andalus.

When Abu el-Ali entered the room, he was carrying the prayer mat. "Did you know," al-Kiran turned to face him as Alansha busied herself preparing food, "that was mine?"

"Yes." He lay the rug along the wall, then clasped his son's elbows in a man's embrace.

"It's from the men," al-Kiran announced proudly.

"You've earned it, I'm sure," his mother rejoined. "Was the Mistress hard on you?"

"Both hard and loving . . ."

"There aren't words." She smiled approval.

"The rabbi . . ."

"You look like you haven't been fed in weeks." Shuffling to the table, a tray in each hand, Alansha cut him off. "What's wrong with the her, Mershi? You said . . ."

"Enough of that, Alansha," his mother snapped. "She has her purposes — and we have ours." Smiling again, she whispered in his ear: "Alansha has worried about you," then louder: "We're all glad you're back with us now."

"She's not to be trusted." Alansha fumed then moved off toward her room, muttering: "Mistress Khayam, she's called now, is she? No Mistress . . ." the rest was inaudible.

Ignoring her, Mershi Kamir pointed to the bread, meat, fruit, and water pitcher. "Are you hungry?"

Seating himself, al-Kiran took a bite of the bread. Remembering the wine the rabbi had insisted he share that noon, near the cypress spring, sopping bread, saying it was flesh and blood — conscious of his father standing behind him — al-Kiran decided there was much he wouldn't talk about.

Watching his mother move about the kitchen, he admired how beautifully graceful she was. He didn't feel like eating. He wondered about Alansha's complaint against the Mistress.

He didn't want to think about it. He wanted to slide back into the security of the home he would soon leave forever. Abu el-Ali put his hand on al-Kiran's shoulder. "We hope the Kirian Rug helped you understand the Orders which unite the Jewish, Christian, and Moslem faiths."

While the sounds of Cordoba floated over the dark outer-walls of the villa, his father guided him onto the patio then toward the lion fountains which guarded the labyrinth.

The moon crescent had disappeared hours before. Bright star-beads studded the sky.

"You'll be dancing soon enough." Abu el-Ali lit the lamp then patted the bench. "Sit beside me tonight."

"What did Ziryab say?" al-Kiran asked hesitantly.

"The Ziryab riddles. He is devoted to the Mistress."

"He was my only friend." Al-Kiran's heart was pounding.

"A good one I suspect." He studied his son before continuing: "He said there was danger, but that you had escaped — more than whole. Do you know what he meant?"

"No." Al-Kiran looked away, thinking that he had brought something of the Mistress with him. "Where was he going?"

"Your mother believes he carried messages to the Eunuchs."

"Mother reminded me of a dancer tonight."

"I first saw her at the Festival of All Faiths," he paused, a new intimacy in his voice, "moving in the snake-line with the other aspirants."

"You didn't know her before that?"

"No. But I was determined to know her then." He sighed reflectively. "During the breaks, when the dancers eat and rest, I tried to get close to her; but, of course, that is forbidden." He glanced at his son. "Watching her move, I was fascinated by her grace and by the power of the dance."

"Was there any talk of the prophecy that year?" al-Kiran hesitated. He still feared that speaking of it out loud would dissipate its power.

"Of course." Abu el-Ali turned to look through the fountains toward the gate to the labyrinth beyond.

"Ben Hebaron says that there will be an actual eclipse and that the dancers will fly as 'blackbirds after the owl.'"

"The owl of objective knowledge." Abu el-Ali nodded. "It's a Sufi formula. Ben Hebaron and ab-Dar Il'ium believe this is the year." Then, standing: "May the vision of Mohammed carry you across the bridge between the worlds."

Turning toward the labyrinth, he continued: "Power flows

with the birds chasing the owl. The dance will take you where it will. May the breath of our prayers support you."

Feeling slightly uncomfortable, al-Kiran asked: "What did you feel when you saw Mother dance?"

"That in her body she carries some deep force." His voice trailed off.

A new sense of identity welling up within him, al-Kiran whispered: "I feel the same when I watch Kristien."

Nodding, then starting to walk, he guided al-Kiran. "Ab-Dar Il'ium introduced us following the dance. I knew, from that moment, that even though I would be a mullah, I would also accept the path of the Sufis — and that, through her, a child would be born to complete what I had seen."

"What of Orwan Oshiwah?" al-Kiran asked, tentatively. "What was, is, she like, Father?"

"I have never met her directly."

"I have dreamt of her." Al-Kiran hesitated.

"A cave priestess — she's violent and mysterious — a teacher like the Mistress of ibn Massara. Did she speak?"

"She said I have been protected by half-truths and she thrust her hand into my chest. She was missing one finger." Thinking of the cave opposite the alcove, he asked: "Is the Mistress related to her?"

As if considering al-Kiran's statements, Abu el-Ali paused, then turned back toward the patio. "There are certain things which are not discussed."

"Is she of the same lineage as my Grandmother?"

"Like your mother, and the Nubian, the Mistress, and your grandmother, follow an older line."

"Oshiwah?"

"The nine-fold Goddess and," Abu el-Ali nodded, "the fourth to the three who have been usurped by men — the shadow which frightens the priests but which must be reincorporated before we can be whole. And," he hesitated, "the Mistress and your mother are true Kirians, true blood sisters."

Al-Kiran was spinning in disbelief and shock.

"We would have told you, but it couldn't be risked."

"Why?"

"If the fundamentalists had known . . ."

"Is that why Alansha is upset?" He was angry and confused. "She knows the Mistress, doesn't she?"

"She worked with Orwan in the training of the sisters." Abu el-Ali paused. "She's quite serious about the food."

"The Mistress fed me," al-Kiran protested.

His father reached out to soothe him. "To the esoteric orders, 'food' is much more than you take in through your mouth. All I can say is that Alansha disagrees about the food." Guiding al-Kiran's gently, he added: "Let's go in."

Mershi Kamir rose from a chair in the corner, shadow around her, her hair auburn, not coal-black like Abu el-Ali's. It curled lightly above her dark eyes, almond shaped and bright. "Are you well, al-Kiran?" She leaned forward, hands on the inlaid table. "Are there many changes since you left?"

"I am different." He hesitated.

Grinning, exuding pleasure, she hummed, her hips swaying, then sang softly, reflecting the words in her movements:

"The birds and the owl sing from the trees.
They fly through the sky black and blue.
Were the ocean so cold, the clouds so gray,
How would the lover find you?"

She came forward and hugged him. He sagged, hoping she would never let go. "Don't fear the dance. Open your heart."

His mind hovered at the mouth of a cave. Two women — the Mistress Khayam behind him, Orwan Oshiwah, ahead — were pointing at his heart. "The Shariah . . ." he tried to speak.

"He wants to know, husband, whether he will fly as the faith of his youth is pulled out from beneath him."

"Or will he fall?" his father whispered. "It's time for sleep, al-Kiran; but listen, first, and consider 'The Song of the Men' — which I recited to you so often as a young boy, barely able to hold your eyes open, and understand:

'Where the wild things grow beyond the desert and the snow
The moon found her wings and cradled the kings
Who were suckled by earth for the promise of birth
That rose with the leaven which was planted by heaven.
But the sun had begun to kill them by its preachings.
From the north they came forth to the west for the test
of the teachings.
But the joy of the south was deep in his mouth
And the star of the east had brought him a feast
So the child of the winds could live through the ends
of the teachings.'

"Now," he laughed gently, "Allah insists upon good dreams.
Just remember: the Dancers are always in prayer."

CHAPTER SIXTEEN

"FINAL PREPARATIONS"

During the final days preceding the beginning of the Festival, al-Kiran did not attempt to see Kristien or ben Hebaron. Although his parents made it clear that there was no need to practice the Shariah, he enjoyed being back to his old routines. At times he was happy, but at certain moments he felt that his world was falling apart. He tried to suppress his memories of the Mistress and Ziryab, and of how al-Mansur was plotting to disrupt the long dance. He told himself that those were matters beyond his control and that ben Hebaron had said he was ready, that he need only relax.

The sun was rising later each morning, deeper in the south. Nights were longer. The moon was a sliver in the western sky at sunset. On the evening of the day preceding the winter solstice, there would be no moon at all.

He sensed that the earth was moving toward synchrony, toward the point when the moon would cover the sun — but didn't think about it. He wanted to accept the assurances that his learning had already occurred, that his knowledge was sleeping beneath the surface, waiting to be called forth.

He helped his parents with the chores. He watched his mother in the kitchen and prayed beside his father on the rug woven by the Kirian Brothers. He walked in the courtyard and found himself sitting in the center of the labyrinth.

Going to bed on the eve of the festival, knowing that the dance would begin the next day at noon and continue through the moment of solstice, al-Kiran breathed deeply. The cold breeze blew through his shuttered window, carrying him into sleep. He awoke, suddenly, in a dream.

He was in the mountains, on a ledge staring at signs in the stone between a sun-swirl and a crescent. Words forming from the signs, he read: "Orwan Kamir Oshiwah al-Kirian."

At that moment Mesire At-Talibin, carrying a torch, walked

out of the cave. Blond and tall, he wore silver armor, a red cross and a rose emblazoned across his chest.

Looking down at his own clothes, al-Kiran saw that he was dressed as an Iman of Ali, and that he wore the insignia of a royal scholar of the Omayyad Caliphate. Reaching up, he realized that his head was wrapped in a turban.

Ignoring al-Kiran, At-Talibin placed his torch in a sconce on the cliff-face, cut a circle beneath the torch with his short Christian sword, then stood back to study the sun and moon symbols on the opposite side of the cave-mouth.

Unsheathing the crescent sword of the conquering Arabs, saying: "This is for the moon and Venus," al-Kiran approached the circle. The scimitar glowed red, like the cross on At-Talibin's armor. The handle burning in his hand, he sliced the pathways of the No'Koonja Naqsch into the stone, joining nine points around the circumference.

Backing away, they faced the cave together. At-Talibin, holding his sword point upward, turned and touched his blade to al-Kiran's shoulder. In the silence, al-Kiran, using his scimitar, did the same, blessing and charging At-Talibin. As the sword and the crescent crossed above and between them, At-Talibin said: "This is the womb of our common heritage."

Al-Kiran responded: "This is the womb of our future," then, startled by an owl, sat up in bed.

Fumbling to light a candle, his mind filled with a vision of the cave to which Mershi Khayam had sent him, in which he had met Orwan Oshiwah, from which he had just returned. He knew that when the sunrise finally came, he would feel no compulsion to prostrate and pray. The rhythms of the faithful would support, but not distract him.

"We were on the ledge. The sun was rising. We turned. We were both wearing the patched robes, the motley, of Taifa ibn Massara."

A rose-blue haze hung over Cordoba as al-Kiran quietly slipped into the garden, past the maze, and through the gate at the back of the Kirian estate. He wanted to walk, to feel the city, to ground himself before his teacher would take him into the world of the long dance.

Winding down the pathways between the adjacent villas, thinking of Kristien, he moved toward the inner city.

From iron-grill baskets, perched like great birds in nests on top of a thousand spiraled minarets, the muezzins were greeting the sun — calling the faithful to prayer. Their chants mixed with the first stirring along the river. A few dogs barked. Smoke trailed upward from chimneys.

The spirit of the city rolled lazily through the domed mosques, the steepled churches, the square and stout synagogues, the madrasahs and colleges, the pavilions, markets, and broad parks, the villas, town houses, gardens, and zoos. He felt it rumbling beneath his feet, yawning behind and within the stones and lumber of the buildings.

Rays stretched from the dappled east. He walked through the Plaza of the Jeweled Mother and into the Street of Astrologers, feeling the sky-dance overhead, the fade of constellations. Light streams meandered slowly back into the dome of the heavens. In the flicker and retreat of the stars, he saw the promise of return — the promise of the eclipse, when night and day would embrace above the dancers.

The sacred dance between sky and earth, between sun and moon, loomed ahead, approached from the horizon, moved across the earth, the sun chasing shadows through the city of many faiths. He stretched to it with his heart as he moved steadily toward the old Arian monastery.

Peacocks squawked along the Guadalquivir, demanding that their keepers scatter more feed across the morning ground. The braying of camels and donkeys mixed with the general squall, like sound clouds in an otherwise clearing sky.

Fish mongers, with their carts, were pushing up the lanes from the docks to the temporary markets, the night's catch displayed on gray planks, the cold sun glistening in rainbows along their sides, eyes watching — an occasional flit along their fins, their bodies snaking beneath the chill breeze.

"Yahweh be praised!" Al-Kiran surprised himself, having used ben Hebaron's expression. Then: "They sacrifice that we may eat. May we do as well." Breathing in the smell of donkeys and mules, camels and barges, produce and cooking fires, he added: "Yahweh and Allah are one."

Moving into the district of the tanners, he relished the pungent afterglow of yesterday's work hung in the air, crisp with the sheen of Andalusian winter.

The lane narrowed and curved into the Square of the Wine Merchants. He walked before store fronts decorated in conspicuous Christian and Jewish motifs. Gazing around the square, he recalled ben Hebaron's observation: "Our sovereign insists that this trade be conducted by those who have not yet converted to Islam. Allah be praised for the good sense and patience of the Omayyad Caliphs."

Inscriptions from the great Sufi poets proclaimed the richness of life in al-Andalus. Pausing before a vintner's shop, reading the lines from a famous celebration of spirit and flesh, he saw himself with Kristien in the Cypress Grove: "May the dancing girl bring me the cup — Companion of my heart, Seeress, bestower of Grace!"

The sun, glowing red with promise, slanted over the adjoining buildings as he moved forward. "There is room here for all faiths," the teachings of ben Hebaron surfaced in his consciousness, "if one has the good sense to not affront the mullahs. But . . ." He came back to the present, thinking of the political crisis already apparent within the city, of al-Mansur lurking at the edge of the inner circle during the selection of the dancers at summer solstice.

"We must reassure the Berber chiefs. We must steady the world and stop al-Mansur," he said out loud, concern in his heart but strangely certain that he was prepared to try, that somehow he and Kristien were the keys.

"I am to look for the boy during the eclipse." His feet scuffed the cobble stones while, frustrated by his lack of knowledge, he struggled to recall the details of the letter.

Walking beneath the morning sky, he wove into an old residential district and was re-assured by the happy chatter of children stirring their parents, within the privacy of their homes. He knew ben Hebaron recognized his struggles and weaknesses, but had confidence in him. Kristien had a special knowledge of the body and its energies, as did Mershi Khayam, and was weaving the bond between them to some higher force.

He remembered Orwan Oshiwah, his grandmother, before whose cave-temple, in the dream world that morning, he had met Mesire At-Talibin, a devotee of the Christian mysteries.

He believed that,although caught in sometimes painful and conflicting loyalties as he sought to do the work of the Mistress, Ziryab was his friend. He, above all others, knew the suffering of friendship. But al-Kiran could not fathom exactly why, or how, and to what effect, these persons were influencing him.

He ran his hand along the walls of homes housing guests for the first day of the Festival, knowing that thousands of additional visitors would pour into the city each day until the climax of the Dance of Created Lights at winter solstice.

"Would you welcome a companion?" Abu el-Ali startled his son as he turned the corner and entered a wider street.

"I was lost in thought, Father. Forgive me."

One hand telling his jeweled rosary, his frame solid and tall, dignified, his robes and turban white, his beard spread over his chest, Abu el-Ali smiled. The tree lined streets were starting to fill with excited hosts and guests meandering toward the central plaza, ready for the celebration.

"I thought we might walk together once more before the dance." Various passers-by, recognizing him, or his status, acknowledged Abu el-Ali. He nodded to them in return.

Walking in silence, al-Kiran felt an emptiness in his stomach, a slight trembling in his legs.

Looking at him, his father smiled. "Eventually an inner fire will take over, but for the present let us talk."

"Will you tell me of al-Mansur, Father?"

Indicating they should sit on a stone bench, Abu el-Ali said: "All People of the Book tend to abstraction."

"What power of thought I once had is now gone." Al-Kiran hung his head. "There is very little that I understand."

Leaning forward, his father responded: "Your training has broken your mind open that your heart might begin to think."

"My heart?"

"We are striving for direct-knowing — in which condition the intelligences of body, heart, and mind are united."

"Ziryab said that I must be willing to die."

"You are dying, all of us are, always." His eyes met his son's. "Be re-born with awareness, so you can act consciously."

"I am conscious of dying, Father."

"That's the first step." Abu el-Ali stood. "Now, choose the means and the meaning of your constant death. Add to that a conscious intention to be reborn."

They walked back through the park and turned toward the Plaza of Angels. "Al-Mansur is but one means of your death." He nodded to a fellow mullah who passed by in the street. "Kristien of Nubia, Mershi Khayam, the Ziryab, ben Hebaron, your friends, your mother and myself — each of us, and everything you have known, is passing away."

His father's words crushed him. A fist around his heart, he whispered: "Then al-Mansur is determined to ruin all that the Omayyad Caliphs have established in our city?"

"Our enemies present us with the work we must do."

"But I don't know how al-Mansur will attack."

"If I knew, I would tell you."

"What do you know, Father?"

"For several years, the All Faiths Festival and the design of the dance have been the subject of discussions between Hasdai ibn Shaprut, Alpha ben Hebaron, Sheikh ab-Dar Il'ium, Moses ben Hanoch, the Royal Uncle, and myself."

"Because of the danger from al-Mansur?"

"And because of the Prophecy. I wish I could have told you more, earlier, but it wasn't possible. The Chamberlain is our concern as much as yours. During the last three days we have been considering what role the Mistress Khayam intends to play." He paused. "As you know, the rabbi is alarmed."

"Is she trying to help us? Mother trusts her, and . . ."

"We can not expect to fully understand," he started forward again, "but we're certain she would not harm you."

Slightly relieved, al-Kiran said: "There was a Christian monk, or warrior, called At-Talibin."

"On discovering that the sorceress had left the tekke, he and ab-Dar Il'ium came immediately to Cordoba."

"Why did she leave?" al-Kiran asked anxiously.

"We don't know what to expect. At-Talibin believes that the Mistress complements us."

They moved past the Plaza of Angels in silence. As birds fluttered in the trees to their left, Abu el-Ali stopped and, looking toward the Arian Abbey, recited: "'By the sacred sephiroth of the Kabbalah, by the names of power and the arcana of fundamental laws, we are drawn each year to our roots in the dance between earth, moon, sun and stars.'

"That's all I know with my head. But in my heart," he turned toward his son, "I know you are ready for the dance."

Sometime later, as they neared the Kirian gate, al-Kiran asked: "What of al-Mansur?" Neither had spoken since they left the park opposite the abbey where Kristien waited.

"He is ruthless and cruel," his father answered as if drawn back from a deep meditation. "Even now a troop of Berber soldiers climbs toward ibn Massara . . ."

Immediately rejecting the image, al-Kiran interrupted: "I dreamed al-Mansur attacked the Caliph."

"He will attack, but it's not certain when, or to what extent he will succeed."

"The Royal Guard will stop him!" al-Kiran insisted.

"The guard is under his command. If it were not for the fact that they still respond to Hakam's presence, it would already be too late. Yesterday he ordered the razing of the Arian Abbey. But today, as you just saw, it still stands."

Flooded with horror, al-Kiran froze. Taking his arm, Abu el-Ali continued: "It was as if Abd-er Rahman had returned, or Othman himself. You should be proud, Kemi."

"What?" Al-Kiran was trembling, full of fear for Kristien's safety. "Ben Hebaron . . ."

"Hakam II appeared, unarmed, and ordered the troops off."

Pulling himself back from the vivid memory of the Berber soldiers sneering at Kristien and suggesting that rabbi should be castrated, al-Kiran asked: "Why then has he not removed al-Mansur from power?"

"Fly for the owl — the fundamental fact of who you are." Abu el-Ali pointed toward their villa. "Don't be distracted by the wolf. Everyone has the two forces inside of them. Affirm. Deny. Then reconcile during the dance."

Before al-Kiran could respond, Alansha came hurrying out of the arched doorway, irritated, calling: "Where have you been, al-Kiran? You have to eat."

They turned through the gate. Alansha rushed him toward the kitchen, obviously determined to stuff him full before releasing him to the dance. Dutifully, if not with actual hunger, he began to eat. After his father retreated to his study, he asked: "Where is my mother, Alansha?"

"The Ziryab was here early." The words hissed in his ear. Suddenly panicked, he turned quickly, fearing that the Mistress had crept up behind him. Backing away, Alansha grinned. Her voice lowered, she whispered: "We're all in it together."

"Ziryab was here?"

"You were gone." She squinted at him. "Now your mother is."

"Where did she go?" His lungs refused to fill with air.

"To meet with the other Mershi. You must listen, Kemi."

"I'm trying to . . ." The words stuttered from his mouth.

"I have told you."

"What?" he was desperate to call back the nurse who had cradled, sung to, and fed him.

"You must prepare." Alansha backed away, softer now. "Eat while I sing, but don't think."

Apprehensive, but instinctively accepting her guidance, he turned back to his food. Busying herself behind him, Alansha began humming then singing the melodies he had been raised on. He chewed slowly. His body settled. He saw himself meeting the Karobla in the labyrinth in his search for the Kirian seal, and heard the songs Ziryab had recited at Taifa ibn Massara, then Kristien singing near the Abbey. He was falling into sleep.

"Not here." He felt her strong arms under his shoulders, pulling him up. She steadied him, moving him toward his room, her words like a lullaby he could barely remember:

"The warmth in her cave
Against the cold and barren wind
Called to Mohammed
Beckoning him in.

He had fought through the winter,
Had led the troops in a rage,
For he was a sinner
Though he was a sage.

She pressed him soft,
Her breasts dark with love,
Her lips warm and moist,
Her heart a black dove . . .

"Sleep now, Kemi," she whispered, laying him on his bed, brushing his hair back, her hand like fire on his stomach, making some sign connecting his root center to the crown above his head, her voice a promise and a release:

"As the white owl of your future calls, the rainbow flock rises. Cross the bridge. Ride the terror in your heart."

Suddenly alarmed that he may have slept through the dance, al-Kiran shot up in his bed. He was uncertain whether he had already been up, early that morning, walking with his father, then eating at Alansha's table.

"Let me help you." His mother smiled as she stood above him. "The rabbi will be here soon."

Hurrying to get organized, reassured by his mother's presence, the words and melody of Alansha's final song floated toward him, swirled in his memory.

"Have you seen the Mistress, and . . . Ziryab?" he asked, trying to sound casual.

Before answering, she handed him the clothes which she was carrying. "They send their love, Kemi." Dark eyes searched his face. Energy flowed from her into him. "But we can't speak now. We must hurry."

"The Nubian?" His heart aching, he realized he had just this one last moment to share with his mother.

Houri eyed, deep and mysterious, she touched her lips to his forehead. Tears streamed down his face. "She is here for you." She touched his heart then backed away. "By her joy and pain, and yours, the two of you will rise."

"When, Mother?" He was nearly frantic.

"At the mid-night sun."

Al-Kiran hurried to dress and groom himself. Ritually, he touched the water from his basin to his forehead, neck, chest, groin, arms, calves, and feet. He wanted to pray, to fall back into the chants and rituals which had steadied his world but seemed so far away and alien now.

Abu el-Ali spoke from the door: "Are you ready?"

Al-Kiran nodded. His father turned and led him down the hall, through the kitchen, where Alansha bowed, her hands cupped over her heart, through the reception room and to the front foyer where his mother waited.

It was mid-morning. Alpha ben Hebaron was approaching beyond the outer gate. Abu el-Ali stepped forward to greet him. Dark and enigmatic, stunning in a mulberry gown, her hair gathered on top, jade stones in each ear-lobe, a nine-pointed star of stretched gold hanging across her breasts, Mershi Kamir walked into the light beside her husband.

Alpha ben Hebaron, in his striped robe, rabbi cap, tough and determined, solid and sure, waited patiently. Al-Kiran moved out of the shadow. The sun, striking his blue eyes, framed his face in the soft gold of a new and unshaven beard.

He wore no jewelry, nor insignia. His blouse, tight hose, and slippers were of black velvet. He swayed up on his toes then settled back, impatient, eager to spring forward.

His long hair hung clean, brushed and shinning against the black of his blouse. The muscles of his buttocks and thighs bulged as he turned and bowed to his parents.

Straightening, he crossed his arms over his chest; then opening them, revealed his heart — accepting and returning their love. His eyes misting, he turned back to ben Hebaron, who unfolded a long forest-green cloak and swung it over his shoulders. Pulling the hood up, he said:

"Blessings, student. We begin," then addressed Abu el-Ali: "Allah works through all of us." Nodding to Mershi Kamir, he added: "By your love he moves through the dark toward the sun." Then, to both of them: "Would you accompany us to meet Kristien of Nubia?"

Bowing, ben Hebaron turned and walked toward the gate, al-Kiran falling in beside him, Abu el-Ali and Mershi Kamir following, joining the thousands of excited celebrants moving toward the Great Mosque and Central Plaza of Cordoba.

Light slanting over the tall trees behind them, ben Hebaron motioned al-Kiran and his parents to wait. Kristien stood at the top of the stairs by the great door to the Arian church. Her white gown flowed downward, fastened with beads from the point between her breasts to just below the crescent between her legs. A silk, rainbow cape, tied at her neck, hung from her shoulders.

When she moved, the mother black of her glistening skin rippled beneath the openings in her dress. At the first gathering, the mounds of her breasts, the milk cups of her nipples, lifted gently with each excited breath.

Ben Hebaron saluted the Arian monk who stood beside her: "By the Order of Melchizedek and Melchiresa, may the promise of the Christ and the Magdalen be realized in your work."

As the monk bowed, Kristien nodded toward the rabbi then swirled, her gown spreading above white slippers, revealing the dancer's sure and graceful step, bells jingling in silver anklets matched to the band about her neck.

His breath catching, al-Kiran watched in awe. She seemed capable of rising into the blue air between the red stones of the church and the green of the trees. Mingled with the crisp pungency of cedar and cypress sap, musk spread from her. His lungs expanded. At each twirl, her agate eyes struck his.

Slowing to a stop, silence surrounded them like birds settled before flight. The sky dome arched over their heads, time suspended. Spreading her arms and rotating again, light flickered through the folds of her cape, revealing the wings of an owl. From the back of the hood, a white mask stared at al-Kiran; from behind the mask, some deeper mystery.

"Who? Who?" she intoned, half-whistling. Almond eyes sparkling, gold rings in her ears, a stud through the flare at the base of her left nostril, she turned back to face them. Flipping her hood down, her hair hung to her shoulders, each plait beaded with small bells, woven with silver thread. Accompanied by soft ringing, she descended the steps.

Turning away upon reaching the ground, in the sun split by shadows from the trees, her cape, folded in now, appeared as a peacock tail behind her. Spinning quickly back to al-Kiran, she whispered: "One of the birds of Isis," then turned to ben Hebaron saying: "Do you approve, Master?"

"Sign of Lucifer," he responded, nodding.

"Of Iblis, in our tradition," Abu el-Ali added, his eyes surveying her, clearly approving her beauty.

"Who so loved God he refused to bow to man." Smiling, Kristien stepped closer. "So it is with my Mistress."

"Until the men are gods." Abu el-Ali nodded.

"And the women are goddesses." She grinned.

"You are indeed beautiful, Kristien of Nubia, and I am honored." He bowed to her.

Dipping down and bending from the waist, eyes lowered respectfully, Kristien touched her forehead to the extended hand. "Mershi Kamir Kirian," she spoke carefully, "I speak to you from my heart." She brought her eyes up before continuing. "Beyond, beneath the outer me, my wise old seer looks out upon the dance with compassion, and a smile. The ancient one waits for the young one to knock upon the door."

Regal, yet with moisture glistening in her eyes, raising the younger woman, Mershi Kamir embraced Kristien, saying: "And both are in you now. Open, Priestess, for we greet ourselves." Holding Kristien at arms length, considering her, Mershi Kamir continued: "A mother bears for the promise of the dance. The desert blooms in the dark. Go now, child and seer. You have my blessings and my love."

At that moment, bells rang from the Arian steeple and muezzins called from minarets for late morning prayer. Mershi Kamir Kirian bent forward and kissed Kristien of Nubia on the forehead. Tears flowed from both women as she said:

"And now I commend to you our son." Backing away, Abu el-Ali at her side, she turned toward the church.

Wrapping a robe around Kristien, protecting her from unworthy eyes, Alpha ben Hebaron accompanied her on one side, al-Kiran on the other. A flock of ravens rose into the blue sky, like a school of fish, veering in a circle above the abbey, then gliding toward the Central Mosque.

While the faithful oriented toward Mecca, al-Kiran robed and hooded in forest green, Kristien in burgundy-red, shepherded by the rabbi, passed through the Plaza of Angels toward the heart of Cordoba, the soul of al-Andalus.

CHAPTER SEVENTEEN

"Sacred Space"

Ben Hebaron ushered al-Kiran and Kristien through the bevies of excited and festive Arabs, Berbers, Jews, Iberians, Christians, Basques (all races, slave and free) gathered in and about the great Mosque, ready for the Festival and Dance prophesied by Mohammed, honored by the Cordovan Caliphs since Abd-er Rahman I, speculating among themselves, eager to witness the enactment, to be a part of the last vision of the Messenger of God.

Steadying his breath, keeping his eyes down, conscious of the Nubian beside him, his teacher's purpose, his parents' support, al-Kiran struggled to concentrate his attention, his excitement mounting at every step.

An Omayyad aristocrat, he saw himself matched to the Nubian slave-princess, both select of the select. He felt other eyes scanning him as ben Hebaron motioned to the dance-masters who, in turn, directed their students into lines of power, describing a pattern about the fountain, a shrine now, in the center of the plaza. Eight couples, female and male, were arrayed to support Kristien and al-Kiran, placed now at the ninth point in the pattern of the No'Koonja Naqsch spread across the courtyard, invisible but alive between the dancers.

The festive assembly milled in and out of the colonnades opening along the side of the Great Mosque and swarmed in slow swirls about the square, a huge and diverse organism coupling and breaking into smaller units, moving through the open arches and around the stalls at the perimeter, buying Cordovan delicacies and greeting each other in excited conversation.

Red, yellow, blue, and green striped tents lined the square — temporary centers of entertainment, meals, and celebration. Musicians strolled about. Lute players accompanied story-tellers and poets, declaiming the histories of the peoples and their own visions of what might occur.

Conjurers and jugglers played to gleeful children, hoisted on the shoulders of proud fathers, applauding. Mothers visited in groups, veils loose beneath their chins, bejeweled and beautiful like multicolored flowers.

The Courtyard of Oranges, home of the sacred fountain, filled with the soft cacophony of a temporary bazaar, sheltered and hollowed by majestic cloisters built from the Central Mosque, enclosing the plaza — a tapestry of worlds, sacred and profane woven together.

Taking all this in, remembering his excitement nine years before when he had walked proudly with his father dreaming that one day he might dance, al-Kiran knew that public music and dancing would proceed apace with and parallel to the ritual, the three day dromenon, eighteen dancers aspiring to ecstatic experience, to the realization on earth of the Prophet's last vision and message, winding like two snakes about the fountain in the center of the Courtyard, covered now by a black tent, a replica, he realized, a lump in his throat, of the Ka'ba at the heart of Islam in the center of Mecca.

Mythic theater, ancient folk tales, gymnastics, wrestling, juggling, as well as recitations from the Holy Koran and the great Sufi poets, would stimulate an ever mounting excitement.

The sacred dancers would steadily progress toward the climax, surrounded by the appreciative congregation of the expanded community gathered for the All Faiths Festival, drawn together in recognition that the Prophet, most blessed of Allah, had promised a "new day" following an eclipse.

Perhaps it would be as the Prophet had experienced on mighty "Thunder-Stroke" — Alborak — the white mule with human face and peacock tail who had flown the Blessed Mohammed, and the prophets before him, to the heavens.

Cordoba was astir with stories and speculations. Persian astronomers had forecast an eclipse at the moment of high noon, on the Solstice. The Caliph had predicted that new mysteries, a new science, and a new world order would be revealed following the long dance. Ibn Shaprut, the Royal Physician, was busy with the arrangements for a written constitution, which would date from that moment. Al-Mansur had advised the Caliph that the dance was a pagan orgy, a ritual of the dark light, which must be stopped.

There were many pieces to the puzzle. Alpha ben Hebaron had insisted that in some sense he and Kristien would fly — but al-Kiran remembered also the threat that at the moment of flight a dark-hook would pierce his chest.

The sun drew toward high noon. Clapping together, the dance-masters broke the nine-pointed star-circle of the aspirant dancers, arraying them now into two lines forming a double arc to the north of the shrine in the center of the courtyard. Mid-way in their lines, al-Kiran and Kristien faced each other, the female dancers with their backs to the shrine, protecting it while simultaneously entreating the men to come to them and through them to the mystery.

His Majesty al-Mustansir Hakam II entered the courtyard from the Mosque. Tall, in white robes, his head bare, his hair falling in golden strands to his shoulders, his eyes as piercingly blue as al-Kiran remembered them from the moment at summer solstice when he was selected for the dance — Hakam II stood between the dancers and the shrine. Subh came forward and stood on his left, Hisham on his right, al-Mansur to the left and behind, and ibn Shaprut to the right and behind.

Holding his hands up to still the crowd, the Caliph of Cordoba turned and pulled the black covering from the shrine revealing — while a startled alarm then awe and amazement swept through the assembly — that the waters of the sacred well had been raised and now pooled into a black stone basin covered by a cap-stone monolith supported by four pillars at the corners. Built on the canon of divine proportion, the shrine looked like, in spite of its weight, it could float.

Arms up, a sudden breeze billowing in his robes, Hakam II chanted the attention of the multitude back to himself, minds fluttering briefly then settling on his voice:

"la ilaha illa-llah
There is no reality apart from Ultimate Reality.

la ilaha illa-llah
As Allah Most Resplendent reveals to the beloved Moses:
'I alone am. There is absolutely nothing
apart from the boundless I Am That I Am.'"

Bowing, touching his forehead to the ground, scattering dust upon himself, then head up, his voice full of authority, Hakam II called the congregation to his words:

"Hear me now, oh ye faithful," as in a sermon, all eyes on him as the Leader of the People, "by the inspiration of Mohammed, Blessed Messenger of God Who Is Male and Female, Divine Androgynous Origin and End of All That Is, these stones are brought here, assembled by Moslems, Jews, and Christians, All Faiths, All Peoples of the Book, brought from the caves of Ronda where the wild boar, bull, and bear dance opposite the fish, so that here we Witnesses, Supporters of the Dance of All Faiths, Believers in the Festival of Created Lights, may bring forth on Earth that which breathes now in our hearts — Blessed Be the Prophet of Allah!"

The congregation responded as one voice:

"Blessed Be the Prophet of Allah!"

"Blessed Be His Consort!" the Caliph intoned.

"Blessed Be His Consort!" came the chorus.

Raising his hands, Hakam II continued: "The muezzins will call the faithful to prayer for sunrise, for late morning, for the harvest of mid-day work, before the setting of the sun, and after nightfall, in the dark — and our prayers will sustain the dancers as they dance for us, that the new world may be born — bear we then the prayers for them!"

"Bear we then the prayers for them!" came the response as Hakam II cupped dust from the cobblestone, spread it over himself, and spun slowly, his eyes surveying the entire square.

"Bear we then the prayers for those who dance for us as we celebrate, as we move through the round of the days and nights of their dance, as we gather in the mosque, sing and chant, care for our families, do what work must be done. Bear we then the prayers for the dancers for they dance for us!"

"For they dance for us," came the response.

"On the third day at high noon, oh ye assembled watchers for miracles, open your hearts, be prepared, enter the silence as these dancers dance for us."

"As these dancers dance for us."

"And so I, Hakam II, lead you by the line of Abd-er Rahman, by the Vision proclaimed by our Prophet at Medina, by the words of the Most Holy Koran, toward the New Day:

la ilaha illa-llah Muhammadun rasulu-llah
Divine Unity alone exists,
eternally revealing the Drama of Love."

Revolving slowly about the square, his eyes fixing on the congregation, each person feeling the sweep of his intention, Hakam II paused to face ibn Shaprut and Subh, then the shrine, then Hisham the Heir, then al-Mansur — hawk-eyed and dark, glaring at the Caliph, a warrior cornered but plotting.

Turning on around, Hakam II faced the dancers. His eyes dancing over them, he spoke:

"The Ka'ba, center of holy pilgrimage, captured by Mohammed for the One God-Goddess, is in your hearts and here now before us. From Adam through Abraham and Christ to Mohammed we come from and return to the Lover-Mother-Child. This earth, all creatures, mated by divine breath, holy and conscious, dances as you dance."

Turning once more, his words hovered beneath the dome of the sky. His arms out, he motioned them downward. All dropped to their knees, foreheads to the stones, while Hakam II withdrew, Subh, Hisham, ibn Shaprut, and al-Mansur behind him, leaving the square in a deep and stunned silence.

Struggling to focus, al-Kiran tried to absorb the Caliph's gestures and statements. He was certain that he had witnessed the first such public sermon in the Moslem world. He had not anticipated that the fountain would be transformed, that the Caliph would instruct the people, that al-Mansur would be brought forward and forced to support the festival.

He knew the celebration would ebb and flow during the festival. Individual dancers would drop out to rest but no one would interfere with or even speak to a dancer. They would weave in geometric patterns across the plaza, the crowd clearing before them. Great drums would provide a heart beat, day and night, as of the earth, life itself, countered by hand-cymbals reflecting the growing and dying moon.

Celebrants from the congregation, from the company of the observers, would add flutes, tambourines, lutes, mandolins, clapping, and their own voices, chanting and singing in support of the dance. The prayers of the community would move through the plaza and into their hearts, sustaining them.

Ben Hebaron had explained that the mullahs, rabbis, and priests had made it clear to their respective followers that during high noon, on the third day, there would be absolute silence. All celebrants would open their hearts in silence. At the moment of solstice, if the prophecy held true, the sun would die, and then be reborn, having copulated with the moon.

He felt his master's hand, saw that he had Kristien on his other side. Raising them together, he led them to the ends of the lines of the dancers. The other masters, each between their students, folded the arc back into the pattern of a snake, males in dark green robes, females in maroon.

He prayed that through its energies they would merge with the earth currents, the glide and movement which would raise their feet in unison and in resonance. Propelled by the need of the community, ultimately, he prayed, they would emerge from the world egg and enter the new order.

Ben Hebaron had said that all dancers had been instructed to think of nothing but the dance, the smooth flow of the body, heart, mind, and spirit prefigured in the angels, inherent in all that is. They would have to struggle with the contra-rhythms of the manifest, to find the balance on which the soul may be developed. Each dancer would merge with all the others in a new level of community, and each would ultimately turn to the opposite gender and experience the transference whereby light and darkness dance together.

No teacher would guide them. The dancers would find the dance themselves, informed by earlier dances and the prophecy, but the patterns would be their own.

During past festivals, dancers had formed squares and stood in trance, never moving until awakened by their masters. Some had touched and been overwhelmed before the final crisis. These matters were for the dancers alone. Each had been appointed. All had devoted their lives to the realization of the dream. He knew none of them would ever be the same.

The crowd hushed, focused on the lines of the dancers — bunched back on themselves now, like a snake ready to strike. The sun shone directly into the plaza. The spectators withdrew to the perimeter, leaving nine masters between nine couples in utter silence. Soon they would withdraw to private rooms from which, in spirit, they would join their students.

The general throng, for the present, simply anticipated the excitement of this greatest of festivals, underpinned with faith, smooth in its execution, beautiful in its rituals.

"One word." From another dimension, al-Kiran brought his attention to the surface, focusing on his teacher. Ben Hebaron had not spoken since the lines were formed. Pulling gently, he backed away, removing the cloaks with which he had covered them on the way to the arena. Al-Kiran's eyes met Kristien's, flowed down her body. She was radiant, shimmering in the light, smoldering with the cold fire of transformation.

The rabbi leaned forward and whispered: "Dance."

At that moment gongs sounded from the corners of the quadrangle. Muezzins from minarets, over the domes and cupolas of the greatest city in the world, called the faithful to prayer. As one body, the multitude fell silent. The sky stretched beneath the golden sun of al-Andalus.

Then, into the silence, the Basque drummers began a slow rhythm. A soft and ancient voice pulsed from within their drums. The dancers moved forward, stepping into a dream, a vision enacting itself in a great circle in the center of Cordoba. Everyone but the drummers and dancers, regardless of faith, turned reverently toward Mecca and prayed.

The Festival of All Faiths, the Dance of the Created Lights, had begun. Al-Kiran Kamir Kirian by Omayyad descent with Kristien of Nubia, Slave-Priestess, moved into sacred space. Surrendering himself to rhythms and purposes greater than himself, his heart yearning for what was to come — he followed a warmth stretched from his body and spirit toward the completion of the dance in the Magdalen-Madonna, Lover-Mother, the other, from and for whom he had been born.

The snake uncoiled on the sacred earth. The golden sun hovered in blue skies and slow swirling clouds. The drums droned. The faithful, of all faiths, breathed together.

Beneath the heart-beat of the drums, another and more ancient heart searched for its rhythm within his chest.

Glancing at Kristien, he knew that this was the dance which would never end. Through the eclipse, he would learn to fly.

They moved steadily, side by side, united by a promise prepared in the womb of time. They defined sacred space by the presence of their hearts, open to the mysteries of sky and earth. They settled into the lines before them, ready for the long search, the greater rhythms which would eventually transform all that they had been or known before.

Al-Kiran — at the end of the male line moving north to the apex from which they would turn downward and inward to pass by the shrine on the west, circling sun-wise in an ellipse balanced by the pattern of the females to the east of the shrine in the opposite direction — ached for Kristien's reappearance. She followed the females mirroring the males from the opposite side in the opposite direction coming back to the point where they would face each other across the distance as across an abyss.

He had no idea how long they had been tracing two eggs on opposite sides of the sacred well.

All the dancers leaned forward from the waist in unison with the heavy beat of the big drums, stamping left foot then rising with a skip-shuffle in unison to the cymbals, crouching to the right, stamping to the drum beat, then rising with a skip-shuffle to the cymbals — dancing in trance.

Turning inward from the top of their ellipses, facing each

other he rose, momentarily conscious, her glance across space a fire-spear striking his eyes as they curved back toward the shrine. Their steps and skip-shuffles coinciding to drum and cymbal beats, he could feel her coming nearer, already part of an entity greater than the individual dancers.

Facing each other, she was sun peering through clouds. Rounding their respective ellipses, they passed the sacred pool, through which they knew each other. Pulled in opposite directions by the male and female orbits, he faced darkness and cold, clinging to her memory, awaiting her return.

Glancing up the line before him, he saw the lead dancers, reaching their respective apexes, break from the former patterns and move toward each other. The drums softened, the accent shifting to the cymbals, they wove to their partners. Folding through the opposite line, they turned once around, facing each other, then spun out in opposite directions.

Kristien approached — the fire of her nearness, when they circled each other, a barrier too hot to pass, the peacock tail trailing her as she spun away. Drawing backwards, caught in the same spin which had drawn the males before him, he followed his line. Looping in a counter-sun direction, they formed a figure-eight. In her line, Kristien was doing the same, but in the opposite direction.

The witness-celebrants cleared paths for the movements of the dancers. Heartbeats entrained to the rhythms around and within them, their pulses synchronized, the female and male lines moved parallel to each other, now in the same direction. They circled left to right, sun-wise, in slow whirlpools to the north of the waters bubbling in the black basin within the dolmen-shrine, the fountain at the heart of Cordoba.

Crouching to the drumbeat, right knee up to his chest, then straightening his back to the cymbal accent, his right foot descending, then the opposite on the left — al-Kiran traced sun and moon swirls on the flagstones of the great plaza. Riding on the surface, seeing himself moving as the others moved, he wondered at how little he had observed, was startled by how remote the festival goers now seemed.

Suddenly, at double pace, the female circle swirled forward around the males. Perceptions bobbing into awareness, he noted that two black lightning bolts flashed in a swastika across the back of the lead female's white cape. The next female wore violet, then in succession: sapphire, blue, gold, green, and pink passed him. Wearing a bright orange-red cape, the next to the last dancer, preceding Kristien, spread her arms. A golden snake rose on its coil. He wished Kristien would spread the rainbow owl across her back.

Iblis hovered in green light, his eyes fiery, beyond the peacock tail trailing behind Kristien. "Cast from heaven, I am the perfect and tragic lover." The words formed within al-Kiran. "I re-member mind-heart perfection, male-female, though doomed to eternal separation. By my mission creatures return to one-body, divine and material."

"For which teaching Hallaj was crucified," al-Mansur's voice enunciated in al-Kiran's left ear. His right side resisting, he stumbled, then regained his balance in the line of the male dancers while the females moved away.

Flowing slowly to the left now, paralleling the mosque on the far side of the shrine, he heard ben Hebaron, a voice within his skull, from some other time yet present: "Iblis inscribed the sacred letters, the ancient alphabets, in our hearts, codes and ciphers toward perfect union — the remembering of the First Cause, the Origin behind Appearance."

The females slowed, synchronized their movements, pacing themselves with the men again. Mirroring each other, in their lines, the dancers traced circles. Then, extending the arcs at the bottom, sweeping out, the lead dancers changed steps, the change spreading like waves through the ripples in a pond.

All were swaying now, left and right: two long steps, then gently shuffling to the responsive cymbals between darker and deeper drum beats. Weird antiphonal whistling of pipes swirled out of the southwest corner of the quadrangle, behind the platform on which the Basque shamans drummed, evoking the counterpoint of the blood-pulse of the earth — the whistles shrill like birds calling from an oasis to the dancers, a long caravan weaving through orange desert sands or through a deep forest, green and dark. They were nearing the call to afternoon prayers, their dance the centerpiece in a mosaic surrounded by celebrants waiting for a miracle.

Something was shifting. Eyes open briefly to the greater congregation, he saw that many of the observers were milling about under the colonnades opening into the cool interior of great sanctuary, the forest of marble columns supporting endless waves of undulating arches beneath which the Moslem faithful would turn their attention toward the other Ka'ba, the one in Mecca — as they had when he had seen his parents and the multitude of the Faithful in his dream before the Karobla had swept up, a huge shadow over Cordoba, flowing from the Central Mosque to the Kirian Seal in his family's garden outside which ben Hebaron and Mershi Khayam had argued, before At-Talibin had come to the Taifa to rescue him.

He felt conscious attention on him from groups forming across the Plaza of Oranges, focusing their awareness on the new movements flowing through the lines and transforming the dancers. And he knew that ben Hebaron was looking into and out of his heart from some place in the near distance, someplace that was other and yet here.

The men dancers mirrored the females, heading in opposite directions, west and east. Turning at a sharp angle back toward the north, their circles, which had become eggs, became triangles. From the apex the leaders turned back, swaying through two steps then shuffling, each line tracing a triangle on the stones in the courtyard north of the shrine, descending toward the sacred pool below and between them.

Each of the men wore black, simple and plain — in stark contrast to the females bedecked with brilliant finery. Al-Kiran was the only blond. His long hair hung over his shoulders. His chest heaved. His eyes focused then faded into the progression of the dance, the shadow of the dancer moving before him. He thought of Kristien following her own shadow. He felt her moving east across the bottom of the geometry of their dance.

Images of the Caliph, and Subh, his favorite, the only Princess of the Royal Harem who had borne him a son, floated up before him, carried by the shaman drums. He saw them in a garden outside the palace across the river, beyond the Alcazar of the Ancestors. Hisham, the heir, held the hem of his father's robe. His mother was distressed, pleading with her master. Al-Mansur was standing in the shadows.

Through waves of darkness, he saw fire rising, heard a man screaming, a mother weeping, then: "Before she converted to Islam, Subh was called Aurora, Goddess of the Dawn." The words floated through him, but he didn't know the source. He sensed ben Hebaron, or was it the Mistress, or his mother? It felt as though someone were whispering to him.

He glanced across to Kristien. She glowed at him as they turned, her eyes sparkling. He wanted to climb into the air to her, reach her in a dimension where they would be all the world. His chest aching, his male member stirring, he coaxed himself back toward the balance between restraint and explosion. The thrust and pull of their energies conscious of each other through the dance, was all he could stand now, he realized, remembering that they had barely begun.

The summons of the high muezzin rang across the quadrangle from the minaret at the south wall of the central mosque and echoed through the city. All around the square worshippers stood straight,arms raised and extended from their shoulders, palms forward, chanting as, a reflection on the pool of phenomena glistening in the afternoon sun, his voice low, al-Kiran sang: "We separate ourselves from ourselves. The god-goddess is here."

"Allahu Akbar! Allahu Akbar! Allahu Akbar!" rippled through the courtyard, through the cloisters, in rhythm to the prostrations and prayers of the Faithful.

Moving forward in the line of dancers, hearing their chants, the point above and between his eyes throbbing, he saw figures crossing a bridge between this sacred space and the sanctuary in Mecca, the faithful supplicants envisioning the Ka'ba, praying to make at least one pilgrimage there during their time on earth;

and he saw the Ka'ba coming toward them, merging with the dolmen-shrine in the center of their plaza.

The stalls of the merchants were still. Outside and within the grand tents, the conjurers, jugglers, poets and story-tellers stood or knelt quietly. He saw his father on the female rug of his beginnings, his mother on the male rug of his initiation in the Cypress Grove of the Great Mother.

"The Phantasmal is the Bridge to the Real." He jumped involuntarily, jerking away from the images floating before him. Ben Hebaron had spoken in his left ear.

"Kirian: The Phantasmal is the Real." His brain pulsed as the Mistress spoke in his right ear. Their voices, like slow lightning, coursed down the caduceus of his back winding from side to side and mixing at the base of his spine.

Soft chanting rose through the general hum of the greater congregation. Kristien faced him from the opposite side. His heart throbbed. He wanted to weep, go to her. Words tumbled through his body, then images. He saw the dancers at ibn Massara, the Mistress hovering above the dais, the ribbon of scripture around the top of the dance hall. Eyes catching, Kristien twirled, spreading her cape: the white mask of the phantom owl, the rainbow wings.

Twirling in the opposite direction, he moved with the males, settling into the two step sway and antipodal shuffle, carried by the drums, the cymbals. From the parapet of ibn Massara, he faced the cave. His heart slowed. He heard the melancholy chant of his friend, the magpie:

"They dream of sacred splendor.
They wake from their deep sleep.
They see the other gender.
They smile and then they weep.

Now the tears are flowing,
Just as the jester sings,

The wisdom in their knowing
Comes through the tears he brings."

The faithful finished their prayers. The gongs rang and flutes fluttered like birds settling, rising, then settling again, along dark branches. The troupe moved forward, swaying, an organism within the larger organism of the Festival of All Faiths.

CHAPTER EIGHTEEN

"First Night"

W e are the Created Lights, all of us!" Glancing about the plaza, al-Kiran was reassured to hear his own voice again. It was late afternoon. Members of the greater congregation were meandering through the stalls and tents. Poets declaimed their stories; the Ulama instructed the devoted in the law.

The dromenon moved fluidly, more relaxed now. Each time around the triangles they traced in the stones, the leaders expanded the corners. Within two more rounds, they described squares, male and female, images of the courtyard itself.

The dance had changed. They began weaving back and forth across the perimeters of the squares they followed — three steps to one side, then three to the other, closer and closer to the power which pulsed through the invisible, untouched channels which carried them forward.

Falling deeper and deeper into the new rhythm of the dromenon's forward thrust, he turned east from the northwest corner. The line of the men stretched along the northern wall of their square to meet the women at the inner corners before turning downward to pass the shrine.

As he anticipated meeting Kristien, he noticed that the lead dancers were turning outward toward the northern gate. Like ships cutting through a flood, they moved into the crowd toward the Pavilion of Dancers, the observers opening a channel before them, while the second in each line turned in, toward the mosque, becoming the new leaders of the dance. Moving forward to meet Kristien, the memory of her caresses pulled him toward the future.

Ben Hebaron had explained that there were no strict rules, that the dancers would establish a rapport with their partners without speaking. He had emphasized the need to pace themselves, slowly building their energies toward high noon on the third day. Caught up in the pulse and synchrony of the dance, he was amazed that the first break had come so soon.

His teacher's explanations were coming back now, opening a channel which had been dry. He had said there could be times when all of the dancers would leave the arena, or sit where they were, resting, or break into small groups. "Don't hurry. Eventually an inner understanding will take over."

* * *

"We become one as we dance for each other." The voice rippled up and down his spine, like a cat's tongue. In a daze, he thought of Kristien. "Where is she?"

He looked around, startled by the shadows. "The drums?" Then he heard them, distant. He had become as unaware of the drums as of his own heartbeat.

The dancer ahead of him, and his partner, had broken off. He had meant to watch for their return. The remaining dancers were circling in a long figure eight, crossing their own lines in the center, the eight of the males reflected by the eight females on the opposite side of the shrine.

He heard the water pooling in the black stone; the buzz and hum of the greater congregation in their excited pursuit of the celebration; the call of ravens, the flap of wings.

"Kristien?" He mouthed her name. Her eyes rose before him. His body hopped. Each of the dancers hopped — a hop, then four steps, then another hop as they followed the loops of the eight, out and around then back to the center.

"I am here." She smiled across the fountain. Water splashed beneath the canopy, in the black stone. She was moving in the line of the females, out and away. "Next time," her voice was within him, "we will be together."

The gongs rang. The sun would be setting soon. The muezzin was calling the faithful from the minaret. Breath, from the earth beneath him, welled up into his chest.

The dancer before him had returned. The moon scythe flickered in the western sky. "Even now," he thought, "She approaches." They moved toward each other at the center then out through the congregation of the faithful (prostrate, building bridges to Mecca, lost in prayers) toward the Pavilion of the Dancers.

He wanted to touch her, to sing images of desert sounds, blood storms beating their bodies together, adding his words to the songs of his teachers. Reaching toward the black princess, Priestess of Oshiwah, carrier of the dark light, he started:

"Let the blackbird know the mountain.
Let the owl lead the way.
The mother . . ."

She spun on him — arms out — knocking him backwards. Her cloak spreading in the lingering light — an owl's face, a white mask laughing, eyes on fire — she moved toward the women's side of the pavilion.

* * *

Since the sunset prayers and his break with the Nubian, al-Kiran had returned to the dance, the rhythms, holding himself back, poised and pensive. It was nearly midnight of the first day. The final prayers were done. The cold lick of the night had settled about the greater congregation.

The starscape spread above the square, a gentler light. They were in a long line, female, then male, circling the Ka'ba of the great Central Mosque, home of the sacred spring, the fountain in the center of the Courtyard of Oranges.

"In the Grove at Marme, near Hebron, where the King and his brother struggled beneath the Terebinth and Kerm Oaks," At-Talibin's voice was in his ear, "the Queen of the Ebonites offered herself as the prize."

He shook his head and concentrated on Kristien. He had followed her since returning from the Pavilion, in the long line, for hours, watching the owl's wings folded in and quiet, moving to the right around the circle, then to the left.

Then she broke off, as had each of the women ahead of her, weaving in the opposite direction. The men kept forward. At the end of his line, he continued the left-hand circle, curling deeper into the unmanifest, "the generative" — according to ben Hebaron's teachings.

The female dancers, beneath the night, circled in the sun direction, steadying the men. "They are the day," he thought. "They push us ever deeper into the dark."

The drums were different now: two counter rhythms beneath his steps. The cymbals had become the lead, a magnet at the end of each phrase. Three short steps, with the drums, then the accent on the cymbal as the women moved in the opposite direction, rounding to the outside of the men — passing, then gone, then passing again in the long dromenon.

The inner and outer snakes, male within female, circled in the plaza through larger ellipses, then smaller, tightened to the source in the center, then expanded. The women pushed the men toward the shrine then pulled them out, their rhythm three short steps to one dominant.

The congregation was hushed now, busy but thoughtful, moving through the tents, in and out of the cloisters, along the colonnade which opened into the sanctuary of the mosque — it's attention to the dancers coming in waves. A seriousness was beginning to tell on the wider celebration. Already the audience was aware, in spurts, as a disorganized body, that a new order was forming, related to this Festival of All Faiths.

* * *

Poised in the darkness toward the morning hope of his prayers, the inner sun to which his heart yearned, al-Kiran wanted to touch his forehead with cold water, ritually cleanse. He was at the far west of the circle.

Kristien, at the end of her line across the fountain, followed the females — then danced toward him, arms up, robe black yet shimmering with all colors, an energy body glowing as fire from a diamond center.

Standing on the lip of the black monolith, across the stone gathering waters in the center, in the shrine, beneath the lintel, she beckoned.

Phantom arms pulled him toward black breasts, stomach,

legs apart, pelvis rolling. He wove behind the men into darkness as, all light, he broke into another body and rose to face her.

Buttocks tightened, his phallus a light sword — every animal within him wailed with excitement. Thighs quivering, sperm rolled within his testicles. Chest heaving, he pulsed to thrust himself into her mystery and lose himself forever in the dance of the first god and goddess.

Clouds covered the sky. Like a black wing over the face of light, darkness fell across the world. They were alone. There were no drums, no heartbeats, no breaths rushing for voice, no words pounding for entry into the world.

He was quiet. She was before him. Her eyes sparkled. She reached across the pool. Their hands approached above the waters. She knelt, bending him forward with her to gaze into the waters. She put her hands into the waters, his following hers. They touched beneath the cool surface. She calmed him, soothing his muscles, relaxing his taunt skin, returning breath to his lungs, sight to his eyes, memory of the dance to his legs. There was no reflection on the surface.

He was in the line of the males, on the east now, smiling across the sacred center to Kristien, Princess of Nubia, who smiled in return then followed the line of the dancers, as did he, ever deeper into the night, toward the dawn.

CHAPTER NINETEEN

"Second Day"

Moving beside Kristien to the Pavilion of Dancers, al-Kiran heard the first stirring among the peacocks in the Royal Gardens and thought: "Like the tail of mighty Alborak, who carried the Prophet," but dared not speak.

The crowd had thinned. Individuals gathered in groups around the tents, idling and huddling at random. While sunrise approached in the east, celebrants flowed back through the great gates into the plaza.

A new rhythm stirred throughout Cordoba. As the muezzins summoned the faithful from the dreams of another world to the splendor of this one, he felt a balance and restraint, a force which could move and withdraw, something within and beyond, independent of, yet intimately identified with his body.

The sky color was gliding toward yellow. The pink of a new sun surrounded by blue spread into the slate of the further skies. The faithful turned east, chanting: "Allahu Akbar! Allahu Akbar! . . ." He glanced up, hearing his mother:

"We are flooded with the promise of light. Light is coming to the dark." Then Mershi Khayam: "She is the consort to Mohammed, Jesus, Abraham, and Adam. Love her as the God loved her. He searches through you. Offer yourself to her." His grandmother responded: "The light of the morning star comes to the waters in the black stone. Oshiwah. Dark dances in the light of the sun." He smiled, pleased, easier in the dialogue of the inner voices, and passed into the silence.

The prayers of the faithful had been completed; the carpets re-rolled and stacked within the cloisters. The greater congregation warmed to the second day. His feet followed the shuffle of the drums, then cymbals.

Again the rhythm shifted. A new group had joined the Basque drummers on their stand, adding dry bones and rattles.

233

Between the steady throb of the deep drums, the new sounds mixed into and spread beneath the dance.

The line of the males met the females in a pass. They pulled their line across the other, leading the dromenon out into a epi-circle. Then they curved back, cording the lines together. The black strand of the males wove through the progression of females, each cape a different color.

They descended toward the shrine, the females straightening their backs on the firm beat, then bowing during the responsive chorus, moving forward. The males bent then straightened, pos-turing in the counter rhythm — up when the females were down, down when they were up.

Circling around the shrine, the women went to the left, the men to the right. At the north point, he met Kristien. The drums were speeding-up then pausing, suspended, stretching to meet the rose-fingered promise of the sun spreading across the Guad-alquivir, through the parks, into the Courtyard of the Dancers. Merchant skiffs passed beneath the Roman Bridge, carried through the gray-blue float of the early morning toward the docks, hovering beneath silver-green sails above the chop of the waters, laden with goods for the second day of the Festival.

Side by side, al-Kiran and Kristien faced the four pillars of the shrine from the north, "at the point," he thought, "where we entered the Cypress Grove, the entry to the labyrinth at home."

Kristien folded her legs beneath her body, her cloak spread about her. Sun glanced off the top of the shrine. The female dancers followed her lead, forming a circle about the Ka'ba. The males stood behind their partners, statues now, facing the stone, like the ancient sisters of Mecca.

He envisioned some cataclysmic event ripping the veil between the worlds, destroying the Ka'ba of the desert fathers — then it's reappearance in Cordoba. Power pulsed along invis-ible lines. Words from his teacher fell like pebbles into a pool, spreading in waves from the sacred spring: "The Ka'ba will disappear during terrible times before the arrival of the male and female guide."

He knew that Mecca had been the mystery center of ancient Arabia, that the Ka'ba contained the black stone of the desert tribes, the talisman engraved with the crescent of the moon and Venus, the Horns of Hathor, the Great Mother.

"The Arabs worshiped Al-Uzza, both God and Issa." At-Talibin was speaking. "Venus kissed the Stone of Kebir, the Ka'ba, before Mohammed conquered the Stone for Allah."

"Rabunni," al-Kiran whispered, "by what right did the Prophet claim the Stone of the Mothers?"

"By the direction of Gabriel," ben Hebaron answered. "Keep your ear to the ground. Pick up the pieces as they fall." The voice pumped within his ear, linked to his heart.

"But . . ." he struggled, his eyes closed now, his mind trying to reassemble the scene where he knew his body slumped behind Kristien, "none of this is in the Book."

"Friday, sacred to Venus, is the day of prayer." Ben Hebaron was speaking. A hush fell over the Courtyard, then even the memory faded, and al-Kiran found himself standing in the Cypress Circle. He was alone, but the voice continued:

"Green, sacred to the Prophet, stands for the World Mother. The Islamic crescent and the scimitar represent her horns, the waxing and waning of the moon, the morning and evening star, the crack between the worlds."

"Did the Nazarene come to destroy the works of the Mother?" al-Kiran asked, his eyes open now.

Turning in the Circle, he looked for his teacher. Behind the stones he saw the other dancers crouching. Behind them — the cypress trees, and yet at some level he could also see the congregation of the Faithful in the Courtyard in Cordoba where he was standing, turning, his eyes blank, his mind on fire.

"Eventually the obvious, which seemed invisible, will be seen." Kristien, kneeling before him, pulled up her cowl. The white mask stared into his face.

Wearing the skeleton of an owl, Ziryab hovered in the trees. His hymn floated through the air:

"To protect the child she carried,
Sarah, that ancient, sacred queen,
Claimed she was not married,
And conjured thus the king.

For Abraham did tithe
To mighty Melchezedek
And Salem was the prize
For whom she did the trick."

Gliding in a circle around al-Kiran, Ziryab grinned. His head, too big for his body, tilted to the side. Pleading at the same time he laughed, his arms were extended, his hands and fingers flicking in flight, shaking something free. His eyes, dark pools, filled with pain and love. Stopping, his voice careful but insistent, he said:

"They came from the desert to destroy the works of the Mother. The scimitar became a sword, the dancing veils of the sacred priestesses became barriers against the feminine. But know," he turned away: "it is with the blessing of the Mother that we exist at all."

Climbing upward, his arms the wings of an eagle, al-Kiran settled on a stone ledge above a sheer precipice.

"Blackbird like me," Ziryab smiled welcome, "this is the Cave of Creative Light. See the Kymerian?" He pointed downward. "See the Taifa?" He pointed behind and above al-Kiran.

His face old and wrinkled, yet like a child's, Ziryab's voice echoed from the cliff: "Now, Kemi, listen:

From the darkest magic cave
Beneath the fairy dell
The goddess in pain does save
The prince from vilest hell.

The haunted clown in motley cried.
He played, but still we grieve.
We see the snake of morning pride.
He prayed, then entered Eve.

These are the tears of widows.
To God they're sacred whores.
They're laid as golden meadows.
Their left as darkened moors.

But though the sun's bright torch can kill
The germ of fertile earth,
The sight of evening still
Can light the moon of birth."

Bowing from the waist, Ziryab spread his arms.

Transforming from owl to cave priestess, Orwan Oshiwah, black, chiseled and majestic, walked toward them, followed by Mershi Kamir and Mershi Khayam, her daughters. Nodding to al-Kiran she sang:

"Upon the cross of matter,
Upon the holy rule,
The god in ragged tatter
Reveals the sacred fool.

The widows filled with tears
Stand just below the rood.
They see him in the fears
Which nailed him to the wood.

So now the jester brings the rings
Which Mary and Jesus danced
Across the bridge on phantom wings:
The Grail, the body lanced."

Cold fire, the echo of a cave tilting the world, a huge shadow, bear or dragon, Karobla brushed his heart. Struggling to focus, he found himself in the courtyard of the Dance.

He was facing the dolmen-Ka'ba, the waters bubbling in dark light. Kristien of Nubia, standing now, sensual, her nipples showing through the white folds of her gown, her hips swaying forward, open, thighs spread, was inviting him. His heart ached as the attention of the other dancers steadied his body.She whirled up, rotating slowly. Worlds faded.

His feet moved forward, carrying him in the line of the dancers, out and around the Ka'ba — nothing in the world but the rainbow wings on her back, the owl-mask hovering over her.

The sun had climbed higher, shining now in pathways over the cloister walls on the east side of the quadrangle. The light rays moved down from the capstone, along the four columns, across the face of the stone, into the waters.

The women sat as guardians about a temple. Circling in the direction of the sun, he was chanting: "Guardians of the Guardians." Drumbeats carried his words, pulsing within his heart like the prayer: "Allah, Most Merciful!" which had carried him to the classes among the trees in Cordoba, then to the Cypress Grove. Now "Guardians of the Guardians" carried him, circling the women, in the Dance of Created Lights.

He followed the males before him. Then lining-up, male behind female in the delicate composite of light and shadow, he began to chant, quietly, the pictures, within his heart:

"Guardians of the Guardians; Dancers in dark light.
Carriers of the Mysteries; Flyers in bright night.

Behold the gold and silver wing.
Uphold the dancers while they sing.
Uphold, we must, the vision ring."

His heart swelled. A tear caught in his throat. He wanted to hold and protect the Nubian princess, the slave-priestess of Isis-Oshiwah. But he stood, then crouched behind her, whispering:

"We yearn for deeper marriage.
We dance and then we swoon.
Our trials light the passage,
Our broken hearts the moon."

He wondered whether Kristien's heart broke toward his, as his broke toward hers, in uneven rhythms. The gongs rang. The muezzins, from their high towers, summoned the faithful. The drums, the cymbals responding, the breath, the slow swirl of prayers, of yearning, faded into darkness, floated in silence, lost in the fold of the mid-day sun.

He floated in, through, and above the blue-sapphire, gold, amethyst, then red, pink and green flame which pulsed within the line of the male dancers circling the females. Occasionally, rounding a corner and rising up, looking across the Courtyard, he could see the old ones of ibn Massara spread around the square, positioned at points describing an enlarged enneagram in the center of which the circle of aspirants breathed, themselves a smaller ninefold star — and in the very center, within the waters, a rainbow light.

At times he felt Kristien's attention upon himself, pulling him gently to herself, his consciousness flickering toward her, his arms spread to embrace her, then letting him float away, moving through the long dance while she sat rapt in meditation, letting him fall into whatever dreams or visions his soul called forth. He shifted between vision and normal consciousness. Each time he seemed to awaken, he wondered how much he would remember.

The afternoon light shimmered on the pillars at the four corners of the shrine: jasper, marble, granite, and onyx, replicating the forest of stone within the Great Mosque, connecting earth and sky. Beyond the priestesses of the dance, sacred waters bubbled in the Ka'ba of their unified vision.

Suddenly, like from a dream, the summons to prayer flooded his consciousness. Sunset was approaching.

He recalled lightning, black wings, silence, the distant roll and crash of thunder. He had been out of his body — some place with Kristien. He was on a bridge, the chant of the muezzin, crossing back through sound and color.

Kristien had been with him. They had spoken of their bodies, like statutes, protected by the other dancers; "and by shepherds," she had said, "in the greater congregation."

CHAPTER TWENTY

"SECOND NIGHT"

The mullahs were spread in a larger circle about their own. His father's voice echoed throughout the plaza:

> "When Earth is rocked in her last convulsion;
> When Earth shakes off her burdens and man asks
> 'What may this mean?' —
> She will proclaim: 'your Lord has inspired me.'"

Ben Hebaron sang in response:

> "La ilaha illa'llah Al-Uzza / God-Issa!
> The treasury of Love is loosed in the world:
> Dancing in desire for the Beloved!"

The sun's parting rays spread across the green and gold onion dome of the minaret rising from the great mosque. Returning his attention to the plaza, al-Kiran saw the dolmen-arch. Beneath the capstone, between four ancient menhirs, a woman was dancing. Oshiwah Goddess, virgin, mother, crone, and lover, danced in the silver rainbow between the stones.

Spreading her wings, she whirled, then rose on her snake tail. A penis throbbed between her thighs, then opened, a cave of return, a mouth between this and other worlds.

Laughing, she sang, as the vision faded:

> "I come to you a maiden;
> I sing to you alone —
> To the fire in the semen,
> At the root of your bone."

The women dancers stood and faced the men. Kristien was before him. One finger, from the long drape of her robe, extended toward his forehead. Her tongue flickered from dark and inviting lips. Her eyes were on fire.

The male dancers approached their partners. The females backed-up, pulling the men in vortices on the periphery about the shrine. Drums, hand-cymbals, reed pipes, tambourines, whistles, rattles, dry bones clicking filled the air.

Then they sat, side by side, facing the dolmen cave, the tomb. Water pulled them toward the crack in the worlds. Venus cast her spear toward the flame of the departing sun.

Darkness descended on Cordoba like a cloak. Curious celebrants stood in bunches about the quadrangle discussing the weird silence which enveloped the dancers.

Their hands touching the flagstones of the plaza, their backs straight — the eighteen aspirants, like gods and goddesses beneath the moonless sky, sat in a circle around the shrine.

Their arms rose from the flagstones outward in unison to either side, suspended momentarily; then upward, breathing in, then down, holding breath, to the horizontal. Breath feathering from the tips of their fingers, they exhaled.

Hands dropped to earth and lay there, as if nursing. Arms rose, extended with drums, whistles, bones clicking, stretching to each other, then to dark sky. The flutter of wings, of young phoenixes, called from beneath the black-purple dome of al-Andalus, calling for rebirth.

Down again, exhaling in a burst at the horizontal, matched now to trumpets and shouts from the audience, rays jumped between feather-tips. Inner light pulsed and leaped in uncommon currents. Mounting rhythms swirled around the circle with the rise and fall of each long sweep of their arms.

The gongs struck. The muezzins summoned the faithful to late night prayer. The followers of Mohammed turned toward Mecca. The dancers continued to chant, light flashing between them while the Faithful spread their rugs, in deep piety, adding their light to the darkness:

"Allula Akbar . . . Allula Akbar . . . Allula Akbar . . ."

Their prayers, the rhythm of their communion with the source circulated out and beyond the plaza — stretching from the inner eye of their rapt attention to the star stone of the ancients in Mecca. From the dark waters bubbling in the black stone in Cordoba, the Faithful danced across the heart-bridge and returned carrying the treasures of Allah and Issa.

Al-Kiran swayed with the slow swirl of the drums. From a still point above his head, he felt energies rising. He saw Andalusian and North African beacons flaring in the darkness, rising from the world to the stars and beyond, spreading in love and submission across the inner planes, food for the journey building within himself and the Nubian princess.

He opened his eyes. All the dancers were swaying, humming around the circle. The women were clapping. The plaza was filled with Moslems facing Mecca, foreheads to the ground, then rising from the waist, foreheads glowing.

Completing their prayers, their pilgrimage to the sacred stone, they turned right, thanking the angels as the Dancers responded: "Allah-Issa — the Beloved Is One , Infinite and Immediate in the Heart."

In the sanctuary of the chosen, a blue flame danced above the black stone, the clear waters, a voice without a body in the center of the Plaza in Cordoba: "Child of the light within dark night." The words rolled within the chant, carried by the drums: "The night is fertilized by bright light."

Secure between the silks and damask capes of the females, al-Kiran faded into trance. The flower petals grown from the congregation of the faithful, the sweet nectar of concentration harvested by the angel bees, spread through his body.

"Oshiwah — Harushsss, to the East you go, to be eaten by a bigger goblin . . . " came his mother's voice. He was at home, sitting in the corner, watching her work the ghosts with her big broom. "Harushsssh, you go to be changed!"

The female dancers were chanting:

"Harushsssh/Oshiwah . . . Harushsssh/Oshiwah
. . . Harushsssh/Oshiwah . . ."

Pushed by the wing of his mother's voice, wind swirled

around the circle. Above drums, flutes and tambourines, shrill whistles and claps, a swirl of dancing lights, another voice sang:

"He is chained to the maiden by the snake born in heaven;
By the tree of his daemon to the earth with his semen;
Through the mists of the ocean in her womb he is swollen;
Beneath her wings begotten in the dance of the coven;
From male the leaven, food for the dragon;
His heart so open, his love an oven;
To her he is token that the dream isn't stolen;
Nor the vision broken of the birth in the dolmen;
For the nine have spoken of al-Kiran Kamir Kirian."

In the hollow about the shrine in the center of the plaza, night wrestlers danced in celebration of Adam and Lilith, of Elohim and the Daughters of Men, of Eve, Cain, Seth, and the two Enochs; of Isis, Osiris, Sarah, Abraham, and Hagar; of Jacob, Isaac, the Three Marys and Jesus; of Mohammed and Aisha, Othman and Nailah, of Ali and Fatima; of Arab, Basque, Iberian, Egyptian, Celt, Roman, Nubian, Berber, Bedouin, Persian, Slav, German, Greek, Hebrew, Turk, Mongol, Frank, Genoean — all tribes and races; Shaman, Christian, Moslem, Jew, free and slave, men and women — children of the gods and goddesses of the dance. They danced.

Then he heard Alansha as he had on the morning following his mother's explanation of the enneagram at the center of their garden — the "Memory of Home." He had followed the Karobla, who had escaped from his dream, into the maze. She was singing from the kitchen window, her song a memory and a revelation, a promise and a warning:

"The prince prayed at the edge of the mountain
While the Lady in Black slept in the den.
The crescent of the Prophet's green chariot
Thundered in the blue sky overhead.

'Stop the world, stop the world,' came the whisper.
The lady rose from her dark bed
Fearing the man for love of her beauty
Had leaped to his death instead."

Lights swirled through the chanting and counter-claps of the dancers. He was being pulled upward in a spiral, a body out of a body. The drums faded. A woman's voice spun him in the dark:

"On the Karobla he returned from the heavens.
The opposite of mighty Alborak he rode,
Messenger to the peoples of the desert,
Through the black winds and cold.

The violence of the sea meets the golden rays.
The wind catches the lad as he falls.
On the wings of our courage love plays.
So goes the song of her laws."

CHAPTER TWENTY-ONE

"WINTER SOLSTICE"

Cymbals and drums curved together through the courtyard.
Each drumming echoing itself through differing media,
repeated and heightened the slow antipodal zikr of the dance.

The rhythm shifted. Gongs rang in the dark rise and warp of
a deeper sound. The sun rose, coaxed back into the sky by the
prayers and hopes, demands and needs, of the night. The moon
trailed the sun — lost in the light streaming in blood rays over
minarets and domes in the east.

The plaza was filled with excited but restrained celebrants
rising from their prayer mats. Emerging from the cracks between
the worlds, two snake lines wove in and about a channel directed
at the Cordovan Prince and Nubian Princess.

The lead female crossed in front of al-Kiran. Slicing him
with white fire, she spun him in place. The male moved past
Kristien, spinning her as al-Kiran spun back from the opposite
direction to face the next female dancer. Hooded and impersonal,
her tongue flicking, her eyes up in her head, hissing, she sliced
then looped out behind him as the male in the opposite line sliced
and spun Kristien.

As each female struck him, sounds exploded — amethyst,
sapphire, blue, then gold up and down his back, within his chest,
his head, his throat, his solar-plexus green, then pink swirling
into orange from black at the base of his spine, smelling of fire. A
single eye flickered, blood-red, throbbing, stretching through the
strained harmonic of his body. Muscles aching, he fought to
remember himself.

The dancers, flickering in slow motion, stamped on the
alternating beat of the gongs. In pain, he heard his father and
mother chanting: "Kirian/Koran . . . al-Kemi/Koran . . ."

Simultaneously, the voices of the rabbi and the tentmaker:"The Koran bursts in splendid light . . . The dark wings of Issa-Christ!" He opened his eyes.

Body undulating, pounding the ground, Kristien stamped toward him, bells ringing on her ankles, nostrils flared, exalted, ecstatic, her breasts and pelvis heaving.

A claw seared into his chest. Stretching for her, he screamed in pain. The other dancers were clapping, each slap between their palms a retort.

He fainted.

Red tongue thrust through a white face, Kristien twirled him. Her voice echoed across the plaza: "Dance, lover. These are the agonies of the Dance."

Exhausted, he was moving toward the Mosque. Across the courtyard, the line of the males was progressing slowly, parallel to the line of females which he followed.

He wailed. A responsive moan rose from the females. The last dancer, in the line of males, turned toward him. Tears streaming down her face, Kristien moved to the line of her own gender, as he did the same.

Winding across the arcade, into the Mosque, beneath fili-greed arches, through a forest of stone columns, they followed a double helix toward the Mihrab, the sacred shell from which Hakam II watched their progress.

Bunching at opposite walls, the snake lines sprang forward spinning before the Caliph. His heart ripping, al-Kiran stretched toward Kristien then exploded upward. Passing the fluted dome, he sailed into the sky.

Below him, he saw his own physical body leading the line of the males, the females being led by Kristien. They were moving back across the marble floor, beneath arches, toward the Courtyard. Above the dolmen Ka'ba, in the blue tongue of a cold flame, red fire from her open mouth, green fumes from her eyes, like the prophet's chariot, or the beast of apocalypse, her huge claws clasped about the black stone as if to protect an egg, the Karobla called after him:

"Who . . . Who . . . in the fires of a dying age, came
first to be your mate? Or is it too late?"

Frightened by the howl of her laughter, al-Kiran struggled
upward. As the dragon re-settled on her dolmen perch, he
remembered her hovering in the pathway before him, phallus
throbbing, hissing: "When you attempt to pass, son of the sacred
mother, we will have our ride." Then, from the distance below,
he was hit by a huge crash, as if the platform of the shaman
drummers, the bone clickers, tambourine and cymbal players,
had fallen — and heard Kristien scream.

Swooping in a circle, al-Kiran searched the Courtyard. In
the distance, above the heads of the confused masses, he saw His
Majesty Hakam II, bareheaded, descending the steps of the
mosque and moving toward the dancers. Suddenly, as near-
observers surged away, al-Mansur, black-turbaned and fierce,
burst through the crowd from the opposite direction. Shouting,
he ordered his men against the dervishes of ibn Massara.

The gongs and drums stopped. Golden hair loose to his
shoulders, Hakam II stood before the attackers. Furious, al-
Mansur, raising his scimitar, raced toward the Caliph. Frantic, al-
Kiran searched for young Hisham.

In a burst of bizarre laughter, the Karobla spit fiery rays and,
spreading her wings, rose above the assembly. Al-Mansur's
sword whirled beneath her shadow. Raging, he advanced. The
Caliph knelt, neck exposed in submission.

Geometric patterns exploded. Blue waves, cold and spiraling, swept out of the west, clashing in orange and black ribbons.
At the far extent of al-Kiran's vision, a huge vortex, a cone
between earth base and moon apex whirled across the plains in
eerie silence toward the city.

In agony, lightning screaming through every cell, his legs
bloody talons, trailing yellow gloss through the chaotic sky
toward the plaza, al-Kiran catapulted downward. Propelled by
drums, gongs, cymbals, the rattling of bones crashing in wild
cacophony, he pierced the ebony cloud spreading from the jew-

eled face of the Dark Goddess and struck al-Mansur, beating him backward.

Sirens pulsed from the black stone within the dolmen. Gold strands spun through the granite-green chariot of the light filled with darkness, the dark within the light. A wailing spread through the city. Panicked pilgrims, animated by dread, turned in confused circles. The Caliph, dazed, rose slowly. Al-Mansur, bloody and stunned, limped away.

Arms out, cape flowing, Kristien ran forward, then flipped up onto the shrine. Venus calling to Mars, she beckoned al-Kiran to follow.

At that moment, the vortex, a shadow-vacuum, slammed into Cordoba. Dogs howled. Horses and camels pulled frantically at their tethers. Thousands of birds flew in startled circles toward storks calling from ancient nests on the highest minarets overlooking the plaza.

Terrified, the faithful prostrated themselves. In utter silence, they bowed to the flagstones in prayer. Hakam II intoned the Judgment of the Last Days.

Whistles spiralled downward. Torches flared within a huge underground cavern. A sacred stream issued from the black hole around which dancers moved in precise patterns.

Arching backward, hair dangling, hands planted, legs wide, entreating entry, her body the earth, Kristien invited al-Kiran as she invited the golden sperm of the sun.

In the rhapsody of sweeping wings beneath the revolving sky, his phallus a flame, wailing and yearning, he followed her onto the dolmen. Her breasts on fire from the dark furnace beneath her belly, she sang:

"From heaven you descend while I rise black and blue.
Alborak's for mule-like men; the Karobla is me and you.
As Eve I build your mansion. I accept your sacred deed.
So come to me in passion. Sow in me your seed . . ."

As the last slice of the sun disappeared into the crimson hole of the moon, her legs encircled him. Mouth to his mouth, womb over his groin, incarnate and whole, she rode him, snake mother, a snake from him into her. Liquid light exploded between them. Al-Mansur fled beneath the radiant shadows.

In the crystal rain, through the prayer-ache and crisis of the miraculous, al-Kiran of Cordoba and Kristien of Nubia rose above the plaza. On a rainbow bridge piercing the Ka'ba of primary mysteries, at the heart climax of the Festival of All Faiths, the sun re-emerged in pieces and darkness gave birth to created light.

EPILOGUE

Something within the space-time continuum yearns for the realization of pure light but is incapable of experiencing ecstatic union except in momentary explosions of the earth-based self. Earth throws the shadow across the moon which reflects primary light from the sun, and we experience it as if the moon dies once every twenty-eight days and is then slowly reborn until it is full and then begins dying, in pieces, once again.

During a total eclipse, for a moment, the experience is reversed. The moon takes the full blast of the sun during broad daylight, the sun disappears behind a hole in the sky, and, for a few terrifying and ecstatic moments the two worlds stand together. Out of such moments, by the interpenetration of normally discontinuous realities, new realizations and aspirations are born.

The general setting in which the story of al-Kiran and Kristien takes place is historically accurate. Many of the greatest Islamic, Jewish, and Christian philosophers, physicians, scientists, theologians, and mystics which the world has ever known, lived and worked in al-Andalus. But fundamentalism was on the rise and when young Hisham became Caliph, al-Mansur was named Vizier, thus effectively ending the House of Omayyad.

As to al-Kiran, the Kirians, ben Hebaron, Kristien, the Mistress Khayam, Ziryab, and at-Talibin, you must judge their value by the measure of your own heart. Nothing about them, so far as I know, is untrue; but you will not find their histories in any other book.

Jay Bremyer